"Steven Young Bear is strictly off-limits..."

Molly pressed the portable phone to her ear as she spoke. "I don't know what to do, Dani," she said.

Her friend's sigh was loud. "Oh, for heaven's sake," Dani said. "Call Steven up and tell him what's going on. He'll understand. He sounds like a really nice guy. Besides, Manning's project may not take that much time."

"Oh, Dani, the way I feel now, if it only took a week, that would be seven days too long."

"Call him."

"I can't. If Steven wants to see me again, he'll call me. I gave him every opening to do so. And if by some miracle he does I'll tell him what Manning said and see how he reacts."

But he won't call, she thought to herself. *Why would he? We're standing on opposite sides of a tall fence that divides two very different worlds.*

Dear Reader,

Montana is the kind of place that inspires a passionate following of people who seek to protect and preserve what remains of the wild beauty of the legendary American West. The Yellowstone ecosystem is very much a part of that passion, and *Montana Standoff* is based on real-life tales of people who have fought, and are fighting still, against the threatening power of Big Money and the government giveaway of our public lands. This story is about ordinary people who are making huge sacrifices and big differences to save the very best of our wild heritage for future generations to enjoy.

Steven Young Bear, the grassroots environmental lawyer who first appeared in *Montana Dreaming* and then in *Buffalo Summer,* believes that a strong enough conviction of the heart can not only move mountains, but save them, as well. His fight seems doomed from the outset, going up against a Goliath of an adversary—a huge, powerful multinational mining conglomerate with a lawyer named Molly Ferguson steering the way toward bottom-line corporate profits at the expense of everything Steven is struggling to protect.

If you think that one person can't change the world, think again. Each and every one of us can make a difference.

Nadia Nichols

MONTANA STANDOFF
Nadia Nichols

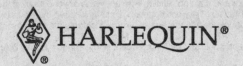

TORONTO • NEW YORK • LONDON
AMSTERDAM • PARIS • SYDNEY • HAMBURG
STOCKHOLM • ATHENS • TOKYO • MILAN • MADRID
PRAGUE • WARSAW • BUDAPEST • AUCKLAND

ISBN 0-373-78032-X

MONTANA STANDOFF

This edition published by arrangement with Harlequin Books S.A.

® and TM are trademarks of the publisher. Trademarks indicated with
® are registered in the United States Patent and Trademark Office, the
Canadian Trade Marks Office and in other countries.

www.eHarlequin.com

Printed in U.S.A.

This book is dedicated to all those ordinary people who are out there fighting to make life better for our grandchildren's grandchildren. Thank you all.

CHAPTER ONE

MOLLY FERGUSON'S AFTERNOON at the law firm of Taintor, Skelton and Goldstein had been relatively uneventful until Tom Miller tapped on the door to her office, leaned his upper body against the frame and gave her a long and meaningful stare. The absence of his usual arrogant smirk put her immediately on guard.

"May I come in?" he asked.

Tom was an egotistical jerk, and Molly's refusal to date him had made things awkward around the office. She'd been relieved to hear that Tom had just accepted a position in a California law firm and would be gone by the end of the month. Molly laid aside the brief she'd secretly been studying in the off chance she might one day be called upon to do something remotely important. "Certainly. What's up?"

He approached her desk with a mysterious expression and a thick file folder in one hand. "We were hoping Brad would be in today, but he just phoned again to tell us he's sicker than ever, and he only just remembered that there's a public meeting he was supposed to attend tonight on behalf of one of the mining companies we represent. Brad said it was no big deal, just a courtesy to inform the local citizens about the proposed mine and all the benefits it will bring to their community." Tom paused for effect and smiled. "Skelton was wondering if you could cover for him."

Molly's heart skipped a beat. Was she hearing him right? Was she actually being asked to do something other than file briefs? After eleven tedious months of being nothing more than Brad's glorified secretary, was she finally going to do some real work? "Of course I'll go," she said, hoping she didn't appear too eager. "What time, and where?"

"Seven in a place called Moose Horn, which, according to the latest census, has a year-round population of twenty-seven adults of voting age." Tom held up the thick file. "You probably won't have to say a word, but better study up, just in case. The meeting's being held at the town office, which is about a two-hour drive south of here. You could hop a commuter flight, but that means you'd probably be stuck in Bozeman for the night."

"I don't mind driving, but that won't give me

much time to look over the file," Molly said with a twinge of anxiety, her eyes measuring the thickness of the folder.

"You'll do just fine." Tom smiled his most charming smile. "Brad says you're up to speed on all the legal issues that might be raised at a gathering like this. You shouldn't have any problems. Moose Horn's town office is also the fire and police station, and the town library is housed upstairs. I'm sure you won't have any trouble finding it. It's probably the only building for miles around. Look for a man named Ken Manning. He's the company geologist and mine rep, and he'll be giving the presentation and fielding most of the questions. We weren't able to get hold of him to tell him you were replacing Brad, but like I said, it shouldn't be any big deal."

"Fine." Molly reached for the file. "I'd better get started, then."

Tom held it beyond her hand. "Sorry about ruining your Friday night. I'm sure you had some plans?"

"John was taking me to hear the Mountain Symphony Quartet at the Pavilion, but I'm sure he'll understand."

"You're still seeing that guy? Is it true that he's been married three times already?"

Molly felt the heat rise into her face. "John's a very nice man. The file, please?"

"Of course he is," Tom said. "He's a very nice man with three divorces under his belt. If you want my opinion, you should be thanking Brad for coming down with the flu and getting you out of that date. And there's still time for you to discover how good a real man can be. I'll be around for another week."

"The file," Molly repeated, and Tom tossed it on her desk with a smirk.

"You lose," he said.

Molly frowned at Tom's departing back. "I don't think so," she muttered under her breath, and then began scanning the first page. John wouldn't be happy. He'd been looking forward to hearing the quartet play. It was almost four o'clock, and he'd no doubt be teaching a music class. She glanced at the phone. No point in putting it off. She wouldn't be able to concentrate until she made the call. She picked up the receiver and dialed. His secretary answered on the first ring.

"John's in the middle of a private lesson with a rather important client," the snooty woman informed her. "Are you quite certain that you wish for me to disturb him?"

"Yes, please," Molly said with as much haughty loftiness as she could inspire. "It's actually really important." She drummed her fingers on her desktop as she waited. And waited…

"Hello?" John's voice was brusque.

"John, it's Molly. Listen, something's come up and I have to attend a town meeting in Moose Horn at seven tonight. I'm afraid we'll have to postpone our dinner, and as for the recital—"

"Moose Horn?"

"Yes. It's a small town about a hundred miles south of here."

There was a brief, chilly silence. "You know I've been planning this evening for quite some time. The violinist was a student of mine."

"Yes, I do know, and I'm so sorry, but Brad's sick and I've been asked to cover for him."

"Tell them you can't."

Molly hesitated. "It's my job, and besides, this is the first real assignment I've had. I need to—"

"I see," he interrupted. "Well, my student is waiting for me."

She flinched at the sound of the phone slamming down and gingerly replaced her own receiver. This wasn't her first glimpse of John's temper, but she decided then and there that it would be her last. She sighed, focused on the first page again and began to read. At five p.m. she replaced the papers neatly into the file folder and tucked it into her briefcase. Time to go. But the brief study she'd given the file hadn't scratched the surface of the vast scope of this mining project. She only hoped the townsfolk wouldn't notice her ignorance. The project ought to be a fairly easy sell. After all, how could anyone protest the creation of hundreds of good-paying jobs and a greatly increased tax base?

She took the elevator down to the lobby and exited the building. Her vehicle was parked in a reserved space, one of the few benefits that came with being the newest member of the firm. As always, she admired her sleek red sports car as she walked briskly toward it, leather briefcase in one hand, keys in the other. She deactivated the alarm and the door locks, and moments later was leaving Helena and heading to Moose Horn.

Molly had moved to Montana after she'd graduated Yale law school and passed the bar exams. Her family was from Boston, a mix of Scottish/Irish immigrants that included a few cops, a few priests and an assortment of outlandish and sometimes feuding clan members who kept life interesting even from so far away. She loved them dearly and missed them all very much, but enjoyed living in the shadow of the Rocky Mountains. She felt like a pioneer of sorts, being both the first bona fide lawyer as well as the first Ferguson to head West. It gave her a legendary status within her family, one that she tried only halfheartedly to dispel on her trips home at Christmas and in June, for her mother's birthday.

Helena was an okay town to live in. Tiny, compared to Boston, but it had all the necessary cultural endowments to keep from being considered…well, to keep from being a town like Moose Horn. Where on earth had they ever come up with that name? She sighed and slipped a CD into the player, cranked the volume and let the little red sports car hit cruising speed on Interstate 15.

STEVEN YOUNG BEAR SLIPPED away from the wedding reception at the Bozeman Grand Hotel with a feeling of relief. The party was still cranking along in high gear and no one noticed his early departure, certainly not the bride and groom, who were swaying in each other's arms on the dance floor. He didn't like weddings. He didn't particularly enjoy dressing up, but his sister Pony had asked him to attend. "It would mean a lot to Ernie and Nana if you came."

And so, he'd attended the wedding of Nana's sister's granddaughter Leona to that fancy-talking owner of Jolly John's car dealership in Livingston. Jolly John Johnson was the grandson of Lane Johnson, the senator who had been instrumental in destroying half of the Crow tribe's buffalo herd under the pretense of protecting the white man's cattle from brucellosis. Unlike cattle, the buffalo had never been proven to carry brucellosis, but

Johnson had ordered the slaughter just to hurt the tribe, and hurt them he had. Of course, that had been twenty years ago and Jolly John had had nothing to do with it. He'd been seven years old. But Steven remembered it vividly. Remembered the sounds of the rifles, the stink of the carcasses, the dark vultures clouding the skies.

And now Jolly John, grandson of Indian-hater Lane Johnson, had married a full-blooded Crow. Life was full of such ironies.

Steven exited the building, surprised and gratified to see that the sun hadn't yet set, and slung his tuxedo jacket over his shoulder as he walked to the parking lot and his dark green Wagoneer.

Moments later he was heading for home. His mood was melancholy. He was tired of weddings. There had been too many of late. An old friend earlier that spring. And the fall before that, Jessie and Guthrie's. He doubted he would ever find the kind of happiness they had found, and the older he got, the less likely it seemed.

Fortunately, Pony had. Strange, how things had worked out for her. Steven would never have imagined his traditionalist sister marrying a white man, yet seeing her with Caleb McCutcheon for the past few months had made him realize how right they were for each other, and in less than a month, they, too, would be married. He was glad for Pony, even if it did mean he'd have to get dressed up in a tuxedo again. She deserved to have the kind of life that Caleb could offer her—the love and the happiness and the freedom from want.

All was truly as it should be. He repeated this mantra silently as he drove, but by the time he reached Gallatin Gateway and turned down the long drive that ended at the little cedar post-and-beam house, he was ready for some time alone to nurse his lonely heart. The last thing he wanted was company, but the first thing he saw as he approached the house was a strange vehicle parked in his drive, and two people, a man and a woman, sitting on his step.

They stood and watched quietly as he got out and shut the Wagoneer's door. The woman was a girl, really, dressed in blue jeans and a baggy sweatshirt, her boyishly short dark hair framing a thin face. The man was older, in his late forties, a lean back-woods type with thick glasses and serviceable work clothes.

"Wow," the girl said as he approached. "I guess you were at a fancy party."

"A wedding." Steven stopped in front of them. "I assume there's a reason you were sitting on my step. I'm Steven Young Bear." He reached out to shake their hands.

"Rob Brown," the man said. "This is Amy Littlefield. We're both from Moose Horn. I'm the first selectman there. We've been waiting here for three hours, hoping you'd get back in time."

"In time for what?"

Brown glanced at his watch. "There's a town meeting being held at seven tonight to discuss the proposed New Millennium mine on Madison Mountain. Are you familiar with that project?"

"Somewhat," he hedged, guessing what was to come.

"We…that is, the citizens of Moose Horn… had hired Sam Blackmore to represent us at this meeting."

"He's a good attorney," Steven nodded, thinking that they'd come to get his opinion on their choice of representation. "Experienced. He'll steer you in the right direction."

"Then, you haven't heard?"

Steven recognized the undertones of darkness in those four words and felt the weariness within him deepen. The day had been long, and it wasn't over yet. "I've been gone all afternoon."

Brown shifted uneasily. "I'm sorry to have to tell you this, but Sam was killed this morning in a single-car crash. He was coming down the access road on Madison Mountain when he lost control of his vehicle."

"Sam's *dead?*"

Brown nodded. "Was he a good friend of yours?"

"I knew him." Steven rubbed the back of his neck, stunned. He pictured Sam the way he'd last seen him, not three weeks ago, on the courthouse steps in Bozeman. Balding, overweight, kind brown eyes and a slow-spoken honesty that made people rethink their negative attitudes toward lawyers. They'd shaken hands and spoken briefly, then gone their separate ways. Sam had a wife and three grown children. "What caused the crash? Do the police know?"

"I don't know. They were still investigating the scene when Amy and I went up on the mountain. We couldn't get anywhere near the site."

Steven dropped his hand, stared out across the valley. Wondered if Sam had felt any different when he got out of bed on the morning of his death. "Hard to believe."

"He was so nice," the girl said. "He really cared about what was happening. And now…"

"Condor International, the mining company that owns the New Millennium project, is sending their geologist to talk to us about the proposed mine," Rob Brown explained. "It isn't really an official meeting. It's more of a courtesy on the part of the mining company, but we wanted to show them we meant business when we came out opposed to this mine. We thought the best way to do that was to hire a good lawyer. So we collected money, held bake sales and bottle drives, sold raffle tickets for a donated Hereford calf. We raised five hundred dollars and then we contacted Sam, who agreed to represent us.

"We gave him all our information. He went up on the mountain several times himself in the past four weeks to see what was happening. I paid him the retainer just this morning and I also gave him all the water samples we'd taken from the area streams. I believe all of it was with him when he crashed his car."

"I see." The great weariness mired Steven's thoughts. He wanted nothing more than to go inside his peaceful little house and close the door. He wanted to tell these earnest people to go away and leave him alone. He wanted to hide away from the mean, ugly world. Sam Blackmore was dead. He'd died this morning, while Steven was readying himself for Leona's wedding to a slick car salesman who had those hokey radio commercials....

"So you need someone to speak for you at this meeting that's being held in..." he glanced at his watch "...a little less than an hour, but you have no money. I suppose you asked around and somehow found out that I was the lowest-paid attorney in the state of Montana, so you staked out my house."

Brown fidgeted, his face flushing. "No. We

called the Beartooth Alliance, the Greater Yellowstone Coalition and the Rocky Mountain Conservancy. They all recommended you highly. They said you were good, that you were a fighter."

"Well, I'm sorry to disappoint you, but I no longer handle active environmental litigation. My fighting days ended two years ago. And besides the fact that I've given up litigating, I have little knowledge of this particular proposal. I'm familiar with the mining company you spoke of, but—"

"Isn't that enough for a start?" Amy asked. "Please, Mr. Young Bear. We're desperate. I know the town of Moose Horn doesn't matter to most of the people on this planet, but to us it's a beautiful place. We live there and we love it, and we don't want to see it destroyed by some greedy mining conglomerate."

Steven shook his head. "I'm sorry you wasted your time."

"But…"

"You'll be late for your meeting if you don't leave right away."

Brown reached for Amy's arm but she shrugged away from him, thin face determined, eyes fierce. "My mother left me her diamond engagement ring," she said. "It's two carats, pear cut. Blue. A beautiful stone. I've had it appraised and—"

"No," Steven said.

"It's worth a lot of money. I'll sell it and you'll have the fee you need. Name your price. Just please come to the meeting tonight. Please, Mr. Young Bear. This means so much to all of us. If you could only walk on that mountain, you'd understand the awful thing that's about to happen to the entire area, and what it means—"

"Does it mean more than your mother's engagement ring?"

"This fight is so much bigger than me," she said without hesitation. "So much bigger than all of us."

Steven felt his resolve beginning to crumble. Ever since Mary Pretty Shield's death, he had deliberately avoided the fights, avoided the risks, avoided the pain of failure. He'd rolled down his shirt sleeves, buttoned his cuffs and toed all the proper political lines. But he would never forget her, or what she stood for. When Amy Littlefield spoke almost the exact same words that Mary had spoken nearly two and a half years ago, it was as if Mary were reaching out from the grave, trying to remind him of what was really important in life.

And there was this truth, too. It was his fate to back the underdogs. All of his life he would walk that path. He'd never be a rich attorney. It simply wasn't meant to be.

"I'll go to the meeting, but on one condition," he relented. "You keep your mother's engagement ring."

Steven declined the offer of a lift to and from the meeting with Amy and Rob, preferring the privacy of his own vehicle, but he had rapidly fallen behind their Dodge sedan and given up trying to keep apace. He felt as though the entire world were rushing by him at breakneck speed, everyone in a hurry to get somewhere, everyone late for something...but what? What drove people to live their lives at such a frenzied pace? Where was the enjoyment in that?

He admired the alpenglow that backlit the mountain range to the west, highlighting those last clear streaks of gold and vermilion before dusk coaxed the stars to shine down out of the night sky, and wondered if the wedding reception was over, if Jolly John and Leona had left for the airport and their trip to Hawaii. Seemed like everyone wanted to honeymoon in Hawaii. If he ever got married, he'd opt for Alaska, maybe. He'd like to see the salmon run by the thousands up some wild, unspoiled river, camp in the shadow of Denali, float a raft down the Yukon...

He sighed and glanced at his watch. Ten minutes to seven. He was definitely going to be late.

MOLLY TOOK THE WRONG TURNOFF outside of Bozeman and was nearly in Deer Lodge before she realized her mistake. She pulled over and studied the road map intently, anxiously nibbling on one fingernail.

In less than an hour, she'd be officially launched as a real, practicing attorney, pacing studiously before the residents of Moose Horn, calmly and succinctly explaining the financial benefits and industrial intricacies of a world they knew nothing of. She'd be skillfully guiding them into a brighter, more financially secure future, and who knows? They might even name their new library after her.

Molly shook her head with a laugh. At this rate, she'd be doing well if she just found the town before the meeting was over. She tossed aside the road map and spun her car around, reversing her direction on a dime with a nickel to spare. She shifted, shifted again, and had the speedometer nudging sixty-five in mere seconds. Lovely little car to drive. It almost made this two-hour road trip fun. The window was down and the cool mountain wind whipped through the car. The road was made to order for her Mercedes, all curves and twists. She came around a tight corner and hit the brakes. A dark green Jeep Wagoneer blocked the road in front of her, traveling at a sedate speed that instantly caused her blood pressure to soar. She was already late for the first important assignment she'd ever had with Taintor, Skelton and Goldstein, and now she was trapped behind some nursing-home escapee.

Another corner approached, and then a brief straightaway beckoned with no oncoming traffic. She downshifted, accelerated and flew past the sluggish Jeep like it was standing still. On the next brief straightaway she pegged seventy and U2 was blaring from the speakers when something struck her cheek just below her left eye. The car swerved as she hit the brakes, slapping wildly as an insect fell into her lap. Her brief, panicked glance identified the insect as a honeybee even as she felt the car leave the road. The Mercedes slid sideways and nosed over into a ditch, throwing her against the seat belt as the car came to an abrupt stop in a thick cloud of dust.

Molly sat for a moment, dazed, then scrabbled to release her seat belt and jump from the car, brushing her hands over her clothes to make sure the bee was gone. She felt her cheek swelling where the bee had stung her. Tires crunched on gravel and she turned, blinking to clear the tears from her eyes. A vehicle pulled over onto the shoulder. The driver of that irritatingly slow Wagoneer she'd just passed emerged, walked around the front of his vehicle and approached the edge of the ditch.

"Are you all right?"

The man had a deep voice, and he was dressed to kill in a tuxedo. His hair was the glossy black of a raven's wing and he had calm, dark eyes and a handsome face. He was certainly not ready for a nursing home, in spite of the way he drove. He was decades away from a nursing home. Eons.

Molly raised a hand to her cheek. "I'm fine," she said as he started down the embankment toward her. "A bee stung me and I went off the road. I'm not sure if I can get my car out," she said as he drew near. She took a step and stumbled into the side of her car even as he reached a firm hand to steady her. Her knees were wobbly and she was sure he could feel the trembling that was beginning to take over her body.

"Easy. Your car looks okay, but it'll need to be winched out of this ditch. I could pull it out with my Jeep, but I'd need to pick up a good tow rope. You sure you're all right?"

"Fine," she repeated. "But I have to attend a meeting in Moose Horn. I was already late when this happened, and now—" She stopped speaking when her voice broke.

"I'll give you a lift," he said. "I'm on my way to the same meeting. We can get your car out of the ditch afterward."

Molly hesitated. She had never before accepted a ride from a stranger, but she trusted her instincts, and they were telling that this man was safe. "Thank you. I'd appreciate that very much."

"Glad to help. I'm Steven Young Bear, by the way," he said, extending his hand.

"Molly Ferguson," she said, liking his warm, firm grip. "Thank you again, Mr. Young Bear. I don't know what I would have done if you hadn't stopped."

THE DRIVE TO MOOSE HORN took fifteen minutes. Steven's passenger sat quietly beside him, reassuring him every time he asked if she was all right. Sporadic conversation centered on getting her car out of the ditch after the meeting. It would be dark. They'd need to either call a tow truck or see if one of the townsfolk had a rope or chain heavy enough to use. "Yes, all right," she murmured repeatedly in response to his one-sided dialogue, nodding her agreement to his plans. She seemed distracted. He noted that her face was very pale and her hands were trembling in her lap, but attributed that to the adrenaline pumped into her system after skidding off the road. He hoped she wasn't going into shock. It was a miracle she hadn't been killed, driving that fast when she left the road. He hoped she'd learned that rural roads and excessive speed were a bad combination.

It would have been impossible to miss the town of Moose Horn, since the road ended at the one and only public building. A cluster of cars and trucks crowded the small gravel lot. Steven parked, got out, went around the vehicle and helped her out. Her hand was ice cold.

"Thank you, Mr. Young Bear," she said, gripping her briefcase. "I was supposed to meet someone named Ken Manning. He should be here, though I don't know what he looks like, and I'm not sure he knows I'm coming, so he probably won't be looking for me...." Her voice trailed off as she gazed at the building.

"I know who Ken Manning is," Steven said, wishing he'd never agreed to come tonight. The very mention of that man's name set his stomach churning. "I'll hook you up with him, but first I really think you should get checked out. I'll ask if there's an EMT present. Usually in a remote place like this, one or two of the townspeople are trained to handle medical emergencies, and—"

"That's not necessary, Mr. Young Bear," she interrupted, her voice strengthening, becoming firm. "I wouldn't classify a bee sting as a medical emergency. Really, I'm fine." She lifted her briefcase and took two wobbly steps before coming to an uncertain halt. Steven took her briefcase out of her hand and encircled her waist with his arm. "Thank you," she said humbly as he guided her into the building.

"You're very welcome," he replied, taken aback by the unexpected surge of protectiveness he felt for a woman he'd only known for the past five miles and twenty minutes. By the time they reached the town office, she was walking unassisted. She paused to take her briefcase from him, smooth her clothing and give him a wan but reassuring smile before entering the room.

The whole town was there. There were chairs, but only enough for half. Rob Brown sat up at the front of the room behind a big desk. Next to him sat Ken Manning, the geologist from the mining company and there was an empty seat to his left. All conversation stopped as Steven led Molly past the crowd at the rear, through the maze of occupied seats at the front, and pulled out the empty chair while Manning stared with obvious dismay, both at Molly and Steven.

"Ken Manning, Molly Ferguson," Steven said when she was seated, giving a brief nod to Manning. "Ms. Ferguson was just involved in an accident. Her car went off the road."

"I'm perfectly fine," she said in a brisk, no-nonsense voice. "Mr. Manning, I'm Molly Ferguson and I'm here on behalf of Brad Little. He was taken ill at the last moment and couldn't make it. He sends his regrets."

Manning scowled, obviously taken aback by the young woman's appearance and her announcement that she was replacing Brad. "I don't recall Brad ever mentioning you," he said, staring briefly at her swollen cheek. He glanced up at Steven. "There seem to be a lot of lawyers going off the road all of a sudden. I heard about Sam Blackmore's accident. I suppose that's why you're here?"

"You supposed correctly." Manning hadn't changed a bit. Same cold eyes, same tight, thin face, same predatory expression. The memories of their past encounters were still vivid enough to rankle. Steven had a sudden fleeting vision of Mary Pretty Shield's naive smile, and the pain was like a knife reopening a freshly healed wound. Steven glanced questioningly at Molly, who gave him another reassuring smile. He shrugged and then retreated toward the rear of the room, aware of the curious stares that followed him. It wasn't every day a full-blooded Crow Indian came to a town meeting dressed in a black tuxedo. It was enough to get a rise out of the sleepiest of attendees, and none of them appeared to be the least bit tired.

There was a big land map pinned to the wall on one side of the room. A blackboard spanned the other and big angry words had been boldly scrawled and underlined in white chalk across the top.

We won't be shafted by New Millennium Mining!

"Thanks for coming," someone murmured behind him, and he glanced around to see Amy Littlefield. "You were so late we were afraid you might have had a change of heart."

"The woman I came in with was just in an automobile accident. Her car went off the road about five miles from here and I was next on the scene. Does Moose Horn have an emergency medical technician?"

Amy shook her head. "Hank Fisher was the best, but he drowned in a boating accident last year. She'll have to go into Bozeman. Is she seriously hurt?"

Steven glanced to the front. "She says she's okay. I suppose I could take her after the meeting. What's happened so far?"

"That guy from the mine, Ken Manning, talked about the project, pointed it out on the map and showed us some pictures of how the inside of a mountain looks and how they go about mining the ore, and then just about everyone here said something against the mine. The woman you came in with—who is she anyway?"

"She's the temporary legal rep for New Millennium mine."

"Oh," Amy said, visibly dismayed. "Well, I guess we should have expected that they'd have their own lawyer."

Rob Brown stood and adjusted his thick glasses. "All right. I guess we've made our position here in Moose Horn pretty clear. We've heard what Mr. Manning had to say about how great this project will be for all of us, but we happen to like things the way they are. We don't want the top of Madison Mountain taken off and carted out of here in big trucks, and we don't want cyanide leaching into our streams and rivers. We don't want our town invaded by construction workers and miners, and we intend to fight tooth and nail to keep these things from happening."

There was resounding applause from the twenty-six other people in the room. When the commotion died, Molly Ferguson spoke quietly to Ken Manning for a moment, and then, at his reluctant nod, she got to her feet. Moving to the wall where the map hung, she stared for a moment, a frown furrowing her brow. At length, she turned to face the population of Moose Horn. She cleared her throat—a small, vulnerable sound in the expectant silence.

"Hello. My name is Molly Ferguson and I'm an

attorney with the law firm of Taintor, Skelton and Goldstein, which is representing this mining project," she began in a surprisingly professional and well-modulated voice that provided stark contrast to her somewhat disheveled appearance. "I apologize for being late, but my car went off the road about five miles from here. I wasn't here to listen to your comments, but Mr. Manning just attempted to summarize them for me. Your reservations regarding this project are completely understandable. It's only natural that you wouldn't want to see the rural character of your town changed or your way of life threatened, but please consider the benefits that would be realized.

"The Sourdough Mining Company stands on firm ground, and has since it was founded in 1877. An estimated one to two hundred *million* dollars worth of copper and iron ore is hidden within that mountain. This project would employ over one hundred and fifty people for ten to fifteen years," she continued, apparently not seeing the confused glances being exchanged by members of the town, nor hearing the undercurrent of voices, one of which muttered, right next to Steven, "Sourdough Mining Company? What the hell's she talking about?" and oblivious to Ken Manning, who had risen half out of his seat behind her wearing an expression that Steven could only describe as ominous.

"These are jobs that would pay employees a decent, livable wage. We're not talking about criminals and hoodlums invading your town. We're talking about honest, hardworking men and women, people like yourselves, who certainly deserve the chance to live a good life.

"And let me emphasize that your fears of pollution are completely unfounded. All of the mine's waste products will be stored in a special reservoir and capped with rock and cement when the project is completed. There will be absolutely no leachate to contaminate your rivers and streams. Engineers have been designing these special reservoirs to protect places like your watershed. It's state-of-the-art technology and absolutely safe.

"The increased tax base this mine generates would allow you to build your own elementary school, house your library in its own building, update your firehouse and your town hall. Businesses would move in to help support the larger population. A gas station, grocery and hardware stores. Moose Horn might actually become a place on the map."

"It already is!" a woman called out.

"Well, no offense intended, but I couldn't find it on mine," Molly said.

"That's no surprise," a man guffawed. "You don't even know what mining company you're supposed to be representing!" The citizens of Moose Horn burst into derisive laughter as Molly Ferguson's face flushed crimson. She turned toward Manning with a stricken expression, but he had slumped back into his seat, dropped his face into his hands and was shaking his head slowly back and forth. Steven moved quickly to the front of the room and the laughter instantly died.

"Good evening," he said in the resulting hush. "My name is Steven Young Bear, and I'm an environmental attorney. I'd like to say a few things if I may. First and foremost, I was deeply saddened to hear that Sam Blackmore was killed earlier today in an accident on Madison Mountain. I've known him for many years, and I was asked to come here this evening to speak on his behalf. There was no time to prepare, so I must ask you to please bear with me.

"Ms. Ferguson has stated that up to one to two hundred million dollars worth of copper and iron ore would be hauled out of here by the Sourdough Mining Company, but unless Ken Manning has changed horses in midstream, I believe we're talking about a different mine and a different mining company here. Ken is currently the chief geologist for New Millennium Mining Company, a subsidiary of the Texas-based conglomerate, Condor International. If what I've read in the newspapers is correct, what they propose to do here is remove the entire top of Madison Mountain and take out between six to eight hundred million dollars in silver and gold.

"I don't know that much about this particular project, but I'm familiar with some of their other mines, and I don't doubt those figures. They've mined a lot of ore out of a lot of mountains in this country. They've left a lot of messes, too. Big, state-of-the-art industrial-mining messes. In Colorado they've left a mess with an estimated cleanup cost of two hundred million dollars after taking one hundred and twenty million in metals out of the land, and a cyanide leak in one of their state-of-the-art reservoirs killed every living organism in a seventeen-mile stretch of the Arrowsink River.

"In New Mexico this very same company filed another claim on public lands and took thirty million out in metals, during which time leaking acid wiped out the entire fishery in the Rogue River. The cleanup cost at this abandoned mine is expected to run close to three hundred million dollars and may become a Superfund site, paid for by our federal tax dollars. That's money out of your pocket and mine.

"Their Soldier Mountain Mine right here in Montana is contaminating the drinking water and causing high cancer rates among the Sioux on the Rocky Ridge Reservation.

"You folks are right to question the wisdom of situating an open pit mine in the middle of a beautiful wilderness area. Madison Mountain deserves better than to be sacrificed to the corporate bank. As a nation we need to speak as one voice to force our government to overhaul the archaic mining laws that allow such plundering of our public lands. We need to start now, today, right here, with twenty-seven voices. It may not seem like much, but it's a beginning. We have a big job to do," he concluded, "and we had better get to it." He returned to the rear of the room to a deafening burst of applause.

Manning rose from his seat as if to offer a rebuttal but the first selectman beat him to the punch. "The next town meeting to continue discussing this proposal is scheduled for September tenth," Brown said. "I hope that Mr. Manning and his attorney will be able to attend. This is the beginning of a process that is new to all of us, and I hope, too, that Mr. Young Bear can guide us through it. Thank you all for coming and for voicing your opinions."

The meeting broke up and there was a slow shuffle of people out the door. Steven looked around for Molly, but she was standing beside

Ken Manning, her face very still and pale as Manning addressed her. He could only imagine what Manning was saying. Rob Brown and Amy Littlefield approached with a score of other people in tow. "So what do we do now?" Brown asked.

"You can start by putting some emergency zoning into place. New Millennium will be looking to house over three hundred contractors in the immediate area. Zone your town to prohibit temporary cluster housing, rapid growth and sprawl. Zone the hell out of it. You say the water samples were destroyed?"

"They were in Sam Blackmore's car," Brown said, "and his car was totaled. It was hauled to a place called Maffick's Salvage in Jefferson. Maybe the samples survived, but…"

"I'll check with the local police," Steven said. "But if they didn't, you'll need to take fresh samples from every year-round or intermittent creek or seep that would be impacted by this mine, and the samples need to be kept in a safe place. They're the most important evidence you'll ever have against this company. And then you need to start making noise. A lot of noise. The more people who know about this, the better. The more press releases that get into the newspapers, the better. Invite heavy-hitting journalists here to tour the site.

"We need to get the Yellowstone Coalition on the bandwagon, along with the Rocky Mountain Conservancy and the Beartooth Alliance. They can all help your cause. I'll do what I can to get the ball rolling on that end. Every phone call can make a difference. If you can do a mailing, do it. Start a petition drive. Get signatures, names and addresses of all voters who oppose the mine."

"We have no money," Brown stated bluntly. "We all work, but our jobs barely put food on the table."

"Money is what a campaign like this needs," Steven said. "You need to find backing. Environmentally friendly businesses, sportsmen and women who hunt and fish this area. Neighboring communities, the tourism industry, the tourists themselves. Anyone who wouldn't want to see this wilderness destroyed and would kick in dollars to protect it. A big coup would be to get a national group like the Sierra Club or the Nature Conservancy on board. I'll make some phone calls to them, too."

"Will you come to the next meeting?" Amy Littlefield asked.

Steven hesitated. He glanced back to Manning, who was stabbing his finger in Molly Ferguson's face, then looked back at the ring of faces surrounding him. Thought about Mary Pretty Shield and the last time he'd ever seen her, the way she'd smiled over her shoulder at him as she walked out his office door. After her death, he vowed he'd never fight these fights again, yet it was her memory that had brought him to Moose Horn. How could he abandon these people now?

"I'll be there." He paused again. "A campaign like this takes over your life," he cautioned. "Going up against a giant like New Millennium Mining will become the longest, nastiest fight you've ever gotten into. The litigation could drag on for years, and I'll tell you this right now. The odds are against you."

"We have to try." Brown looked around at the ring of hopeful faces as they nodded their assent. "We *have* to."

CHAPTER TWO

MOLLY STOOD OUTSIDE the door of the town hall building, hugging herself against the cold and shivering in spite of her resolve to appear stoic, as the people filtered slowly from the building. Ken Manning had just blasted her with both barrels, not that she could blame him. She'd failed her first official assignment for the law firm quite miserably. "That was quite a circus act, Ms. Ferguson," he'd stated bluntly as the meeting adjourned.

"I'm sorry." It was all she could think to say.

Manning had frowned. "Quite frankly, I'm sorry, too. It's a disgrace when a multibillion dollar corporation like Condor International is handed legal representation of your caliber, especially from a firm that's done plenty of profitable business with us in the past and should know better."

"Mr. Manning, really, I'm so sorry. I was informed about this meeting an hour before I had to drive down here. An associate somehow gave me the wrong file to study, and—"

"So I noticed," he'd said. "Sourdough Mining?"

"I...I'm not exactly sure where the company is based out of, but they mine copper and iron ore and—"

"I also noticed that you arrived here with the opposition's attorney. Is that another one of your questionable strategies?"

Molly had struggled to maintain her calm. "As I explained earlier, my car went off the road five miles from Moose Horn. Mr. Young Bear was kind enough to stop and offer me assistance. I accepted his offer of a ride. As a matter of fact my car's still in the ditch..."

"How very unfortunate for you," Manning said, as he pulled on his overcoat. "You made a mockery of my project at this meeting, and you can be sure that I'll be calling Jarrod Skelton first thing Monday morning and letting him know what I thought about your performance."

Without another word he'd turned and left her standing behind the desk, her left cheek throbbing and her job in very dire straits. Finding the door was a matter of following the cold draft that wafted in from outside. There she stood, shivering, searching her pockets for a tissue and praying that Steven Young Bear hadn't left yet, because she was pretty sure none of Moose Horn's decidedly hostile citizens were going to offer her a two-hour courtesy ride to Helena.

"You think you're going to win, don't you?" Molly turned to see a gray-haired woman flanked by a male companion. "You think you're going to tear our beautiful mountain apart."

Molly flinched at the aggressiveness in the older woman's voice. "Well, I..."

"Excuse me, please, ma'am." Steven Young Bear appeared beside her. "This woman was recently involved in a car accident and needs immediate medical attention. I'm sure you'll allow me to see that she gets it." His hand on her elbow gently but firmly propelled her past the blur of faces and into the darkness. Moments later they were leaving the town of Moose Horn, and she couldn't wait to be rid of it.

For a while they drove in silence, and then Molly said a heartfelt and humble, "Thank you for rescuing me once again. That was without a doubt the most humiliating experience of my life. When you walked up and began to speak..." Her voice faltered and she gazed at the tunnel of road illuminated by the Jeep's headlights. "I wish I could have just disappeared."

"I'm sorry. My intention wasn't to make a fool out of you."

"You didn't have to," Molly said. "I did that all

by myself. A colleague of mine was supposed to cover this meeting but he got sick at the last minute. Another colleague asked me to go in his place and gave me the wrong file to study. This was my first real assignment, my first chance to prove myself to the firm, and I sure as hell dropped the ball." Molly drew a deep breath and tried not to let the tears that were stinging in her eyes get the best of her. This wasn't the end of the world, or the end of her career as a lawyer. She would explain to Skelton what had happened, and he'd understand, give her another chance.

But what if he didn't?

"I think you should get checked out at the hospital in Bozeman," Steven said. "Just to make sure you're all right."

"For the hundredth time, I'm fine. The only thing that was seriously hurt tonight was my ego."

He said nothing to this, just drove on, while Molly slipped off her shoes, massaged her aching feet and wondered how she would ever save face after such a disastrous performance. The Jeep slowed and pulled over onto the shoulder, nosing downward just enough to illuminate the ditch. She stared at her car and felt a deepening sense of despair. "You're lucky you weren't seriously hurt," he said, startling her out of her morose reverie. "Well, it's pitch dark, I don't have a tow rope, and you shouldn't be driving even if I could pull your car out of the ditch."

"I'm perfectly capable of—"

"It's way past suppertime," he said. "Let's get something to eat and worry about your car tomorrow."

She hesitated. "That sounds nice, Mr. Young Bear, and you're right, I'm starving. But I'm sure you'll understand why I really don't want to be seen in public. If you could just drop me off at the hotel by the airport in Bozeman, I'll order up room service tonight and have my car towed out of the ditch in the morning."

"You're forgetting one small matter," Steven said. "The bee that stung you left its stinger in your cheek."

Molly raised her fingertips to touch the spot gingerly. "How do you know?"

"I saw it," he said, and pulled back out onto the road.

STEVEN YOUNG BEAR TOOK HER to his house in Gallatin Gateway. She sat on a sofa in the living room while he mixed her a gin and tonic. He refused all offers of help and so Molly allowed herself to be tended to by a man she hardly knew. She felt so inexplicably comfortable in Steven's presence that it seemed the most natural thing in the world to be curled up here on his sofa. He came out of the kitchen and pressed a cold glass in her hand. She sipped. Beefeater. Schweppes. Big slice of lime. Delicious.

"Thank you," she said, but he was already gone. She heard noises behind her in the kitchen. Pans rattling. The sudden poofing sound of a gas burner being lit on a cookstove. Not only was he disconcertingly handsome, but she was finding that there was far more to him than met the eye. He came back into the living room and set a plate down on the coffee table. "Appetizers," he said. She picked up a thin sesame-seed cracker and nibbled. Tried a piece of sharp cheddar. Sat back and closed her eyes, wondering if all this was real or just a dream. Moments later, she heard the snap and crackle of a fire in the fireplace, smelled the fragrant tang of wood smoke and sighed with something very close to contentment. She was far happier curled up on this sofa than she would have been listening to a Stradivarius violin. She heard Steven enter the room and sat up. He was holding a small basin and a pair of tweezers.

"Hold still," he said, as he set the basin down and bent over her. "I'm going to remove the stinger and dab this poultice of baking soda and water on your cheek. It should help with the swelling."

She held obediently still for his first aid. "Thank

you," she repeated when he had finished. He didn't reply, but went back to the kitchen. Soon she could smell intriguing aromas. He returned and laid another log on the fire, then disappeared back into the kitchen and made more domestic noises. She thought it was extraordinary that a man she hardly knew was cooking supper for her, especially under the circumstances. She took another sip of her drink and touched her fingertips to the poultice that Young Bear had applied to her swollen cheek. He was right. It already felt better.

"I hope you like shrimp curry," Steven said, coming from the kitchen with a plate of food and setting it onto the coffee table in front of her.

"Never had it," Molly admitted. "I'm a corned-beef-and-cabbage kind of a girl, but it smells wonderful." She set her drink down, picked up the fork he'd laid beside the plate, and in a matter of minutes had cleaned it of the last grain of rice.

"More?" he said.

She sat back with a flush of embarrassment at how quickly she'd devoured the meal. "No, thank you. That was delicious and once again I can't thank you enough." She hesitated. "Forgive me, but I have to ask. Do you always wear a tuxedo when you go to public hearings?"

"Only when they're important," he said.

Molly laughed. "I have only one more favor to

ask. Could you please call me a taxi to take me into Bozeman?"

He picked up her plate and took it into the kitchen. "You're welcome to stay in the guest room," he said over the sound of running water. "Tomorrow's Saturday. Most law offices are closed, but the auto parts store will be open and we can pick up a tow rope. My Jeep should pull your car right out of that ditch."

Molly sat up, gripping her gin and tonic and wondering if she'd heard him right. "That's way too much to ask," she finally managed to say. "I'll just take a taxi to the airport hotel. You've done more than enough as it is." She rose to bring her glass into the kitchen but he beat her to it, appearing in front of her, taking it out of her hand, and replacing it with a plate.

"Finish off the rest of the curry so I can wash the pan, and I'll fix you another drink," he said, as if offering her a fair trade.

Molly sat back down, plate resting on her knees. She should insist that he call her a taxi, but the combined lure of the cheerful fire in the fireplace, the peaceful ambience of the house, and the company of this extraordinary man won out. "Thank you, Mr. Young Bear."

"Steven," he corrected. "And you're welcome."

STEVEN POURED HIMSELF another cup of coffee, dropped back into his chair and bent over the text he was studying. He took a taste of the strong black brew, read for a little while and then glanced up at the kitchen clock. Nine a.m., and not a peep from the guest room. He didn't know if he should be relieved or concerned. Perhaps she was a late sleeper, or maybe she was allergic to bee stings and during the night had slipped into an irreversible coma. He walked into the living room, where he paused for a long moment outside the guest-room door, listening. Nothing. He gave a light tap. No response.

"Molly?"

Silence answered him and his anxiety deepened.

The door opened smoothly when he turned the knob. She was lying on her back with the covers drawn up to her chin, fingers curled around the edge of the blanket, and red hair hiding the pillow beneath its fiery cascade. Her eyes were closed and she was breathing evenly. He closed the door, satisfied that she was alive but wondering how to wake her. He had work to do. He wanted to get her situated in her own world again so that he could concentrate on formulating a battle plan to fight this New Millennium Mining proposal.

In the kitchen he lit the propane burner and put the cast-iron pan over it to heat. Within moments, thick slabs of smokehouse bacon were beginning to sizzle. The sweet hickory aroma mingled with the sharp, rich fragrance of fresh-brewed coffee. Surely the smells of breakfast cooking would rouse her from slumber land.

In the meantime, he'd keep studying.

MOLLY WAS IN ATHENS, standing among tall, bone-white pillars. A long gown of the finest silk whispered in the breeze off the Aegean Sea and brushed against her long, slender legs. Her magnificent hair was long and thick, the deepest chestnut, just as she'd always wanted. His was a shade of ebony that shamed the night and his eyes were dark, as they were in life. He lifted a powerful, beautifully muscled arm, beckoning her to the top of a mountain where men swarmed like ants carrying rocks out of a shaft and running to the bottom. Thousands of rocks being carried by thousands of men, all of them running, running....

"They're stealing our soul," he said in his deep, masculine voice. "They're killing our mountain."

Her mother was calling her to breakfast. "Molly? Time to get up. Rise and shine, lass, you're burning daylight."

Molly's eyes flew open. She stared up at the blur of white ceiling, moved her head toward the rectangle of light in the unfamiliar room. Her momentary disorientation was quickly replaced by the pleasant memories of the night before. She relaxed and stretched beneath the covers. It was so quiet here, and so gloriously peaceful. The smell of bacon tantalized, and her stomach growled in response. She pushed the covers off and sat up, reaching automatically to try and subdue her wild hair. Hopeless.

She stood and went into the bathroom, stared at her reflection in the mirror. Her face looked almost normal. The swelling had gone down overnight, but there was no mistaking where she'd been stung. She sighed with relief and glanced down at the vanity. Steven had left her a brand-new toothbrush and tube of toothpaste. She brushed her teeth, washed the baking soda poultice off her cheek, and was drying her face on a hand towel when she heard a knock.

She padded barefoot across the room and opened the door. Nothing. The knock came again and she realized that there was someone at the front door. She waited a moment for Steven to answer it, but apparently the loud spatter of frying bacon had drowned it out. Still holding the hand towel, Molly crossed the room, slid back the dead bolt, and opened the front door. Sunlight spilled over her bare legs but the chill air negated any warmth. She blinked with surprise as a very pretty young woman with eyes and hair as black as Steven's stared back at her.

"Yes?" Molly said. "Can I help you?"

PONY YOUNG BEAR was struck speechless by the sight of the woman who stood in her brother's doorway, dressed in what she had to assume was one of Steven's white shirts…and apparently little else. The young woman's hair was a shoulder-length flaming mass of curls that took on a life all their own. Her left cheek was red and slightly swollen, and she was holding a hand towel as if she'd just come from the bathroom.

"I… I'm here to see Steven," Pony managed to say, wondering if the poor woman was a victim of domestic violence. Steven was always rescuing people from less fortunate circumstances.

"Oh." The woman lifted one hand in a futile attempt to corral her hair. "He's cooking breakfast. I'll tell him you're here. And you are…?"

"His sister."

"Oh! Well, please, come in…."

"Pony?" She heard Steven's voice as he appeared in the entryway, holding a spatula. "You're just in time for breakfast," he said, his expression betraying nothing. "This is Molly Ferguson. Molly, my sister, Pony." Pony shook hands with the redhead, whose grip was surprisingly firm.

"I'm pleased to meet you," Molly said. "And now if the two of you will please excuse me…"

Pony noticed how Steven watched the young woman walk across the living room. Then he turned back to her with a faint grin. "Nice legs, huh?" he said.

"Steven, why didn't you bring her with you to Leona's wedding?"

"Because I only just met her last night."

"Oh." Once again she was struck speechless.

Steven drew her inside and closed the door behind her. "So. What brings you to my humble abode?" he asked as he returned to the kitchen to turn the bacon.

She trailed after him, noticing the drink glasses on the coffee table in the living room. She looked at her brother. "I just wanted to tell you that you looked really handsome in that tuxedo."

"You told me that yesterday."

"I wanted to ask you if you could wear the same thing on my wedding day."

"You already asked me, and I told you I would."

Pony sighed. "All right. I was worried about you. You were so quiet, and you left the reception so early."

"We're talking about Jolly John Johnson's wedding reception. At least I went, didn't I? And I'm always quiet, remember?"

"Yes, but yesterday was different." Pony sat on a stool at the counter and teased her brother with a smile. "Today, though, I can see that you're doing okay."

"Yeah. I went to a bar and picked up a woman. I did good, huh?" He grinned over his shoulder. Steven lifted the bacon out of the pan and laid it on a paper towel. "How many eggs do you want?"

"I can't stay. I don't want to interrupt anything."

Steven drained the bacon fat from the pan. "You're not. She got stung in the face by a bee yesterday and drove her car into a ditch. I offered to give her a ride home from the public meeting in Moose Horn which, by the way, we both attended. As it turns out, she's the New Millennium Mining Company's legal rep and she lives in Helena. You see? No hanky-panky going on." He gave her a long significant stare and then repeated, "How many eggs?"

"One. So, she's the high-priced attorney representing the corporate giant, and no doubt you're representing the penniless environmentalists."

"Some things just never change. Over easy, or sunny-side up?"

"Over easy." Pony rested her elbow on the counter and her chin in the palm of her hand. She gazed speculatively at her brother. "And so. She spent the night?"

"It was late by the time the meeting adjourned. We were both hungry and she needed some first aid. Today we'll pull her car out of the ditch and she'll be on her way. Story over."

Pony smiled as she slid off the stool. "Chapter one is over," she corrected. "I'll make the toast."

MOLLY'S CAR WAS OUT of the ditch by eleven. The day was a beautiful blue-and-gold celebration of September, and though Molly was a city girl, she found the mountainous terrain compelling. She was almost disappointed when Steven's Jeep pulled the Mercedes onto the roadway so easily, and she almost hoped he'd find something wrong with it, some reason why she couldn't possibly drive back to Helena.

"She's as sound as a dollar," he said, levering himself out from beneath the vehicle where he visually checked the oil pan and the undercarriage. "These German cars are built like tanks." He stood, dusted off his hands, and gave her a look she couldn't interpret. "You shouldn't have any trouble driving home."

Molly rummaged in her purse and peeled out a hundred dollars in an assortment of crumpled bills. "For food, first aid, and lodging," she said, extending the offering. "I can't thank you enough for all you did."

"I don't want your money," Steven said.

"Please," she pleaded. "If you don't take it, I'll spend the rest of my life feeling guilty for taking advantage of your incredible kindness."

"I helped you out because I wanted to," Steven said. "The only thing you should feel remotely guilty about is trying to sell the citizens of Moose Horn on a project like New Millennium Mining."

Molly felt the sting of his words and replaced the money in her purse. Her chin lifted. "You see things a little differently than I do, Steven, but there's nothing wrong with giving fair representation."

"How long have you been working with mining companies?"

Molly's chin crept higher and she felt her cheeks flush. "Eleven months."

"Ah," he said, as if her answer had effectively ended the conversation. He turned toward his Jeep.

"Listen, I know how you feel about New Millennium," Molly said, "but technology really has made great strides. Responsible mining companies have learned from past projects how to better protect the environment. Times have changed."

He glanced back. "Mining companies don't give a damn about the environment or the resident human population, and they're powerful enough to break all the laws and get away with it. The profits far outweigh the cost of a good conscience or the fines levied against them."

"It's not like that," Molly protested.

"Isn't it? You have a lot to learn. Maybe you should take a look at one of Condor International's mines that's currently operational to know that some things will never change. The Soldier Mountain uranium mine would be a good example of their ethics."

"Where's that?" she said, embarrassed once again by her ignorance.

"Just east of the Rocky Ridge Reservation on federal lands."

"Show me."

"It's a long drive."

"You said I have a lot to learn. I'd better get started, hadn't I? When can we go?" Molly knew she was being blatantly forward, but she also knew she wanted to see this man again, very much, and he wasn't trying to make that happen. No doubt he thought she was as incompetent as the rest of them did. Well, she wasn't, and somehow she had to create the chance to prove that to him.

"You should see the pit on a weekday, while they're working it."

"All right. How about this Wednesday?"

Steven hesitated. "You don't really need me

along. Your credentials will get you through the gate."

"Yes, that's true. I could go alone, or I could ask Brad to take me. Brad's already shown me two sites and both were very interesting. He pointed out what he wanted me to see, told me what he wanted me to know. If you really want me to understand this issue from *your* point of view, you need to do the same. I really want to see both sides of this coin, Steven. It's important to me, and it should be equally important to you. Thursday?"

"I don't know," he hedged. "I'll have to see what's on the books."

"Tomorrow, then…?"

"Tomorrow's Sunday. You wouldn't get the full effect."

"I have an incredible imagination."

He hesitated again, obviously reluctant to commit.

"If we leave here by 9:00 a.m., we should be in good shape, time-wise. I'll pack the lunch, buy the gas, and drive." She tossed her purse onto the passenger's seat and climbed into the Mercedes. "I live at 244 Prospect Street, apartment four. Brick building, second-floor walk-up," she said, turning the key in the ignition. The engine purred smoothly to life. Steven stood watching her, hands shoved in his jacket pockets, wearing the same inscrutable expression. She eased out on the clutch and the Mercedes moved forward. "Thanks again for everything, counselor," she said, hoping he'd respond with something like, "See you tomorrow."

But he didn't. He just stood in silence and watched her drive away.

THAT AFTERNOON, as soon as she arrived back in Helena, Molly arranged to meet her best friend at their favorite café. Though the wait wasn't long, she'd already shredded four paper cocktail napkins into confetti before she spotted Dani breezing through the door. "Thanks for coming so quickly," she said as her friend dropped into a chair across from her.

"No problem at all. I happen to be starving, I didn't eat breakfast this morning, so this works out well for me. What's up?" She leaned forward suddenly, eyes widening. "My God, what happened to your face? Did John *hit* you?"

"If you're referring to my cheek, it's just a bee sting. Waiter? Another mai tai cocktail, please."

"They don't serve mai tais here," Dani said with an exasperated shake of her head. "Are you all right? When did you get stung?"

"Yes, I'm fine, and they serve mai tais here now. I just taught the bartender how to make one, and it's delicious." Molly glanced around to make sure no one was listening and lowered her voice. "Dani, I need to ask you a big favor."

Dani's eyes narrowed. "From the telltale glow, I have a feeling this favor has something to do with a man, but if the man is Stradivarius John, the answer is no."

Molly was startled that her agenda was so obvious. "This isn't about John."

"Good. Who, then?"

"I met someone last night, at a public hearing," Molly said.

Dani shrugged out of her blazer and draped it over the back of her chair. "Was this before or after the bee sting?"

"Almost simultaneously."

"What's the favor?"

"Could you please lend me your emerald earrings?"

Dani laughed and looked around for the waiter. "Hurry with that drink."

"This is serious, Dani. With any luck, I'll be spending the day with Steven tomorrow and I want to look especially nice, so any advice you have on what I should wear would be most appreciated. Fashion is definitely my failing."

"Yes, I know that, but you've never taken my advice before, especially regarding fashion."

"I always listen to what you have to say."

Dani nodded her thanks to the waiter who delivered her drink. "No, you don't. I advised you not to date John, remember? He was just one month divorced from his third victim when he asked you out."

"Well, yes, you did warn me," Molly admitted, beginning on another cocktail napkin, "but he seemed nice, and it's not like there was anything serious between us. We went out once in a while, that's all. It was better than eating dinner out alone, and I wasn't looking for anything more serious than that. At least, not until yesterday."

"Okay, so John's history. That's a relief. You got stung by a bee and met an incredible man at the same moment, and you're thinking you may have just experienced love at first sight. Am I right?" Dani's voice was as cynical as her expression.

Molly sat back in her chair, exasperated. "Are you going to help me or not?"

"Are you going to tell me the whole story from the beginning?"

Molly did, speaking bluntly and not sparing herself in the least. "So you see," she concluded, "I had no idea that Steven was the attorney representing the citizens of Moose Horn, and I made a complete idiot of myself in front of him...and in front of everyone else, too, for that matter."

"Moose Horn?" Dani raised her drink for a taste

and grimaced. "Uck. What on earth did you tell the bartender to put in this concoction?"

"Skelton will probably fire me after this."

"It isn't your fault that Tom gave you the wrong file. What a rotten thing for him to do! I warned you about that guy, too, remember?" As Dani spoke, she held her glass up to the light to study the contents. "He used to work with the Downing firm, but they dismissed him after several clerks complained of sexual harassment."

"He's asked me out a couple of times," Molly admitted. "I think giving me the wrong file was his way of getting back at me for not saying yes."

"Slimy creep," Dani said, trying another sip, making another face. "He's the one who should be fired."

"Actually, he's being transferred, but I really don't want to talk about Tom."

"No, of course not. You want to talk about the wonderful man you met last night. Steven. Continue. You made an idiot of yourself, and then what happened?" Dani looked around again and waved to the waiter. "I'll have my usual," she called across the small room. "The avocado, vegetable and sprouts wrap, no mayo." The waiter waved back, acknowledging the order from across the small room.

"He rescued me from the hostile citizens after the meeting and gave me a ride to his place…"

"Hold on. Do I really need to hear how he had his way with you on your first unofficial date?"

"…because my car was stuck in a very deep ditch, which I drove into after being stung by the bee, and it was late, so he thought it would be better to pull it out in the morning, after…"

"After he seduced you," Dani finished.

"He fixed me a drink, fed me dinner, let me sleep in his guest room, cooked me a delicious breakfast in the morning, and pulled my car out of the ditch. He wouldn't even take gas money from me. I thought all the knights in shining armor died in King Arthur's time, but I was so wrong."

"Hmmmm." Dani frowned. "This sounds serious. And you're spending the day with him tomorrow?"

"Well, maybe. It's not exactly a date. More like a professional courtesy. He might take me to see what an open pit mine looks like."

"Wow, sounds romantic. When will you know if this *professional courtesy* is a happening thing?"

"If he hasn't arrived at my apartment by 9:00 a.m., I guess it isn't. But I want to look nice just in case he does, especially after how I looked yesterday."

Dani drummed her fingers on the tabletop. "So let me get this straight. You want to wear my emerald earrings to tour an open pit mine with a man who already sounds like he's afraid to commit?" She shook her head. "I don't think so, Molly. 'Nice' doesn't include a pair of two-thousand-dollar gems going on a 'maybe' date that's more like a professional courtesy. Besides, it isn't a woman's jewelry that catch a man's eye."

"That's easy for you to say," Molly gestured with frustration. "Look at you. The way you dress, the way you do your hair, the way you walk. Everything about you is naturally perfect. You're the outdoorsy Julia Ormond of the estate-planning world. You'd look glamorous in a sweatshirt and blue jeans. I'm not that blessed." She leaned forward intently. "Look, I know I'm acting a little bit out of character, but this is important. I'm twenty-six years old and I've never felt this way before. I may never again meet another man that makes me feel this way."

Dani gave her a bemused look. "Okay. I'll help you coordinate an appropriate wardrobe for possibly viewing an open pit mine, but we'll save the emerald earrings for your first definite dinner date. Deal?"

Molly sighed with relief. "Deal."

STEVEN SAT at the kitchen table gazing down at the open page of an environmental law handbook but he wasn't concentrating on the text. He was thinking about the handful of people in Moose Horn who had the nerve to stand up to a multinational conglomerate and say "No!" loud and clear, knowing they'd probably be bulldozed into the next century. He was thinking about money. It took lots of money to wage a successful campaign, and money was always hard to come by. He would make a series of calls first thing Monday morning and get things going on the financial front, but it would be tough because the times themselves were tough, and purse strings were drawn pretty tight in an uncertain economy.

He was thinking that in the morning he would have to drive to Helena to pick up Molly and take her to view one of New Millennium's mines. He turned the page of the textbook and wondered why the idea of spending the day with Molly Ferguson didn't bother him. It should. It wasn't as if he'd volunteered his time to further her education. It wasn't as if he'd asked her to go on the trip. He should be thinking about ways to get out of it.

But he wasn't. He was thinking that it would be good to see her again, though he couldn't for the life of him fathom why. He shook his head and sighed and tried to focus on the page, but all he was seeing was Molly Ferguson, remembering the bravado that didn't quite mask her shyness...and the glory of her beautiful red hair.

CHAPTER THREE

BY NINE MINUTES past nine o'clock the following morning, Molly's morale had hit an all-time low. Steven Young Bear wasn't coming. She'd known all along that he wouldn't. And why should he? He had no obligation whatsoever to help her out any more than he already had. She'd made a fool of herself yesterday, putting him on the spot, pressuring him that way, and now she was paying the price. Not only was she probably going to lose her job because of her poor performance at the Moose Horn town meeting, but she'd messed up any chance she might have had to further her acquaintance with Steven Young Bear. She'd asked him to do something he obviously hadn't wanted to do: chaperone her on a field trip to an open pit mine. If she'd asked him to dinner, he might have said yes. It would have been a far more diplomatic move, since, after all, she owed him one. She could have offered him a good, old-fashioned Irish corned-beef-and-cabbage feast.

Instead, she'd behaved just like one of those

brassy, forward women her mother so disapproved of. Twenty-six-year-old Molly Ferguson, lonely and desperate, had flung herself at a man who had ever so politely tried to brush her off. She had humiliated herself by allowing her impulsive emotions to get in the way of reason and logic.

She paced the confines of her apartment, thinking about all the awful dates she'd been on since her father had reluctantly allowed her to go out with boys at sixteen. She'd said yes to every invitation to go see a movie, not because she liked the boy but because her father was so overprotective. But the truth was, most of the time she'd secretly wished she were ensconced in her room reading a good book. Then later, when she was all grown up and in college, she'd gladly spent all of her time in the dorm, studying. Studying was a good excuse not to suffer through another boring date. She'd given up on dating until John had pestered her into a routine of having dinner with him on weekends he was free… and even those dates with John sometimes had her thinking about the current book she was reading, or the files she was working on in the office.

Not John's fault, really. She'd been totally focused on attaining her law degree ever since she could verbalize what she wanted to do with her life, and after getting her degree she'd been totally focused on becoming as competent a lawyer as she could. But moments after meeting Steven Young Bear, her law degree and her career were suddenly no longer enough to sustain her. She'd known Steven for less than a day and already she wanted more out of life than going to work every day, spending long hours at the office, and coming home to an empty apartment.

Much more.

Molly marched to the kitchen, ignoring the packed picnic basket that silently mocked her on the counter. She'd clean the apartment. Lord knows it could use it. She'd start by washing the windows, her most dreaded of all chores. She reached for a roll of paper towels, retrieved the glass cleaner from beneath the kitchen sink, and snapped on a pair of yellow latex gloves. She was halfway through the third window when a firm knock at the door startled her. She paused and smoothed her hair off her forehead with the back of her hand. "Who is it?"

"Steven Young Bear."

Molly crossed rapidly to the door, snapping the dead bolt back and releasing the security chain. She opened the door wide, still clutching the spray bottle of window cleaner and the crumpled wad of paper towels in her yellow-gloved hands. He was *here,* standing right in front of her, within arm's reach. She had to look up to meet his eyes.

Handsome and rugged in blue jeans, flannel shirt, sheepskin jacket. She fought to catch her breath and steady her racing heart. Miracle of miracles, Steven Young Bear had actually come.

"Sorry I'm late," he said in that deep, masculine voice. "I misjudged my driving time."

"Oh, you're not late at all." Flushed with embarrassment, she stripped off the gloves and motioned him in. "Have you had breakfast?"

"Yes, thanks. We should get on the road right away. It's a long haul."

"Of course. I'll just grab my jacket...." She snatched the picnic basket off the counter, feeling awkward and shy. "Okay. I'm ready."

Minutes later they were heading north toward Havre. Steven was driving, though she'd tried to persuade him to let her take her car. "No, thanks. Government studies have proved that red sports cars are involved in more accidents than any others," he said, deadpan, thus ending any further conversation about who would drive. She sat meekly in the passenger seat, hands folded in her lap, gazing out the window and reminding herself that she was a grown woman, not a giddy high-school girl with a crush on the captain of the football team. *Remember, you're Molly Ferguson, corporate lawyer at least for another day, and this isn't exactly a date,* she told herself firmly.

"You must hike," Steven said suddenly, and she glanced over at him, startled. "Those hiking boots of yours look like they've traveled up and down some pretty serious mountains," he said, eyes fixed on the road.

"Yes, they sure have." She peered down at them, flexing her ankles back and forth and silently thanking Dani.

"What's your favorite climb around here?"

"Actually, I haven't decided yet," she said. "What about you?"

"I've only climbed one mountain around here. *Cante Tinza.* Brave Heart Mountain. I went there on a vision quest and stayed up there for three days."

She shifted in her seat, glad to change the subject. "What's a vision quest?"

"It's a ritual period of solitary fasting in a sacred place that puts you alone before the Great Mystery, ready to make contact with the Higher Power and become one with the universe."

"That sounds like pretty serious stuff. Did you make the proper connections?"

He shook his head. "I got really cold and tired, and on the fourth day it began to rain and sleet, so I walked back down the mountain and went home. I guess the spirits didn't want to talk to me."

Molly studied his expression, searching unsuccessfully for the humor she heard in his voice. She looked out the window again and sighed. "I have a confession to make. These are my ex-roommate's shoes. Dani hikes and climbs all the time, she's a regular mountain goat, and when I told her we were going to look at a mountain, she took it upon herself to dress me appropriately for the occasion."

"You look very nice."

"Dani's my fashion consultant. She's descended of old French nobility and knows about such things, but I'm the daughter of an Irish laborer and a Scottish dreamer, neither of whom paid the slightest attention to what was in vogue. They were too busy trying to raise a bunch of wild kids." She heard his laugh for the very first time. It was a deep, sexy laugh that made her feel more like a giddy high-school girl than a corporate lawyer.

Molly stretched her legs out, flexed her ankles again in their stiff leather hiking boots. She longed to sit closer to him and trace the powerful curve of his shoulder with her fingers, breathe the intoxicatingly masculine scent of him. She'd never felt this way around John, or any other man, for that matter. It was with great effort that she forced herself to look out the windshield and not at Steven. "I think I'd like to climb a mountain some day," she said, watching the scenery flash by. "Just to see what the view's like from the top."

THEY REACHED THE MINE east of the Rocky Ridge Reservation at a little after 1:00 p.m. The name of the mine was displayed on a large sign at the base of the gated road. "Soldier Mountain Mine," Molly said, drawing her knees up on the Wagoneer's bench seat. "How do you suppose it came by that name?"

"Supposedly, a cavalry detail on a routine patrol was wiped out near here by the Sioux back in the 1870s. The story goes that a few of them escaped to high ground and made a stand there. Since this was the only high ground around, I guess that explains it."

"Did any of the soldiers survive?"

"Not according to history."

"Hmmm. Well, unless the guard opens the gate for us, it looks like we're in for a long and sneaky walk."

"There's no guard at the lower gate," Steven said, putting the Jeep into park. He reached into his hip pocket and pulled out his wallet. "Wait here."

Steven picked the lock on the gate in minutes, and he closed it behind them after driving the Jeep through. When he climbed back behind the wheel, Molly studied his impassive features. "So, what other tricks do you have up your sleeve, Young Bear? And how did you know there wouldn't be anyone in that guard house?"

"I've been here before on a Sunday. The Sioux on Rocky Ridge wanted to shut this mine down, and I was one of the people who tried to help them do it. It's polluting their drinking water and making them sick."

Molly frowned. "But if it's really doing that, why is it still in operation?"

Steven shifted into low gear. "Because the people drinking the water and getting sick are Indians." He drove slowly up the gravel road, not wanting to kick up dust and tell the whole world they were there. When he was almost to the very top, he cut the engine and they sat in silence while the ever-present wind rocked the heavy vehicle. They were hidden from the upper guard house and parked on the very edge of what to Molly appeared to be a huge, funnel-shaped crater with roads carved into the sides, spiraling around and down toward an unseen bottom far below. The magnitude of the drop-off gave her a frightening sense of vertigo, even while sitting within the safe confines of the Jeep.

"Ugly, isn't it," Steven stated. "This is what's left of a mountain, the highest point in fifty miles. Now it's a big poisonous hole in the ground." A dust devil swept across the bleak landscape in front of them and spiraled out over the pit, losing energy and vanishing in an amorphous puff of reddish soil. "This open pit mine is the same kind of operation your client plans for Madison Mountain."

Molly had never seen an open pit mine of this magnitude before. She gazed down into the crater. "Perhaps we just have to accept the fact that sometimes what's necessary to advance civilization isn't necessarily beautiful," she said.

"Perhaps," he mildly agreed. "But the cancer rates on this reservation are thirty times the national average. The drinking water is so bad that mine officials won't touch it. They buy their water. They have it hauled in by the truckload because they have the money to do that."

Steven was staring out the windshield with a calm expression on his face. Molly clasped her hands in her lap and struggled for a logical rebuttal, but she had no idea what to say. She felt the rift between their worlds widen until the wind that rocked the Jeep seemed to blow its lonesome chill through her soul. "This mine employs a lot of people from the reservation," she pointed out. "They don't have to work here, they choose to. Doesn't that tell you something?"

"Sure," he nodded. "That tells me that they're desperate enough to poison their grandchildren in order to feed their children."

"Maybe you're wrong," she said. "Maybe it's not the mine that's polluting the water...."

He turned his head. His dark eyes were inscrutable. "I could take you to the reservation and introduce you to some families who live there, who drink from the river. We can take samples of the water back and have them analyzed. There are government maps that show the movement of ground and surface water from the mine into the river. I'll show them to you and you can draw your own conclusions. You can even drink some of the water if you like. It's free. The tribe doesn't charge for it."

Molly felt an uncomfortable warmth rise in her face. She dropped her eyes. "That would be interesting, but we really don't have the time to go there today."

"No, I didn't think so," Steven said.

"We could plan another visit," Molly said, her face burning. She sat through an awkward silence, struggling to find a way beyond it. "Look, Steven, I'm fully aware that there's a lot I don't know yet, but I'm willing to learn. That's why I'm here with you today."

Steven started the Jeep and let the engine idle for a few moments before putting it into gear. "Let's find a prettier place than this to eat our lunch," he said.

The place they found wasn't all that pretty, but it was protected from the chill winds that swept out of the northwest, and the Milk River ran past it. The hollow he chose on the riverbank cupped the afternoon sunlight. She carried the basket of food to the place where he had spread his jacket for her to sit. "You'll be cold," she protested.

"Not here. Sit."

She sat, opened the basket, and began taking out the lunch she had packed for them.

"I hope you like deviled ham." She held out the sandwich and their hands touched as he took it from her. His fingers were warm and hers tingled where her hand had met his. "I didn't have much in the cupboard. Chips, pickles, two cans of cola." She glanced up, unnerved by his closeness and by the steadiness of his gaze. She adjusted her sunglasses. "You're staring."

"Sorry." He sat cross-legged on the dry grass and looked out across the river while he unwrapped his sandwich. Unseen on the highway above them, vehicles hurtled past with high-pitched whines. "We're sitting in the middle of the Lewis and Clark Trail," he said.

"Really? Wow." She looked around, seeing nothing extraordinary. "So how did you happen to get involved in environmental litigation? Did you always want to be an attorney?"

"The only burning ambition I had while growing up was to get off the reservation. As soon as

I graduated high school, that's what I did. I headed west, worked odd jobs when I ran out of money, and ended up pumping gas in a little town north of Seattle. Lots of logging trucks gassed up there. Big trucks carrying big trees, so big that sometimes only one log would fit on the truck. One day after work I caught a ride on a logging truck heading back into the woods. I wanted to see what those trees looked like before they were cut down."

Molly held her sandwich in her lap. "Were they redwoods?"

Steven nodded. "I stood at the base of one and listened to the roar of the wind blowing through the crown some two hundred feet above me and all of a sudden I saw things differently. I saw the stumps, what was left of the old-growth forest. Trees, forests thousands of years old, wiped out just like that. A little later I ran into a bunch of tree huggers staging a demonstration and volunteered to handcuff myself in a human chain around one of those trees to keep it from being cut. Needless to say, we were all thrown in jail, and while there I decided maybe it was time for me to do something more meaningful with my life than pump gas into logging trucks. So I went back to school, majored in environmental science, went to law school, and here I am."

"Here you are," Molly agreed. "Still fighting for the trees and the mountains." She studied him for a moment. "Tell me about your family."

"I have three younger brothers who live with their families on the res. Until this past spring, Pony was teaching at a reservation school just outside Fort Smith. Then she took a summer job working for Caleb McCutcheon at his ranch outside of Katy Junction, managing his buffalo herd. It sounds storybook, but the long and short of it is, they fell in love. They're getting married in another month and starting a special school right on the ranch for troubled kids."

"I think that's wonderful. Your sister seems like a very special person. Those kids are lucky to have her. What about your parents?"

"Both dead. My father was a steelworker. He fell off a scaffolding while on a job in New York City. We were still pretty young when it happened. My mother never recovered from his death. She died two years later and we kids were parceled out to relatives. My old aunt Nana took all us boys, and Pony was raised by our grandmother, who taught her the old ways."

"I'm sorry about your parents," Molly said. "I can't imagine not growing up with mine. In fact, I can't imagine ever being without them, even when I'm in my nineties." She paused in the act of peeling the plastic wrap from her sandwich. "Tell me about Ken Manning. Obviously the two of you are acquainted."

Steven took a bite of his sandwich and watched a flock of birds skim across the surface of the river. He popped the top of his soda can and chased the sandwich down with a big swallow. "I've known him for several years now. We've crossed swords on more than a few occasions. He's wealthy and high powered, and has strong connections with the Mountain Militia."

Molly raised her eyebrows. "Oh? What's that?"

"An organized citizen's group that holds regular meetings to discuss things like local politics, government at the federal level, and semiautomatic assault weapons. They have close ties with the National Federal Lands Conference and the Wise Use Movement, both borderline right-wing antienvironmental lobbies funded by oil and mining interests."

"Well, the odds are I'll never sit next to him again at any public hearings after my last performance, and anyway, my client's lifestyle is none of my business. I'm merely representing his company's interests." She narrowed her eyes. "Semiautomatic assault weapons? Dare I ask what connection they have to local and federal government?"

He glanced at her long enough for her heart rate

to accelerate, then took a bite of the sandwich, chewed with a contemplative expression. "Good sandwich." Took another bite and washed it down with soda, then set down his soda can and leaned toward her. His strong fingers swept a curl of her hair back behind her left ear. He was so close that she could smell the scent of his skin, and the brush of his fingers against her ear made her catch her breath around a fluttering drum of heartbeats. She suddenly hoped beyond hope that he would kiss her, but he didn't. Instead, he sat back and regarded her with those calm dark eyes. "I've been wanting to do that ever since that very beautiful curl escaped from your very beautiful braid," he said.

She laughed shakily, her heart hammering. "Thanks. I need all the help I can get when it comes to controlling my hair."

"As far as the militia is concerned, guns and politics sort of go together out here. Some folks still regard this as the Wild West. I was threatened once after speaking at a public hearing against the proposed logging of a wilderness area that had been burned in a forest fire. The proposal hinged on an upcoming house vote for managing public lands, so naturally everyone in the environmental camp was fighting to swing the house in favor of protecting the wilderness. I happened to be spearheading the environmentalists. This big guy with buzz-cut hair got right in my face and told me if they couldn't beat me at the ballot box, they'd beat me with a bullet."

Molly paused, the sandwich halfway to her mouth. "You're not serious."

"The militia can get pretty nasty."

She lowered the sandwich. "If you don't mind my asking, what's wrong with logging a burned forest?"

"It was in a designated wilderness area, and they wanted to build major logging roads to access the standing timber. A lot of the trees weren't dead, and even if they were, fire is all part of the natural process. Big permanent logging roads aren't."

"So you risked getting shot just to protect a bunch of scorched trees?"

"It's the principle of the thing. You have to pick your fights. I thought we might win that one."

Molly took a small bite of her sandwich and chewed, frowning. "So what happened?"

"Money and politics happened. The logging industry won the vote, and the big roads went in. The trees are all gone now, and soil erosion is silting up the spawning grounds in the river. The same old story is being played out in other places, too. It's hard to stand up to big industry."

"People need jobs."

"What kind of jobs will the loggers have when the last tree has been cut?"

Molly saw the rift widening between them again. "You think the mining industry is a greedy monster, don't you?"

"I think we need to start treating this planet with greater respect, as if the future mattered."

"Do you have any children?"

He drained the last of his soda and lowered the can. "Is this a loaded question?"

"Not at all. I'm just curious."

"No children, never been married. You?"

Molly shook her head. "But I understand how people feel about bringing jobs into a community. I understand the importance of putting food on the table when you have children to feed. A mine on Madison Mountain will bring a lot of good paying jobs into that depressed area. It will make life better."

"Better for whom? The people who live there now, who love the place just the way it is, or the people who would move there to get the good jobs? And how do you tell the people who live there now that their depressed lives are about to change for the better, when their lives are already just the way they want them to be?" He reached for the picnic basket and peered into it. "Did you bring anything for dessert?"

Molly sighed. "No, sorry. We can stop for an ice cream on the way back. I know a great place just outside of Helena that has the best double-fudge chocolate-chip ice-cream cones on the planet."

STEVEN DROVE DOWN THE HIGHWAY toward Helena wondering how accurate his gas gauge was. He'd never redlined it before. He'd always paid attention to things like how much gas was in his vehicle before taking a long trip, but for some reason this time he'd spaced it out completely. The last thing he needed right now was to run out of fuel.

"I'm sorry, Steven." Molly was tucked beneath his sheepskin jacket, gazing out the side window. "It seems like I have to say that an awful lot when I'm around you."

"For what?" Steven said. She'd just finished telling him all about her family. Her mother and father. Her brothers. Her aunts and uncles and grandmothers and grandfathers, the place in Scotland where her ancestors were buried near the ruins of a crumbled castle, and the old Roman sword her great-great-grandfather had plowed up in his Irish potato field that her father still had. It was a colorful history, and he couldn't imagine why she would be apologizing for it.

"For being so argumentative. I practically forced you to take me to see that mine, show me something relevant to the New Millennium project, tell me important things, teach me what I need to know so I won't make a fool out of myself again, and all I wanted to do was defend the mining industry because I happen to represent it. I'm sorry."

"My intention wasn't to put you on the spot."

"I know that. And I really do want to go back and visit the reservation when we have more time." She shifted, turning to face him. "I keep thinking about that guy that threatened to shoot you," she said. "And the fact that Ken Manning might be associated with that group. And the fact that such groups even exist."

"I guess everyone needs a hobby," Steven said. The engine faltered and a fist of anxiety clenched in his stomach. Just one more long uphill, one more mile...

"I was threatened once, too," she said as if recalling some long-buried memory. "Not quite as violent as your threat, but it was scary."

"Oh? Where?" Foot off the gas pedal now, coasting down the hill...

"In high school, by three big, tough girls. They cornered me once after freshman gym class in the locker room and said I was a witch, told me they were going to cut all my hair off and light it on fire. My hair was a lot longer back then, and if anything it was even redder than it is now."

The Jeep felt like it was hitting invisible barriers as the carburetor began starving for fuel. He could see the gas-station logo up ahead. "What did you do?"

"I told them if they gave me the scissors I'd cut it myself and they could do whatever they wanted with it. I didn't care. So they gave me the scissors and I cut my hair really short. Things were progressing nicely but just when I was almost finished, I nicked my hand with the scissors and made it bleed. And although I'm a strong person, I have one awful weakness. I faint at the sight of my own blood. So down I went onto the bathroom floor, out like a light. Caused quite a commotion at school, but those girls never bothered me again." She paused and frowned out the windshield. "Do you think we'll make it to the gas station?"

"I hope so. I don't feel like pushing." He lost the power steering when the engine died and had to wrench the wheel hard to guide the Jeep up to the gas pumps. Never again in a million years would he be this lucky. "What did your parents have to say about all that?" he asked as they coasted to a stop.

Molly smiled. "My mother cried and my father was so mad he called the school and threatened a lawsuit. My brothers made fun of me, like they always did, but in the end, I survived."

"You have beautiful hair. Those girls were just jealous." Steven got out and filled the Jeep's tank. Then, when they were back on the highway just south of Fort Benton, he said, "Forgive me for asking, but with a weakness like fainting at the sight of your own blood, how did you ever manage to survive growing up in a family with all those brothers?"

"It wasn't easy," she admitted. "I was unconscious throughout most of my early childhood years."

He laughed. "You'll have to tell me where this famous ice-cream place of yours is."

"It's just before we reach Helena." They sat in silence for a while with just the whine of tires on the highway in the background. Molly shifted in her seat, facing him again. "What does your girlfriend think about what you do?"

Steven switched on the headlights. "No girlfriend. Makes things a lot easier."

"I suppose it would, especially if you're getting death threats from a radical right-wing militia group."

"That was over two years ago. What about you?"

"My death threats were all in high school."

"I mean, your boyfriend."

She stretched her legs and sat up a little straighter. "No serious boyfriend. I was too busy going to college and law school and passing the bar exams and trying to impress the law firm that finally hired me on. No time for matters of the heart."

"Must get kind of lonely from time to time."

"Sometimes," Molly admitted. "But mostly I've been too preoccupied to notice." She shifted in the seat again and he felt her eyes studying him. "Of course, that could all change in a moment's notice," she said. "We never know when we're going to meet that special someone that tips us right over the edge."

"I guess not," Steven said. She was so young, so naive, so painfully innocent. Still believing in that dream, still waiting for true love to tip her over the edge. But no boyfriend? That surprised him, given her natural beauty and lively personality, though he did understand about the rigors of law school. He'd spent all his time immersed in textbooks, struggling to make passing grades. Dating had been the farthest thing from his mind. He glanced at her briefly before focusing his attention back on the road. Her features were soft in the dusky light, her eyes dark, mysterious hollows in the milky paleness of her face.

"Whenever I see an old couple strolling along,

holding hands, I know that someday I want to have a relationship like that," she said, looking out the side window. "I want to be holding my husband's hand when I'm eighty years old, and still thinking of him as my lover and my best friend." She was quiet for a few moments and then he felt her eyes on him again. "I learned a lot today, Steven," she said softly. "Thank you for your patience with me."

WHEN STEVEN PULLED UP in front of Molly's apartment building, her heart rate accelerated with anxiety. Their time together was rapidly running out and in spite of her attempts to reach a deeper level of communication with him, he had remained impersonally friendly. She felt vulnerable and foolish for confiding her feelings about true love, yet in spite of Steven's maddening reticence, she found him very easy to talk to. She only wished he would reveal a little more of himself, and show a lot more interest in her. But unless he suddenly opened up in a big hurry, it seemed their nonexistent relationship was about to come to an abrupt end.

"Would you like to come in?" she said, a clumsy shyness nearly overwhelming her ability to speak. "I owe you a meal, and I'm a great cook, especially if you like boiled cabbage. You could admire my original Remington print while I prepare you an authentic Irish supper."

"Thanks for the offer, but I'll have to take a rain check," Steven responded. "It's getting late, and tomorrow's a working day for the both of us." He climbed out of the Jeep, opened her door, and took her hand to help her out, something no man had ever done before and he'd already done twice. He walked her up the flight of stairs and when she fumbled with the key, fingers trembling with nervousness, he took it from her, opened the door, and handed it back without a word.

She hesitated in the doorway, desperately trying to think of a way to keep this from being a forever goodbye. Was it possible that love at first sight could happen to one person, while the other remained indifferent? Was it possible that Steven didn't feel any of that special chemistry that flowed between them at all? "Thank you for the ice-cream cone."

"You're very welcome."

Another painful pause. "If I can't convince you to come inside with promises of boiled cabbage and Remington prints, I guess this is good night, Steven Young Bear." She hoped on the one hand that she didn't sound as desperate as she felt, and on the other that he would sweep her into his arms and kiss her breathless.

"Good night, Molly Ferguson," he said as he turned away.

"Wait," she said, taking an involuntary step after him and damning herself even as she did. "Aren't you going to ask what my thoughts are about New Millennium Mining after today's field trip?"

He paused, glancing back. "I know what they are."

"But..." She floundered in another wave of shyness. "Aren't you going to try to change my mind?"

His eyes were impossible to read. "No," he said.

She clutched her keys tightly, sharp metal biting into her palm. "So, that's it? You drive me to this open pit mine, show me how ugly it is, tell me that it's killing a lot of people, and then you bring me back here and say good night. No closing arguments?"

"No closing arguments."

She took a step back, thrown completely off balance by his candor. "Well, okay, then, counselor. Thank you again for everything, and good night."

"Good night, Molly."

She leaned over the stairwell and watched him walk down the stairs. He was a powerful, graceful man. Completely confident and self-possessed. She yearned for him to stop and look up at her with a parting promise that he'd call her again very soon, but he didn't. "I had a really good time today," she said, but she spoke the words very softly, breathed them, really, and if he heard them, he made no response.

BACK IN HIS VEHICLE, pulling away from the curb, Steven grappled with a bewildering tangle of emotions he'd never felt before. What was it about Molly Ferguson that grabbed him and wouldn't let go? She wasn't the sort of person that he should be the least bit attracted to. She didn't share or even understand his feelings about protecting the environment. To him the word *gold* brought images of cyanide heap-leaching pits and poisoned waterways, whereas Molly heard the word *gold* and thought *jewelry*. There was absolutely nothing about her that should appeal to him…and yet he had very nearly taken her up on that offer of an Irish supper.

Was he *that* lonely and desperate that he would try to put the moves on a fellow attorney who had asked him as a courtesy to show her what the New Millennium mine on Madison Mountain would look like? She was a young and inexperienced intern just trying to understand the issues, and he had very nearly taken advantage of her. Dangerous stuff, especially when they were both involved in what could become a nasty bit of litigation between mining and environmental concerns. A definite conflict of interest.

The drive to Bozeman was filled with a silence so oppressive that Steven turned on the radio, and while the nonstop cacophony bombarded him, he wondered what Molly was cooking and which of Remington's prints she had on her apartment wall, but most of all he kept wondering what it would have been like to kiss her.

He had wanted to. Back at the picnic spot when he smoothed that stray lock of hair behind her ear, he had wanted to kiss her. Standing outside her apartment door, saying good-night to her just a few moments ago, he had wanted to kiss her. Perhaps now was the time in his life that he needed to go to the mountain on another vision quest. Perhaps now he needed to fast and suffer several long, cold sleepless nights in order to drive the heat of this red-haired white woman from his blood.

Or maybe all he needed was a little time to regain his equilibrium. If Manning had his way, Molly would be removed from any association with the New Millennium mine project and Steven would never see her again. They certainly didn't live in the same town or travel in the same social circles. This strange, wild fever she'd ignited in him would slowly subside. All he needed was a little time....

He reached his house in Gallatin Gateway by nine-thirty. He was hungry and looked in the refrigerator for something quick and easy. There was a fair assortment of things he liked, but his eye was arrested by a small green cabbage in one of the vegetable drawers. He used cabbage frequently as an ingredient in salads and stir-fries, but he'd never regarded it as the main course. He pulled it out and hefted it. Minutes later it was quartered and boiling in a covered pot, and the kitchen filled with the strong, steamy smells of what he assumed was a classic Irish meal.

He ate at the kitchen table with the ever-present law books laid out around him. He first tried seasoning a cabbage wedge with salt, pepper and butter. Then he retrieved a bottle of French dressing and doused another wedge and tried it. Italian on the third. Plain vinegar on the fourth with a glass of red wine. He ate the entire cabbage.

Without a doubt, it was the worst meal he'd ever voluntarily consumed.

He took this as a sign, and instead of taking the memories of a wild redhead to his bed, he took one of his books and studied until well past midnight…but his dreams betrayed him in the early hours of the new day.

CHAPTER FOUR

MOLLY WAS CALLED on the carpet first thing on Monday morning by Mr. Skelton, one of the firm's three senior partners. She tried not to be intimidated by the fact that he was wealthy, successful and one of the most eminently respected members in a law firm she had barely managed to hire into. She stood before him in his office, determined to be professional. "As I've already explained, Mr. Skelton, it was an extremely unfortunate set of circumstances," she said. "I was asked just three hours prior to that public meeting if I could temporarily replace Brad as New Millennium's legal representative, and I studied the file up until I had to leave for the meeting. Unfortunately, it just so happens that Tom Miller gave me the *wrong* file."

"Ken Manning is demanding a written apology," Jarrod Skelton said in his stern yet patronizing way, pushing out of his dark green leather chair. "Molly, surely you can understand the position I'm in." Skelton had gained weight recently, and his vest strained to hold its own against his pampered paunch. He tugged at it self-consciously as he rounded his desk. "Don't take this personally. You understand that we have to appease him. New Millennium is a subsidiary of Condor International, and they've been one of our biggest clients for several years. It's an extremely important and profitable account for us."

"I'm fully aware of that," Molly said, "but I can't help but take this personally. This was the first real project I've been entrusted with since I was hired, and I wanted to make a good impression. I wanted to prove my worth to you. The car accident was unavoidable, but I can't explain why Tom would give me the wrong file to study. Sourdough Mine and New Millennium are pretty far apart in the file cabinet. Have you asked him about that?"

"I just came from his office. He explained that a clerk must have misfiled the papers in the wrong folder, and he never thought to check the file's contents before giving it to you."

"Perhaps that's what happened, but I don't think it's fair that I should take all the blame."

"Mistakes are made," Skelton said with an impatient gesture. "Unfortunately for you, that seems to have been the case, and somehow we must atone for it. Besides, Tom's leaving the firm. If we tried to implicate him in this matter, it would make you look even worse. We have to appease Ken Manning, and he's asked for a written letter of apology from you. Brad's meeting with him for lunch. He said he'd deliver it for you."

In the silence that followed, the perfectly modulated and rhythmic cadence of Skelton's twenty-thousand-dollar custom-made cherry grandfather clock gave a beat to the time it kept. Ticktock, ticktock. Never varying, always the same, the clock gonged on the hour and half hour and the entire office measured their day by the time it kept. Molly listened to the clock as heat climbed into her face and wished that her Irish temper wasn't so blatantly visible, but she could see no reason why Tom shouldn't share the blame, even if he was leaving the firm. Or better yet, shoulder all of it, since Molly was sure he'd switched files on her deliberately. But clearly, Skelton had already decided what the course of action should be, and she was in no position, as a lowly intern, to second-guess him.

"I could deliver the letter myself," Molly said. "Wouldn't that be better, Mr. Skelton?"

"I got the distinct impression from Manning that he'd rather not see you again. I'm sorry, Molly. Brad's meeting him at two at the club. If you could have the letter ready…?"

"Of course," Molly said. "I'll get right on it."

Her throat squeezed up around her final words and she left Skelton's office, her eyes stinging with tears. She mustn't let him see her cry. Crying was for weak, silly women and she was neither weak nor silly, just spitting mad. She retreated to her office and closed the door behind herself, sinking into the chair behind her desk and clasping her trembling hands atop it. For a long while she was unable to do anything but seethe, yet somehow she had to compose a note of apology to that awful Ken Manning, and to do that she had to quell her murderous thoughts about Tom Miller. She drew a shaky breath and brought up the writing program on her computer. Fingers poised over the keyboard, she eyed the blank screen and the blinking cursor as if both were mortal enemies.

"Dear Mr. Manning," she began. "Please accept my deepest apologies for…"

For what?

"…for allowing myself to be so deliberately and cruelly deceived by my colleague, Tom Miller, whose immature and reprehensible actions caused me to fail you so terribly at the public meeting in Moose Horn Friday evening. Apparently he thought substituting the wrong file for me to study was fair payback for my repeated refusals to date him, which no doubt bruised his glorified male ego."

She scrutinized the words and tried to calm her pounding heart. She deleted the entire opening and sat for a few moments more, thinking about her mother and father and how devastated they would be if she was fired from this prestigious law office after bragging about her to all their friends and acquaintances nonstop for the past year.

"Please accept my deepest apologies for failing to represent you adequately at the public meeting in Moose Horn on Friday evening. I was ill prepared, and can offer no excuses that could possibly forgive such a blatant transgression on my part.

"Furthermore, I also apologize for being late to the aforementioned meeting and for arriving with the attorney representing the citizens of Moose Horn.

"In closing, Mr. Manning, I hope you understand that my actions and behavior yesterday evening were no measure of my usual standards, nor did they represent in any way the excellent legal representation consistently provided to both you and your parent company by the law firm of Taintor, Skelton and Goldstein.

"With utmost respect and deepest apologies…"

Molly closed her eyes, rotated her shoulders and took a deep, even breath. Steven had said that Ken Manning was involved in the Mountain Militia. She wondered if that organization had a Web site, and if it did, what it would be like. Just the idea of Ken Manning being connected to a militia was a little frightening. Semiautomatic weapons, Steven being threatened. She wondered if Mr. Skelton knew....

JEFFERSON WAS A TWO-HORSE TOWN, and Steven had no trouble finding Maffick's Salvage, the garage where Sam Blackmore's ruined station wagon had been hauled. "I've done a preliminary autopsy on the wreck," Maffick said when Steven asked about the station wagon. "The police asked me to give it a once-over, but everything seemed to be in working order." Maffick wiped his greasy hands on a rag he pulled out of his hip pocket. He was lean and wiry, in his early sixties, with faded blue eyes and three days growth of a beard that was mostly salt with a dash of pepper. "Take a look if you want. A lot of folks've already come by. They like to see the blood, I guess. I should charge admission, make some money. It's out back of the garage. Can't miss it."

The station wagon was a crumpled mess. Windshield missing, roof flattened onto the backrest of the seats, and a lot of blood in the driver's seat. Steven wasn't a physician but he did know that dead men didn't bleed. The crash hadn't killed Blackmore right away, though it seemed impossible he could have survived it long enough to bleed that much.

Maffick was working on salvaging the starter out of an old pickup that looked like it couldn't possibly have anything useful left on it. He shook his head when Steven asked him about finding anything inside of the vehicle. "Nope. The police must've took out all his personal belongings before I hauled it here. Nothing left but the blood when I got it."

The sheriff's department that had responded to the crash was twenty miles north of Jefferson, and when Steven knocked on the office door, the sheriff himself opened it, sandwich in one hand, chewing. "Sorry to disturb your lunch," Steven said as he introduced himself. "I phoned you earlier this morning about Sam Blackmore."

"Oh, sure," the sheriff said around a mouthful, opening the door wide and motioning him in. He extended his hand. "Conrad Walker." Walker was close to Steven's age, in his early thirties. Medium height and build wearing a tan uniform, big badge and pistol holstered on his hip.

"I was wondering what happened to Sam Blackmore's digital camera, his briefcase, and the water samples that he was carrying."

Walker frowned. "What?"

"Did you search the interior of the vehicle at the crash site?"

"Of course." The sheriff stood a little taller, immediately on the defensive. He laid the sandwich atop a wrapper on his desk. "When there's a death involved, we follow strict procedure. There was no camera, no briefcase."

"What about a container filled with vials of water?"

"No. His wallet was on him, and some loose change in the ashtray. There were a few pieces of junk mail, an empty paper coffee cup, and a sandwich wrapper from Happy's Hamburger Joint."

"Any money in the wallet?"

"Thirty-six dollars in various denominations and a Susan B. Anthony coin."

"Did you examine the vehicle at the crash site?"

Walker's flush deepened. "Of course."

"Might you have been distracted by having to deal with the body?"

"Is this some kind of cross-examination?"

"I spoke to a person who claims that Sam Blackmore had a digital camera, five hundred dollars in cash, and a case of water samples with him in his vehicle on the morning that he crashed."

"Maybe he went somewhere before he drove up on the mountain." The sheriff shrugged. "But I can tell you this. There was nothing in the car with him but what I told you."

"What time did you reach the accident site?"

Walker thought for a few moments. "Just past eleven."

"Was the vehicle's engine still warm?"

"I…" The sheriff began to look embarrassed and shook his head. "I don't know. I didn't check. Maybe someone else did…."

"Who discovered the wreck?"

"One of the contractors driving a dump truck. It was just lucky he spotted it, the damned thing was way over the embankment, buried in the trees. He called for help on his radio and stayed until we arrived. We closed the road down shortly after that, once all the contractors were off the mountain."

"Do you have the dump-truck driver's name?"

"Of course, and the written statement he gave if you'd like to read it."

"I would. Where was Blackmore's body taken?"

"St. Mary's in Bozeman."

Steven nodded. "You saw it, of course."

"Yeah." The sheriff hooked his thumbs in his belt. "You wouldn't have been able to recognize him, even if he'd been a close friend. Poor bastard."

"Do you know if the hospital performed an autopsy on the body?"

Walker shook his head again. "I don't know. I mean, as far as we knew, it was just an accident, that's all."

"You think he was killed in the crash?"

Walker stared for a moment and then barked out a laugh. "What kind of a question is that? Of course he was killed in the crash." He paused and his eyes narrowed. "Why, you think there was foul play involved?"

"Blackmore had a briefcase, a digital camera and some important water samples. Where are they now? He was carrying a five-hundred-dollar cash retainer that he'd just received from the citizens of Moose Horn. What happened to that? There are some questions that need answering, that's all."

"Well, I can't say what happened to his stuff, but it was clear enough to me that he was driving too fast down that access road. Some people don't realize that loose gravel acts just like ice under a vehicle's tires. He came to that sharp corner and skidded right off the edge of the world. Murder?" Walker shook his head. "Excessive speed is what killed him."

AT THE HOSPITAL IN BOZEMAN, Steven learned that Blackmore's body had been released that same day to the funeral home and that a cause of death had been established. "Massive head trauma," the pathologist told him. "I estimated the time of death at somewhere between 8:00 and 9:00 a.m., but that's just an estimate. The postmortem was routine and uninvolved. I wasn't looking for anything suspicious, just blood-alcohol levels, other drugs, routine stuff we check for in all car-accident victims."

Steven mulled over the evidence on his way to the office and sat for a long while at his desk, jotting down what he'd learned and then studying his notes. He glanced at the phone several times and then finally threw down his pen and called information. "Butte," he said to the operator. "Sam Blackmore, Esquire."

Moments later a woman answered. He asked to speak to Mrs. Blackmore.

"This is she," the woman replied quietly.

Steven drew a steadying breath. "Mrs. Blackmore, this is Steven Young Bear. I'm an attorney and I knew your husband. I was very sorry to learn about his death."

"Thank you."

"Mrs. Blackmore…" he began, rubbing his forehead as he fumbled for the right words. "Mrs. Blackmore, according to a witness who saw Sam before he drove up to Madison Mountain, he was carrying his digital camera, some water samples taken from the Madison Mountain watershed, five hundred dollars in cash, and his briefcase. The police found none of these things in his vehicle after the accident. Did he, by any chance, stop at home or the office and leave any of it behind?"

There was a long pause. "No, no, I don't think so. None of it's here, at home. I haven't checked his office yet, this has all been such a shock, but I will, Mr. Young Bear."

"I'm sorry," Steven said. "I know this is a terrible time to be discussing these things—"

"It's all right," Mrs. Blackmore interrupted in a voice that trembled with emotion. "I understand what you're saying, and I won't lie to you. Sometimes I've imagined just this sort of awful thing happening to my husband. He fights for unpopular causes, just like you. My husband spoke of you often, Mr. Young Bear. He admired you greatly, and shared your passion in protecting the environment."

"Did he say anything to you about why he was going up on Madison Mountain? Was he meeting someone there?"

"No. That is, I don't know. Sam would never deliberately withhold things from me, but we were both so busy that sometimes..." Her voice halted around a surge of grief. "I'm sorry," she managed to whisper.

"Mrs. Blackmore, if you should find any of the missing items at his office, or see a five-hundred-dollar deposit on a bank statement, or remember something he said that might be pertinent, or if you need anything, any legal advice, anything at all, ever, please call me. Day or night. I'm in the phone book."

"Yes. I will," she choked out. "And thank you, Mr. Young Bear. Thank you for caring. His memorial service is being held this Wednesday."

"Yes. I saw the notice in the newspaper. I'll be there." Steven hung up the phone and dropped his head into his hands with a heavy sigh. Talking with Sam's wife, and her gentle, grief-filled voice, had left him feeling worse than ever about Blackmore's untimely death. Maybe the sheriff was right. Maybe Sam had just been driving too fast. But the murder of Mary Pretty Shield had made a cynic out of him…and Ken Manning was a dark and powerful common denominator.

MOLLY WAS SITTING at her desk, miles in arrears of researching upcoming litigation for fellow attorneys lucky enough to actively practice law, and at the moment, not really caring. Her eyes were riveted on the computer screen and her finger was on the mouse, scrolling down and down, reading about the Mountain Militia that Steven Young Bear had told her about. She was learning all about a group of people who took themselves way too seriously, and took the constitutional right to keep and bear arms to a whole new level that was radical to the extreme. When her phone rang, she was relieved to tear her eyes away from an entity she wished she'd never discovered.

She reached to pick it up. "Ferguson."

"Ms. Ferguson, this is Ken Manning. I was hoping I'd catch you in your office."

Molly's heart skipped several major beats. There was no way he could possibly know what she'd been doing. She cleared her throat and closed the computer screen, as if he might somehow catch a glimpse of it through the phone line.

"Hello, Mr. Manning. What can I do for you?"

"Brad gave me your note when we met at the club this afternoon," he said in a smooth, professional voice. "He's asked me to consider allowing him to keep you as his assistant in researching and presenting New Millennium Mining's proposal to the people of Moose Horn. He feels it's an important process for you to learn."

Molly could think of nothing remotely intelligent to say in response, and after a brief pause Manning continued.

"I agreed, on the condition that you act as his assistant and nothing more. In any public forum or interview with the press, he would be the one to speak on behalf of New Millennium. Are you following me?"

"I understand, Mr. Manning," Molly said, feeling that passionate Irish heat sweep up into her face.

"You should know that I only agreed because Brad insisted you're the best intern he's ever had."

"That's kind of him to say so," Molly replied, glad that Manning couldn't see her expression.

"Brad doesn't feel there'll be any problems with the permitting, in spite of the opposition from the townspeople."

"I'm sure he's right. Twenty-seven people can't possibly stop an eight-hundred-million-dollar project."

"No, but with the proper guidance they could slow things down considerably and cost us a lot of money. Steven Young Bear is a formidable opponent, and he's caused a lot of trouble for us over the years. Which brings up a certain contingency," Manning continued in that smooth, polished voice. "I would expect you to avoid any personal contact with him until this permitting process is wrapped up."

Molly's hand tightened on the receiver. "Mr. Manning, I can assure you that my professionalism is beyond reproach and I would never discuss New Millennium's business outside of this office."

"I'm not questioning your professionalism, I'm laying down the ground rules. Young Bear is connected with the radical environmentalist movement in these parts. They're an anti-industrial, pro-environment group who believe that God is nature and nature cannot be defiled at any cost. These people would halt progress and sacrifice civilization to protect a tree. They choose land over people, mountains over people, and wildlife over people. I prefer that any attorney representing my interests not conduct personal relationships with radicals like that. I'm sure you can understand where I'm coming from. Just being seen with him in public would paint you with the same brush."

Molly recalled Steven's comments about starving the grandchildren to feed the children, about fighting a proposal to build logging roads into a designated wilderness area, about voluntarily handcuffing himself to a redwood tree to keep it from being cut. He was definitely pro-environment, but she would hardly consider him a dangerous radical. "If you consider Young Bear to be a serious threat, then these radicals, as you refer to them, must make sense to someone."

"Both the Environmental Protection Agency and Bureau of Land Management used to be staffed by spineless puppets, and Young Bear knew how to pull all their strings. He'd use any legislation he could to throw up roadblocks.

"Fortunately, the current administration's

holding strong against that kind of environmental arm twisting, but make no mistake, Young Bear's the most dangerous adversary we have. If he had to choose between saving an ancient redwood tree or saving your life, he'd choose the tree because to him that tree represents God, whereas you?" Manning's voice roughened with emotion as he concluded, "You're just a goddamned human."

THAT EVENING Molly lay on her living-room sofa, portable phone pressed to her ear. "I don't know what to do, Dani," she said. "A part of me wants to call Ken Manning back and tell him he and his New Millennium mine can go to hell, but assisting Brad with the permitting process is the most important project I could be involved with right now, and it's the only way for me to save face after that disastrous Moose Horn town meeting."

"Did Manning actually say you weren't to see Steven? Did he out-and-out forbid it?"

"He made it very clear that if I decide to work as Brad's assistant there can be no contact with Steven on a personal level."

"Do you *want* contact with him on a personal level? I mean, you haven't said a thing about him since last Saturday. The two of you spent the entire day together, and you haven't mentioned a word about it. I know that as your best friend in the whole world it's probably none of my business, but what happened?"

"I told you that it wasn't a date. And nothing happened."

"Baloney," Dani said. "I may not be in the room with you, but I know you. You have pathos and heartache written all over you. Tell me everything, or I'll never let you borrow my emerald earrings for that first dinner date."

"Nothing happened," Molly repeated. "He showed me the open pit mine, and it was ugly, which was about what I expected. Afterwards, we found a place to eat our picnic lunch. We stopped for an ice-cream cone at that little stand north of town, and then he brought me home."

"That sounds nice. Then what?"

"He walked me to my door, like a true gentleman, whereupon I asked him in for an Irish supper."

"Surely not," Dani protested. "I thought you said you *liked* this guy."

"Like him?" Molly knew the word *like* didn't begin to describe her feelings. She could still feel the warm tingling where his fingers had brushed her ear. "I don't think I've felt this way about anyone before. Not that it matters. He declined the invitation. And it's just as well that the night ended that way. Steven's strictly off-limits until this New Millennium project is pushed through."

Dani's sigh was loud in Molly's ear. "Oh, for heaven's sake. Call him up and tell him what's going on. I'm sure he knows how political things can get. He sounds like a really nice guy and I'm sure he'll understand. Besides, the permitting process might not take that much time."

"Oh, Dani, the way I feel right now, if it only took a week, that would be seven days too long."

"*Call* him."

"If Steven wants to see me again, he'll call me. I gave him every opening to do so. And if by some miracle he does, I'll have to tell him what Manning said and see how he reacts to that. But he won't call. Why should he? We're standing on opposite sides of a tall fence that divides two very different worlds."

STEVEN STACKED the supper dishes in the sink and reflected on how long the day had been, how drawn out and stressful and how unprofitable. He had neglected his other paying obligations and given all of his energies to a cause that promised no monetary compensation whatsoever. Wealth would elude him as long as he continued down this path, but wealth had never been his motivation. He had a nice house, one he'd helped build himself, but he'd nickel-and-dimed it, and he'd be paying down the mortgage until he was an old man. His Jeep was an extravagance he sometimes regretted when the monthly payments came due, but the reality of it was that he needed dependable transportation in a county that dished out six months of nasty winter weather. He was getting by, but it was a constant struggle.

Attorneys like Molly Ferguson lived on a different level. They breezed through their days confident and secure. They shopped with impunity and drove fast, fancy cars. And yet…what made her so different? What was it about her that had tangled his thoughts so? Why did he glance at the phone and wish it would ring because she had decided she missed him and needed to hear his voice?

Steven squirted a generous dollop of dish soap into the sink and ran hot water over the dishes. Better to let them soak for a while. Lasagna was a messy cleanup job. He turned off the tap, paced to the living room and then back into the kitchen to stand near the phone. He dug in his jeans for his wallet and pulled her business card from it. Stared at her name and the numbers listed beneath it, home, cell and office. She had beautiful red hair, intelligent hazel eyes and freckles that she tried futilely to conceal. She worked for a law firm that represented mining companies desecrating the natural world for short-term material gains. She was without a doubt the most compellingly beautiful yet hopelessly incompatible woman he could ever imagine himself pairing up with.

He picked up the wall phone in the kitchen and dialed her home number.

MOLLY SET THE CORDLESS PHONE aside after speaking with Dani. Her mood was no better, in spite of Dani's efforts to cheer her. The world was definitely a dark and dreary place. She closed her eyes and took a deep breath, released it. Deep breathing was supposed to be very therapeutic. She'd recently read that most people never drew a deep breath. They spent their entire lives shallow breathing, thereby considerably stunting their oxygen exchange capabilities, which correspondingly lowered their mean intelligence level. Or something like that. She drew a deep, even breath and held it until her lungs began to burn....

The phone rang beside her, startling the breath from her lungs, and Molly glanced at the clock on the wall. Nine o'clock. It was probably her mother, who always called right about this time. She hadn't been sleeping well lately, so Molly had told her that whenever counting sheep didn't work, she'd bore her into dreamland with one of her long-winded, one-sided and oh-so-boring conversations about day-to-day life as a first-year attorney. Molly reached for the phone. It would be good to talk to her mother, who somehow always managed to brighten the darkest of her days. "Once upon a time, there was a little girl who thought she could change the world by becoming a lawyer," she began by rote.

"Molly?" a deep and familiar voice said. Definitely not her mother.

Molly's eyes shot open and she sat up with an audible exhalation of air. She spun around and dropped her feet to the floor with a thump, hoping he hadn't heard that loud and undignified gasp.

"Oh, hello, Steven." Spoken in a cool, aloof and perfectly professional. She couldn't let him guess how desperately glad she was that he called. "I thought you were my mother. She always calls at this time of night."

"And you tell her a bedtime story?"

She closed her eyes, savoring the sound of his voice, which held an undercurrent of humor. "Something like that. What's up?"

"Did you happen to see the Sunday paper? There was a brief article about New Millennium and their proposed project on Madison Mountain."

"Really?" Molly was surprised. "No, I didn't, and nobody at the office mentioned it. Pro or con?"

"Neutral. Just states the facts. Are you still working for Taintor, Skelton and Goldstein?"

"Yes. And Manning's agreed to give me one more chance as Brad's very silent and mostly invisible assistant." She hesitated for a moment. "He doesn't like you very much, Steven. In fact, he regards you as a radical environmentalist."

He laughed. "No doubt he warned you that if we shared a ride again, or even spoke on the phone, he would consider it an act of treason on your part."

Molly closed her eyes and felt the sharp pain knife through her heart. "He said I could have no personal contact with you as long as I was representing his interests."

"That sounds like Manning."

"This permitting process probably won't take long," Molly said, but the words had an empty ring.

"Permitting processes can take years, especially when they're challenged. When it's over, maybe you could show me how you manage to boil a cabbage so it's edible," he said.

"I'd like that," she said, her voice barely above a whisper. "I'll even show you my original Remington print. And Steven? I'm sorry."

"You have to do what you think is right. You shouldn't have to apologize for that."

"Maybe, but I'm still sorry."

There was a long pause. "Me, too."

Molly set the phone down again and sat for a few moments, recalling every word of their conversation and trying to convince herself that it wasn't the end of the world. Steven certainly hadn't called just to tell her about a brief blurb in the newspaper. He'd called because he wanted to talk to her, which was a good thing. A great thing. And he was sorry that they couldn't see each other on a personal level until New Millennium was up and running. But what if the permitting process took years? If Steven was successful in spearheading strong opposition to the Madison Mountain project, it very well could. She pushed to her feet and padded into the kitchen to make herself a cup of tea, as if that might help fill the emptiness she felt inside.

CHAPTER FIVE

WHEN THE PHONE RANG the next morning, Steven had just stepped out of the shower and was barely one cup of coffee into the day. He picked up on his bedroom extension, hoping it would be Molly calling to tell him that she was dropping the New Millennium proposal because she couldn't stand the idea of not being able to show him how to cook a proper Irish meal that very evening.

"I'm sorry to call you so early, Steven." His sister's familiar voice came on the line, "but I need a huge favor from you."

"It's six-thirty, Pony. That's not exactly early."

"I thought lawyers did the nine-to-five thing."

"Lucky lawyers, maybe. Does this huge favor have anything to do with your wedding?"

There was a pause followed by a sigh. "Steven, we need a holy man."

"I thought you picked one already. Nana's brother."

"He can't do it. He's in the hospital. His asthma…"

"Too many years working in the mines."

"And so," Pony said, matter-of-fact. "We need someone else."

"And so," Steven echoed. "Naturally you called me, thinking I could pull the very best one out of my hat."

"We're doing the seven sacred steps. Our vows are written, and you happen to have close ties to the very best holy man alive."

"Pony…"

"Luther Makes Elk would do it, if you asked him. I know he would, even though Caleb is a white man." Her voice was determined.

"You would have *Luther* perform your ceremony? I thought you didn't like him."

"Why would you think that?"

"Because he didn't come to your fund-raiser for the school when you advertised that he would. He stood you up."

"Yes, but Steven, he is the holiest and most powerful of the Crow Indians. Of course I would have him perform my ceremony. And after all, he *is* your adopted grandfather."

He couldn't suppress the deep laugh that erupted. "Seven sacred steps?"

"Seven."

"Okay. I'll try and find him, but he's a shape-shifter."

"So are you. Thank you, Steven." But she didn't say goodbye or hang up. He stood dripping on his bedroom floor, phone to his ear, waiting patiently. "How is Molly?" she finally said.

Steven grinned, mystery revealed. "The real reason you called is because you're curious about my love life."

"As your sister, I have a right to be curious."

"Molly's fine, though I haven't seen her since the rules were laid out to her by her boss about consorting with the enemy camp. Are you disappointed or relieved?"

"I want you to be happy."

"Even if my happiness comes with red hair and white European ancestry?"

"Yes, even if. Caleb and I are having a barbecue this Saturday to celebrate the official opening of the school on the Bow and Arrow, and since you are responsible for making the school a legal entity, you have to come."

"Is that an order, or an invitation?"

"The barbecue begins at two and there is plenty of room for you to spend the night. Bring Molly."

"She won't come. She can't. She's been forbidden to have any contact with me as long as she's representing New Millennium Mining. It's a con-flict-of-interest thing."

"What does that mean?"

"It means if we get together on a personal level we might try to influence each other's thought processes and opinions, or accidentally divulge confidential information, and by doing so compro-mise our client's interests."

"You would never do that. Molly will come if you ask her. When do you think you'll be speak-ing to Luther Makes Elk?"

"When would you like to have an answer from him?"

"Steven." Pony's voice held an impatient edge.

"He doesn't have a phone, and he lives a long ways from here. He might not be home if I go to visit."

"I need to know, Steven. It's very important."

It was his turn to sigh. "Then I'll find him."

MOLLY BIT THE END of her pen and gazed out her office window. Noon, and after two hours she was no closer to providing Brad with the paperwork he needed to push forward with the permitting process for New Millennium mine. Her mind was definitely not on her work. She was thinking about Steven, wondering what he was doing, and if he was thinking about her even a fraction as much as she was thinking about him. She had glanced several times at her phone even though she knew calling him would be considered a crime punishable by death in Ken Manning's rule book.

And *why* was she wasting so much time thinking about a guy who probably didn't give a hoot about her? Except…except the way he had sounded when they'd last spoken on the phone, she was certain that he felt something, too. Maybe for him it hadn't exactly been love at first sight, but… She turned her eyes back to the computer screen with a frustrated sigh, thinking about New Millennium and the Sioux dying of cancer on the reservation near the mine Steven had taken her to see. What was the name of that place? Rocky Ridge? She typed in a legal search engine, entered her password, and within moments had forgotten all about her duties as Brad's assistant. The guilt she felt was fleeting. This was important, too. She needed to find out all she could about New Millennium Mining and its parent company, Condor International, because Steven would most certainly be using their every past environmental transgression as ammunition against any future projects on public lands. The better prepared they were, the better their chances of swaying the citizens of Moose Horn in their favor.

She hoped she wouldn't find any past transgressions. Condor International was a multibillion-dollar conglomerate with a very heavy-hitting reputation. Just because Steven had listed a string of past violations didn't mean they hadn't already been resolved in environmentally correct ways. Somehow she had to make Steven see that it was okay to take minerals out of the earth, that it could be done in a responsible fashion and that the land could be reclaimed and made as good as new when the project was complete. She had to make him understand that big business cared about the environment, too, and wasn't the greedy, heartless monster he made it out to be.

And so she began her Internet odyssey into the legal maze, when what she really wanted to do was pick up the phone and ask Steven if he missed her as much as she missed him.

STEVEN SPENT MUCH of the morning making phone calls from his office. He scratched out some of the names, underlined others and wrote brief notes around a few. All in all, he made pretty good headway in getting the ball rolling from a financial standpoint against the New Millennium Mining proposal. He'd just hung up from speaking with one of the bigwigs at the Wilderness Society and was staring at his notes when the phone rang. It was Amy Littlefield.

"We just sent out a mailing, like you suggested," she said. "A one-page summary of what's happening, and when the next public hearing is."

"Good. The more people who know, the better. We need to start collecting water samples. The ones Sam had with him in his car are definitely missing, along with his digital camera and the money you gave him as a retainer. And just this morning I uncovered an interesting glitch for New Millennium. The road they're building to the mine site hasn't yet been legally permitted. I filed an injunction two hours ago to stop them from using it or continuing the construction process until approval is granted through the proper channels."

"You mean, they built that huge road into a national forest without permission?"

"The permits are in the works, but yes, it would seem they've jumped the gun."

"Then no more traffic, no more trucks, and no more road building," Amy said heatedly.

"As soon as the injunction is enforced it will stop, but only temporarily," Steven said. "Everything will continue just as soon as the permits are in place."

"But they should be fined and punished," Amy protested. "Isn't someone supposed to be watching them?"

"The Forest Service, the BLM, and the Department of Environmental Protection are all federal watchdogs, but sometimes these things fall through the cracks."

"Or are deliberately ignored. I don't see how you can be so calm about it."

"This sort of thing goes on all the time," Steven said. "After a while it becomes the norm for powerful companies to bend the law and pay the fines when they're caught doing it."

"You mean *break* the law, don't you?" she said in a caustic voice.

"I've informed the newspapers, and several journalists were going to look into it. Violations like that could work in our favor if they generate publicity. Everything that brings the project in front of the public eye will help us at this point."

He heard Amy heave an exasperated sigh. "We're going to hold a bake sale to try and raise some money, and one of the local ranchers is donating a beef cow for us to raffle off." Her voice was flat with discouragement. "That isn't going to bring in a whole lot of cash, probably not even enough to pay you for attending that first meeting, let alone the second one, but we hope you'll come. It's the only chance we have to present a united front and put up a good fight."

"I'll be there," Steven promised.

He stared out the window after hanging up the

phone, thinking about fundraising, or trying to, but a certain red-haired woman kept distracting his concentration. He thought about the barbecue Pony had invited him to at the Bow and Arrow, that beautiful ranch on the edge of the Beartooth Wilderness, and the next thing he knew he was pulling Molly's card out of his wallet and dialing her office number. She answered on the first ring.

"Ferguson."

"Young Bear," he said, following her brusque lead. "I'm calling to invite you to a barbecue being held this Saturday at the Bow and Arrow."

"When?" No hesitation whatsoever on her part.

"Two o'clock."

"How do I find this place?"

"When you get to Katy Junction, take a left. You can't miss the ranch sign. It's about eight or ten miles from town."

"I'll be there," she said, and abruptly hung up the phone. Steven held the receiver to his ear for a few moments more, wondering how Pony had known that Molly would say yes, when he'd have bet his bottom dollar she'd politely refuse. He shook his head, marveling. Must be a woman thing.

MOLLY GLANCED FURTIVELY out her open office door. Life went on as usual in the corridors. No one was watching her or hovering near her door, eavesdropping. No one suspected that she had just been speaking with the firm's evil archenemy, making plans with him for a Saturday rendezvous at a ranch called the Bow and Arrow.

She drew a deep breath and tried to remember that she was supposed to be working while she was at work, but she couldn't concentrate. Steven Young Bear had just asked her on a date and she'd said yes. She'd said yes in spite of the fact that she wasn't supposed to see him, consort with him, talk with him, laugh with him, and certainly not fall in love with him. In spite of the fact that when she agreed to act as Brad's assistant, she'd sworn off all but professional contact with the opposition's lawyer. On the other hand, attorneys represented clients, but the clients didn't control their attorney's private lives. As long as there was no breech of contract, as long as they both acted professionally, as long as their private lives remained separate from their professional lives, there was no conflict of interest. What harm could possibly come from going with Steven to his sister's place for a barbecue?

She jumped out of her chair and paced to the window, gnawing at her fingernail. No harm would come. No one from the office would ever know. Certainly Ken Manning would never find out. She would meet Steven there and they would have a good time and then she'd come back home.

"Molly? Do you have those papers for me?"

Brad's voice startled her and she whirled around with a surge of guilt. He was hovering in her doorway, file folder in one hand, tie loosened, top buttons of his white shirt undone, hair tousled. He looked like he'd been busting his butt on the New Millennium permitting process and fully expected that she'd been doing the same.

"Ah, well, no, not exactly. Brad, could I speak with you for a moment?" His expression changed from intense to questioning, but he stepped into her office and waited. Molly crossed to her desk. "I've been doing some research and I think that you should be aware that Condor International is in court right now on four different EPA violations with two of their other mining subsidiaries, and if I can dig this stuff up in such short order, you can be sure Young Bear's all over it."

"So?"

"Well, I'm just pointing out that if push comes to shove, these pollution violations at other mining operations aren't going to look very good for our client. Two of the violations are so bad they've been proposed as Superfund sites."

Brad stared at her for a few moments more and then shook his head with a laugh. "Sometimes I forget how new to this you are. Don't worry about stuff like that, just get those papers together. We have to fast-track this permitting. The courthouse rumor mill has it that Young Bear filed an injunction this morning. He's just getting started making our lives miserable."

"How so?"

Brad shrugged. "He's shutting down the mine road, which is just bullshit theatrics on his part. The road permit's not approved, but it will be in a matter of a few weeks. Everyone knows that, including Young Bear."

Before she could respond, Brad left. She stood for a moment by her desk, thinking about what he'd just said, then glanced at her computer screen. After a moment, she sank down in her chair and tapped in another legal search engine. She still had plenty of time to get the paperwork to Brad before the end of the workday and plenty of questions she might find answers to on the Internet. Brad's comments had done nothing but increase her growing sense of unease. She had initially intended to sleuth out information she could use as examples to show how New Millennium's proposed mine would benefit the tiny community of Moose Horn, but the deeper she dug, the more confused she became.

Four days from now she would be joining Steven for a barbecue on the Bow and Arrow Ranch. Ethically she knew she couldn't discuss any of this with him, but morally she wanted to. She wanted to believe that economic health did not necessarily preclude environmental health, and that the two could and should coexist in a progressive society. That the New Millennium mine could bring a huge windfall to a podunk town like Moose Horn. That change was necessary, growth was necessary, and that a static environment was a dead environment. But as she scrolled through the endless list of violations and the repeated warnings and fines levied by the EPA against the Soldier Mountain Mine and three others owned by Condor International, she began to wonder if her righteous beliefs had any validity at all.

STEVEN LEFT HIS OFFICE EARLY to notarize and file some papers at the courthouse, and then, pausing on the courthouse steps, he thought suddenly about Luther Makes Elk and Pony's request to engage the old man's services for her upcoming wedding. The September afternoon was gentle and golden, and the fumes from the traffic swishing past made him long for the clean smells of blue sage and empty space that surrounded Luther's little shack. He glanced at his watch. It was getting late. He would be even later getting home if he made the side trip to see the holy man.

His adopted grandfather was a traditionalist elder who had once led the Crow into a battle that couldn't be won; a spiritual battle against the white missionaries who had sought to erase the culture, traditions and religion that made the Crow people what they were. It was an ugly battle that Steven Young Bear had no intentions of ever fighting, and yet, such was the irony of life. A step taken away from one place might very well lead back to it in the end. He'd been on the rez the night that Luther Makes Elk was arrested six years ago for leading the traditionalists in a ghost dance and prayer to return to the old times. Steven had been visiting Pony and his aunt Nana and at their insistence he had accompanied them to the ghost dance. In spite of his resolve to remain apart from it all, he had been mesmerized by the rhythmic heartbeat of the drum, by the star-studded night sky, by the sweet-spicy aromas of the sage and sweetgrass smudge.

He had felt as far removed as he could ever be from the white path he had chosen to walk as he watched the ritual dance, and yet it was that very path that had saved Luther Makes Elk in the end, after the blue lights and the sirens, after the forced dispersal of the traditionalists because of the lateness of the hour and the nervousness of the white farmers who lived on leased reservation lands.

At Pony's desperate urging, he had gone to visit Luther Makes Elk at the jail, to talk with him and explain why he had been arrested for accosting an officer of the law with his ceremonial drum, and ultimately, to post the bail that freed the old man. He'd even driven Luther back to his run-down shack in the foothills, not too far from where Pony lived. He had tried to leave then, but Luther Makes Elk had taken out the pipe and made a ceremonial smoke to share with Steven, and a young man did not show disrespect to an elder, especially a holy man.

Steven had reluctantly shared the pipe. After a contemplative pause, Luther had nodded and said, through a curl of blue smoke, "You walk a different path, but one day, your blood will be important to you again, and when that day comes you will become a great man." Luther had handed him the pipe and Steven had smoked. "I will have you be my adopted grandson." Luther had nodded again.

Steven had hidden his dismay from the old man. He did not want to be Luther Makes Elk's adopted grandson, but neither could he insult him. "I would be honored to call you grandfather," he'd said.

Luther had drawn a thin-bladed skinning knife from a sheath at his belt and drew a shallow cut across the heel of his hand. He handed the knife to Steven, who did the same. They clasped hands, blood to blood, and that was how Luther Makes

Elk, the legendary Crow holy man, became Steven's adopted grandfather, and why Steven, instead of heading home at the end of the day, was pointing his Jeep east, toward the reservation, to ask Luther if he would bless Pony's wedding to Caleb McCutcheon. Steven wasn't sure what Luther's answer would be. Luther had never before blessed the union of a white man to one of his own, and had said many times that he never would.

LUTHER MAKES ELK was not surprised to see Steven. "I cooked enough supper for you," he said by way of greeting as he stood in the doorway of his shack and watched Steven approach. His deeply wrinkled face was impassive yet his sharp black eyes missed nothing. "But you came too late," he added. "And so. The food is cold." He motioned Steven inside.

The sun had long since set and the air was growing chill. "I can't stay long, Grandfather," Steven said. "I came to ask a favor."

Luther paused on his way to the little propane stove in the corner of the one-room dwelling. "Sit and eat." He motioned to the only chair drawn up to the small metal table and Steven obediently sat. "I have gathered some things for your vision quest. An eagle feather. Four hardwood twigs to mark your place on Brave Heart Mountain. Red is the color of the cloth I tied around the twigs. Red seemed right somehow." He nodded. "Some bags of tobacco. Sage and sweetgrass for your smudge." He lifted a pot from the stove and set it in front of Steven. "Eat as much as you want," he said.

Steven took the offered spoon and pot of stew and dipped into it. "Grandfather, my sister Pony is marrying a white man. His name is Caleb McCutcheon and he owns the Bow and Arrow Ranch outside of Katy Junction."

"I got your traditional clothing, too," Luther said. "It's in the sack with everything else. You will need these things so the spirits can find you better. We will smoke the pipe together before you go. You can take the pipe with you. It is blessed."

Steven swallowed a mouthful of the stew. He glanced down at the pot, which was nearly full, then raised his eyes. "Grandfather, have you eaten?"

The old man nodded. "Twice, already. I waited, but like I said, you were late." His black eyes narrowed. "You don't like it?"

"It's fine." Steven took another reluctant bite.

"We should have a sweat-lodge ceremony," Luther said, "but there is no time if you are going to climb the mountain before dark."

"Grandfather, I can't go on a vision quest tonight. I have to work in the morning."

"You can't do your white man's work when your spirit is confused. You need to climb the mountain and let the Great Mystery explain itself to you and take the red fire from your blood before it makes you sick."

"I'll go as soon as I can, but it can't be tonight." Steven pushed the stew aside, realizing the futility of trying to explain the white man's way to an old traditionalist. "Pony wants to do the seven sacred steps at her wedding. The vows are already written, but she needs a holy man. She was hoping you might agree to conduct the ceremony."

Luther glanced down at the pot, and then at Steven. "I got to thinking about Johnny Bird, and I wondered, where did he get that meat? Johnny doesn't hunt. But then I tell myself, the meat is a gift. And so. I made a stew from it." He shook his head in faint apology. "It isn't very good, is it?"

MOLLY WAS PACING HER APARTMENT, microwaved dinner untouched, when the knock came at her door. She flung it open and pulled Dani inside. "Steven's invited me to the ranch where his sister lives this coming Saturday," she blurted out, slamming the door behind her startled friend.

Dani raised a hand to her temple as if momentarily lost in thought. "Wow, that's great, Molly. The way you sounded on the phone I thought maybe you'd been fired from your job or disfigured in a horrible car accident. Couldn't you have hinted at the good news and spared me losing several years of my life on the drive over here?"

"They're having a barbecue."

"You're kidding. What will those crazy ranchers think of next?"

"You're my wardrobe expert, my fashion adviser. Advise me."

"What time of day?"

"Two."

"Gee, that's a tough one. Appropriate attire for a ranch barbecue. Let me think." Dani's eyebrows drew together in an exaggerated frown. "Wait," she said, face clearing as she raised her hand, pointing to the sky. "I'm having a vision. Levi's. Cowboy boots. Nice leather belt. White linen blouse, dark gray or paisley tailored vest. Minimal makeup, maybe one or two pieces of jewelry, simple earrings, and I don't mean my emerald ones. Not appropriate for a ranch barbecue."

"What should I bring?"

"A couple of nice bottles of wine and a copy of your résumé."

Molly paced to the window, stared out into the darkness. "I know I shouldn't be going. I promised

I wouldn't see Steven other than professionally, and I should have said no when he asked, but I just couldn't. I'll take my chances and hope I don't get caught." She turned. "That's awful, isn't it?"

Dani smiled. "That's good. There's hope for you yet. And don't look so glum. The ranch owner might take pity on you and give you a job mucking out horse stalls or branding calves after you've been fired from that high-and-mighty law firm of yours."

STEVEN LISTENED to his phone messages when he got home that night. There were a few from colleagues touching base on various legal issues, a briefly worded message from Sam Blackmore's widow stating that Sam's digital camera, the water samples, the money and his briefcase were definitely missing and she had reported them stolen to legal authorities, and another from Conrad Walker, the sheriff who had conducted the preliminary investigation into Sam Blackmore's death. "Thought you'd want to know," Walker's rough voice said. "Blackmore's widow is pushing the district attorney for a forensic autopsy even though the medical examiner's preliminary findings turned up nothing suspicious."

Good news.

He pried off his shoes, retrieved a beer from the

refrigerator and padded into the living room to read the newspaper when his phone rang. "I'm sorry I was so abrupt on the phone today but I was afraid someone in the office might overhear," Molly said, and his heart jumped with gladness at the sound of her voice.

"How do you know your home phone isn't being tapped?" he said, dropping onto the couch.

"Somehow I don't think I'm that important."

"Oh, I don't know about that," Steven said, surprised at how easily the words came, and how much he meant them. Her soft laugh was followed by an awkward silence. "I'm glad you're going to the barbecue," he said.

"I'm glad you asked me." Another long pause, and then she cleared her throat. "Steven, maybe I'm way out of line bringing this up, could you tell me why there's no public record on file of any lawsuit being brought against the Soldier Mountain Mine by the tribe on the Rocky Ridge Reservation?"

Steven felt a jolt of surprise. He took a sip of beer to give himself time to collect his wits. "No," he said.

"But you told me that there was a lawsuit, and you helped them fight that battle."

"Yes."

There was a long silence on her end and then the soft sigh of defeat. "Okay, then. Here's an easier one for you. Can you tell me if there'll be dancing at this barbecue?"

"Probably. My sister likes to dance."

"Do you?"

"I didn't inherit the talent that she did, but I can do a passable Texas two-step."

"What's that?"

"That's a mandatory dance movement for anyone living west of the Mississippi."

She laughed again, and the warm sound made him smile. "I guess I have a lot to learn about this western stuff," she said.

"I'll teach you the two-step if you teach me how to cook a cabbage."

"Deal," she said. "Is this a casual event?"

"Everything at the Bow and Arrow is casual. It's a great place. You'll like it."

After they'd said good-night, he sat in silence for a long time, the newspaper lying forgotten on the couch beside him. He sipped his beer and stared at the wall and wondered why she'd asked him about the Soldier Mountain lawsuit. He'd only brought her there to show her what an open pit mining operation looked like. Her question had startled the hell out of him. He hadn't figured on her being interested in the plight of the Sioux who lived on Rocky Ridge and the uranium mine's long list of environmental violations. He hadn't even considered the possibility that she'd investigate the lawsuit. She'd already run into a major roadblock. Better to let her hit every wall and travel down every dead end until she gave up searching for the answers. Better to let her go on believing in truth and justice, law and order, and the sanctity of human rights, because when those beliefs died there was nothing left to hold on to.

He knew that better than anyone.

CHAPTER SIX

MOLLY DIDN'T SLEEP WELL that night. Just hearing Steven's voice had had the most disturbing effect on her. It wasn't enough to be talking to him on the phone, she wanted to be sitting with him in his cozy little living room, snuggling up next to him on the sofa, resting her head against his shoulder and gazing into the fire as he spoke. She knew it was nothing more than pure chemistry that she was experiencing. Pheromones. Wasn't that what those chemicals that attracted the opposite sex were called? What else could it be to have addled her head so completely? She hadn't known Steven long enough to be head-over-heels in love with him, and two people could hardly be more at odds when discussing big business and the environment.

She took her restless psyche to work and spent Wednesday morning compiling more of Brad's paperwork, but could find no satisfaction in it. She worked straight through lunch, using the time to catch up on filing and answering long overdue correspondence. Boring, routine stuff, not the sort of courtroom drama she'd imagined in law school. She kept glancing at the Internet icon on her computer desktop and reminding herself that she had stopped chewing her fingernails when she was fifteen.

Skelton stopped by her office later that afternoon. "Good job smoothing Ken's feathers," he said by way of greeting. "How's the permitting paperwork coming along?"

"Actually, there's been a bit of a snag." Molly rose from behind her desk, remembering at the last moment to slip on her shoes. "It's in regards to the access road being built on Madison Mountain. We just received this with the morning mail." She plucked the certified letter off the top of her desk and extended it to her boss. "Young Bear's filed an injunction in federal court to stop all work on the road. He alleges that New Millennium did not follow due process of the law and obtain the proper permitting before beginning road construction."

Molly paused for a moment while Skelton unfolded the letter, waiting for a reaction that never came. "It just so happens that he's right," Molly continued. "I phoned Mr. Manning earlier, and he admitted that since there was little reason to expect any problems, work on the access roads should proceed concurrent with the filing for permits and both he and Brad gave the go-ahead for that to happen. Mr. Skelton, is this normal procedure? When I advised Mr. Manning that the road work should be stopped immediately, he just laughed."

Skelton gave the letter a cursory glance before setting it on her desk. "Brad already informed me about this. It's no big deal."

"No doubt the newspapers will print something about it."

"Newspapers have to print something, or they'd go out of business pretty quick. That's small potatoes."

Molly took a deep breath. "While I was doing some research for Brad on this project, I did a quick background check on some of Condor International's other subsidiaries and discovered that this firm also represents the Soldier Mountain Mine near the Rocky Ridge Reservation. Didn't the Sioux try to shut it down two years ago?"

Skelton's expression remained neutral. "Two and a half years ago Soldier Mountain applied for a ten-year permitting extension to continue mining uranium. Young Bear alleged that the mine was contaminating the tribe's drinking water and he tried to block the extension by pushing to legislate tougher clean-water initiatives. Fortunately for us, he failed," he said. "*That* was a tough fight.

This project on Madison Mountain is all about gold and silver. You should breeze right through, fair sailing all the way."

"I haven't a doubt of it," Molly agreed, "but I'm also fairly certain that all our client's dirty laundry is going to be aired by Young Bear at these upcoming public hearings. That's why I need to understand what happened at Soldier Mountain, so I can prepare Brad with a rebuttal. But Mr. Skelton, the funny thing is, all I've been able to dredge up are a few brief newspaper blurbs. The files at the federal courthouse are sealed up tight. There isn't even a statement of claim for public consumption. I've never encountered this kind of a roadblock before, and the court clerk I spoke with was most unhelpful."

"Don't worry about Soldier Mountain," Skelton said with a dismissive wave of his hand. "Young Bear won't bring that up at any public meeting. He's just lucky that ill-conceived lawsuit of his didn't land him in jail." Skelton glanced impatiently at his watch. "I'm late for an appointment," he said, and left her office without another word.

Molly returned the file to the cabinet and sank back into her chair, kicking off her shoes and dropping her chin into her hand. She frowned as she gazed across the room. What had Skelton meant about the Soldier Mountain lawsuit landing Steven in jail? Could it have anything to do with the brief newspaper blurb she'd stumbled across in her Soldier Mountain research about Steven's legal assistant, Mary Pretty Shield? The newspaper had merely related her name, her age and that she'd been found dead beside a river on the reservation. Tribal police had treated her death as an accidental drowning. There was no other mention of her except an even briefer obit two days later.

She wondered if she dared ask Steven about Pretty Shield. It would be a strictly professional inquiry, of course, but what if she didn't like his answer? She had an uneasy feeling she wouldn't. It seemed the harder she tried to enlighten herself in preparation for these public hearings, the more dirt she uncovered. She didn't like dirt. She liked things to be clean and neat and predictable. She liked it when the good guys wore white hats and won every fight.

Molly closed her eyes with a soft moan and felt the beginnings of a bad headache gather like an impending storm in her temples.

Saturday. Oh please, please, come quick....

STEVEN HAD JUST RETURNED from Sam Blackmore's memorial service and was working on a real-estate transfer when Amy Littlefield called his office. "They're still using the mining road," she blurted angrily into the phone. "I just came from there and those great big yellow dump trucks are still going up and down, just like they owned the place. I thought you told me you filed an injunction to make them stop."

"It takes time to serve the papers," Steven soothed. "They'll stop soon."

"I didn't see anything in the newspaper this morning."

"Maybe tomorrow," Steven said.

"We've been talking about blockading the road," Amy said. "We could make up a bunch of signs, call the media, drive our cars over there and set up a roadblock. That would get their attention, and maybe even get us on television."

"Actions like that can turn violent pretty fast. I'd advise you to stay away from the access road."

"We have to do something. It isn't right, them breaking the law that way and nobody stopping them. We can't just sit here and let them get away with it."

"Give it another day," he said. "Sometimes the wheels of justice turn a little slow. Try to be patient."

He hung up and glanced at the clock. Eleven forty-five. It felt later than that. He hadn't slept a wink last night. All he could think about was Molly, and Saturday and how far away Saturday was from Wednesday. His phone rang again. It was Pony. "Did you get a chance to see Luther Makes Elk?" she asked.

"I saw him Tuesday night."

"Well?"

"He thinks I should go on a vision quest."

"Steven, what did he say about my wedding?"

"He seemed to know about it already. Did you tell him?"

"I didn't dare. I know how he feels about mixed marriages. Did *you* tell him?"

"That you were getting married?"

"Steven! What did he say? Will he do it?"

Steven paused. He thought back to Monday night and remembered what he could of the strange conversation. "Come to think of it, Pony, I don't think he really gave me an answer."

"That is *not* funny."

"Okay, here's what I'll do. I'll stop at his place again on my way to your place on Saturday and I'll get a definite yes or a no from him. I promise I'll pin him down and I'll give you his answer at the barbecue."

"Bring him with you," Pony urged. "There will be plenty of food and he will have a chance to meet Caleb and make up his mind one way or the other. Once he meets Caleb he'll agree to our wedding, I know he will. How could anyone not like that wonderful man?"

MOLLY WAS ON HER WAY to the copy room when Brad intercepted her in the hallway wearing an apprehensive expression. "Thought you'd want to know. I just fielded a call from a journalist who writes for the Bozeman *Sentinel*."

"About the nonexistent road-building permits for the mine?" Molly guessed.

"Yeah, only there's more. The rumor is that because the trucks are still rolling in spite of the fact that the injunction was filed yesterday morning, the citizens of Moose Horn are planning to blockade the road."

"When?" Molly said.

"This afternoon, probably even as we speak. The journalist said she just got the heads-up from the woman who's spearheading the citizens group. Amy something-or-other."

"Littlefield," Molly supplied. "Can't we get Manning to stop the truckers and close down the road before the media jumps into this? We don't need this kind of publicity."

"I can't get hold of him. He's not in his office."

"Then I'll bring a copy of the injunction and go myself," Molly said.

"It's an hour's drive just to get to Bozeman," Brad pointed out.

"True, but it's only a fifteen-minute flight," she rejoined. "I can rent a car when I get to Bozeman."

Seeing his reluctance, Molly reached out to touch his arm. "Brad, isn't it our responsibility to represent our client's legal matters and to provide a visible presence in controversial public arenas? Shouldn't one of us go? There could be trouble."

"Look, I doubt anything will come of this. I'd go myself, but I'm meeting a client for lunch. Maybe we should just sit this one out. You could keep trying to reach Manning." He hesitated. "I don't know if you should go down there, Molly. You know how Ken feels about you speaking in public...."

"I'll try him on my cell phone on the way to the airport, and if he wants to take over, that's fine with me. And don't worry. If Manning doesn't show up, I'll restrict my conversation to the truckers and contractors and stay out of the spotlight. Please, Brad, let me go." Molly was swept with a sudden, fierce need to fly to Bozeman, but her motives weren't nearly as noble as she had led Brad to believe. She wanted to see Steven. If he heard about the planned blockade, he'd go just to prevent any trouble—and she'd make sure he heard about it. This was a perfectly legitimate opportunity to get to see him before Saturday. No way was she going to pass it up.

"Okay," Brad said. "You can go. But keep it low key. This is really no big deal."

THERE WERE DAYS WHEN NOTHING of a man's life measured up, and this was one of them. Steven had worked hard to reach this place, this plateau of professional respectability. He liked his office with the Ansel Adams prints on the walls, the battered old oak partners desk, the distant view of the Gallatin range. He liked it most of the time, but today he felt trapped within its walls. There was always so much paperwork, and he disliked paperwork. He was sick of rewriting real-estate deeds. He was tired of doing the same things over and over again, even though he knew what he was doing was good, the way it had been good when he'd helped Jessie Weaver write all the conservation restrictions into her ranch deed before she sold the Bow and Arrow to Caleb McCutcheon.

But today it wasn't enough that he was helping to protect everyone else's special places. It wasn't enough that he was helping Amy Littlefield and her small army of citizens battle a huge multinational corporation. He wanted something more. Something much more. He wanted to see Molly Ferguson so badly that he couldn't eat a bite of his lunch. So badly that when the phone rang he picked it up and said, with uncharacteristic bluntness, "Yes?"

"Your phone manners are getting worse than mine, Young Bear," Molly's voice came over the line. "Listen, I'm calling you as a professional courtesy, just in case you didn't already know. The citizens of Moose Horn are apparently planning to block the access road to the New Millennium mine."

"I know. Amy called me earlier. She was upset that they were still using the road, but I told her to be patient and give it another day."

"Well, she didn't take your advice. They're not waiting. They're going to block the road today."

Steven lurched forward in his chair, clutching the phone to his ear. "When?"

"Right now, or so the journalist covering the story just informed us. I'm about to board a commuter flight to Bozeman, and Steven? I'm bringing a copy of your injunction with me just in case there's any trouble with the contractors who're working on the road, but if you're free…"

"Does Manning know?"

"I'm not sure. He's not answering his home phone or his office phone. He could be at the mine site already for all I know. Steven? I have to go. My plane's boarding."

"Molly?" he said, but he was talking to static.

He fished a card out of his wallet and dialed the number on it. It was Amy Littlefield's home phone, and not surprisingly there was no answer. He then dialed up the sheriff's cell-phone number and on the second ring Conrad Walker's gruff voice answered. Steven succinctly related what Molly had told him. "I'm on my way, but you're a whole lot closer, and I'm afraid there could be trouble."

"Damn," Walker said. "Figures this'd blow up on my day off. I'm standing in the middle of the Yellowstone River in a pair of waders with a fly rod in my hand."

Steven slumped at his desk. "Could you send someone just to make sure nobody gets hurt?"

"I'll call dispatch, get my deputy up there. And I'll be there myself just as soon as I can."

Steven hung up the phone, grabbed his keys and left the office. As the door shut behind him, he reflected on the irony that not moments ago he'd been wanting to escape the confines of these four walls. He'd been wanting desperately to see Molly. Now he was free of his office and on his way to a place where she would be, but instead of feeling exhilaration, he was filled with adrenaline fueled by cold, hard fear. Even at top speed, which at times wasn't very quick at all given the nature of the twisting mountain roads, it took him nearly forty minutes to reach the dirt road that the mining company had built to access the top of Madison. By that time he'd calmed his fears. By the time Molly arrived everything would be over. She wouldn't be caught in the middle of things. She'd be safe. She'd be okay.

But what if…?

Steven slammed on the brakes coming out of a sharp turn and the Jeep skidded sideways, coming to a stop scant inches from the rear bumper of a huge dump truck. As he climbed out of the vehicle, the reason why it was blocking the road became apparent. Several vehicles were parked abreast facing down the mountain access road. There were about twelve people standing in front of the these vehicles, holding signs saying things like Stop Stealing Our Heritage! and No Permits = No Road = No Permission To Pass!

There was a dump truck parked facing up the mountain, and one visibly agitated dump-truck driver the size of Paul Bunyan standing in front of his truck and holding an industrial-size tire iron in two large fists. No deputy sheriff on the scene. No Sheriff Walker. Looked like Steven was going to have to keep the peace. Great.

"Okay," Steven said, walking between the opposing forces. He stared the trucker in the eye. "These folks are no threat to you. There's no need for violence."

"There's no need for them to be blocking the road," the trucker said, his face dark with anger. He was a brute of a man with a huge beer belly, but most of the meat on him looked formidably powerful.

Steven reached inside his jacket pocket and withdrew his own copy of the injunction. "In point of fact, this road was constructed without the permits required by the U.S. Forest Service and Bureau of Public Lands," he said. "These papers were filed yesterday in federal court to stop all road-building activities until the permits are approved."

The trucker flicked his eyes over the sheaf of papers Steven extended. "I don't give a damn what those papers say. I'm being paid to do a job, and I'm doing the job. No one from the mine has told me to stop, and they're the ones who sign my paycheck. You'd better tell these tree-hugging idiots to get out of my way, or sure as hell someone's gonna get hurt."

"You should turn your truck around and go," Amy Littlefield yelled out heatedly, advancing a few steps with her sign. "What you're doing here is illegal and you should be arrested and thrown in jail. This is public land you're desecrating, it belongs to all of us, and you have no right to be tearing it up."

"Amy," Steven said, trying to catch her eye and give her a warning head shake, but she ignored him, her eyes bright and cheeks flushed with righteous anger.

"Look, lady," the trucker said, emphasizing his

words with the tire iron, "what I'm doing here is earning a living. I got kids to feed, and I don't give a rat's ass about much else. Now I'll say this just one more time. Move, or I'm gonna start busting some skulls."

Steven stepped between the trucker and Amy. "You may want to think about the repercussions of doing that," he said. "If you hurt anyone, you'll definitely go to jail, and you won't earn much of a living there. Take a look behind you. See that van with the satellite dish and the Channel 6 logo that just pulled up behind my Jeep? You bust any skulls and you'll be doing it live, for public consumption on the evening news."

The trucker glanced behind him, his expression changing as the van disgorged a newscaster and videographer, both of whom hit the ground at a trot. "Looks like I'll be on the evening news anyway."

"Probably," Steven said, "but you could make things really bad for New Millennium if you play the part of a thug. Put the tire iron away. Think about your kids. Do you really want them to watch their father being hauled off to jail on prime time?"

"Come on, hurry up." They heard the shrill command of the newswoman to her videographer as she raced toward them. "For the love of Pete, turn that damn camera on!"

The trucker glanced over his shoulder one last

time, wavered, then tossed the tire iron on the ground. "Ah, shit," he said, disgusted.

Another vehicle approached from the main road and Steven recognized Sheriff Walker emerging from a pickup truck. He was dressed in faded blue jeans, sneakers and a black police-issue ski jacket. Steven's relief was tempered with disappointment that Walker hadn't arrived in a cruiser with its siren blaring, wearing his official uniform. He felt a hand touch his arm and looked down at Amy, who grinned triumphantly, still brandishing her sign.

"Looks like we're going to get that publicity you said was so important," she said as Walker approached the scene. He came to a halt and flashed his badge and ID briefly for the benefit of all to see.

"Sheriff Walker," he announced. "Someone care to tell me what's going on?"

"These people blocked the road on me," the trucker said. "All I want to do is my job, and they won't let me."

"This road was built illegally and that man has no right to be driving his big dump truck over it," Amy cried.

"That the truth?" Walker said to Steven, who was spared from having to explain by the deep rumble of what sounded like a fairly large convoy of industrial-size vehicles coming down the mountain road toward them. Everyone turned at the sound. Steven shouldered through the group of citizens, edged between their cars and looked up the access road. Walker came to stand beside him, and the reporter and her accompanying cameraman trotted up as the sound grew ominously louder and the earth began to tremble underfoot. The first vehicle loomed into view around the sharp curve and Steven saw Walker instinctively reached for the butt of his revolver even as he heard a most unladylike expletive from Channel 6 TV's roving reporter, Melissa Sue Pauley.

"Run for it!" she shouted.

Instead, Walker drew his pistol and stood his ground beside Steven in the middle of the mountain road while the gigantic dump truck growled in low gear toward them, followed by a fleet of others. "Sorry it took me so long to get here," Walker apologized over the sound of the engines. "My deputy was responding to a traffic accident out on Puma Ranch Road and it took me a while just to get out of those damned waders." He held up his badge as he spoke and waved it back and forth above his head, and when this had absolutely no effect he shoved it back inside his jacket and leveled his gun in both hands. "Okay, Young Bear," he shouted, his voice nearly inaudible over the roar of the big motors. "There's backup from

Bozeman on the way, should be here any minute, but what do you suggest we do in the meantime?"

"We hope they stop," Steven shouted back.

But they didn't even slow down. The lead truck came straight for them, and they heard Melissa Sue Pauley shriek out, "No, you lame-brained idiot, keep the camera running! Get this footage. *Get it!*"

Steven wondered what the cameraman would get, what the nightly viewers would see as they sat in their warm living rooms and watched the world from a safe distance. Would the cameraman capture him and Walker being squashed beneath the aggressive and totally intimidating tires of an entire squadron of monstrous dump trucks? Common sense told him that he should leap aside and let these behemoths mow down the barricade of civilian vehicles. Common sense was a good thing and it came in handy at times like this, but the sheriff obstinately stood his ground. Ninety feet shrunk to fifty in a heartbeat, and just as Steven decided to forcibly pull Walker aside, the sheriff fired a single warning shot into the air.

The response of the truck driver was to lay on his air horn and accelerate, two rash and fool-hardy actions that caused Walker to lose his temper. For a shocked moment the sheriff stood in disbelief, and then, with the bumper of that massive truck less than twenty feet from him, he leveled his pistol and emptied the remaining five rounds into the truck, judiciously avoiding the driver and scaring the hell out of all the onlookers. The truck veered sharply to the left and came to an abrupt halt. The door wrenched open and the trucker jumped down, eyes wild.

"You okay, Clyde?" he bellowed, walking forward. "They hurtin' you?"

"Hands in the air, you stupid bastard! You are under arrest!" Walker shouted, moving to block his advance.

"They got a camera, Reggie," the first trucker called out. "They says we'll be on the evening news."

"You okay, Clyde?" the second trucker repeated as if his comrade hadn't spoken, still advancing toward Steven and the sheriff.

Without a moment's hesitation, Walker reached under his jacket and pulled out a pair of handcuffs. He handed them to Steven. "Cuff that damned idiot when I say so," he said, and before Steven could respond, Walker moved forward, a soldier marching resolutely into battle.

"You! Turn around! Hands in the air. I won't say it again," he barked out with great authority.

He didn't, either, because at that very moment the big trucker called Reggie reached out, wrenched the empty pistol from Walker's hand and tossed it aside. He then lifted the sheriff and effortlessly threw him to the ground as well. "You okay, Clyde?" he said for the third time.

Walker scrambled to his feet and tackled Reggie from behind with the athletic finesse of a professional linebacker. They fell together in a heap on the flinty soil. "Cuff him now! *Now!*" he shouted to Steven, who had absolutely no idea how to get the cuffs around Reggie's wrists while the sheriff was grappling with him on the ground. *"Cuff him!"*

Steven hovered, leaned forward, jerked back, felt a hand grab his arm. Clyde loomed beside him. "Don't hurt Reggie," Clyde said. "He's just trying to protect me."

"Talk to him, then, tell him to stop!" Steven said. "Tell him he's beating up an officer of the law!"

"Stop, Reggie! You're beating up an officer of the law!" Clyde said, but it was too late. The sheriff, with his ineffectual blows, had gotten Reggie mad, and Reggie had commenced to beat on the sheriff with those big fists. Steven reached down, still holding the cuffs, took a handful of Reggie's shirt and jerked backward, trying to pull him off the sheriff. The next thing he knew, stars were exploding in his head and he was flat on his back, spitting blood. He struggled to his knees in time to see several other truckers trotting toward the melee. Good, he thought. They're big enough to break up the fight. He lurched to his feet just in time to be knocked down by Reggie's elbow as the trucker drew his arm back to hit the sheriff yet again. Another explosion of stars. He lost the handcuffs, was searching for them when a boot caught him in the ribs. Didn't see it coming. Flat on the ground again, dirt in his mouth, ears ringing with shouts and curses. Wondered if it wouldn't be wiser to stay down, but he rolled onto his knees. Had to help the sheriff. Reggie was out of control....

Afterward, Steven would wonder how he ever managed to survive that unfortunate day. He would later watch the complimentary copy of the tape that Melissa Sue Pauley had sent him with her thanks for helping her be nominated newswoman of the year, and he would wonder how *anyone* had survived. Over and over, with a kind of morbid fascination, he watched the unedited footage, feeling the same numbness come over him each time, the same overwhelming sense of his own foolishness. He saw himself trying to drag Reggie off Walker in the early moments, then trying to parry the blows of another trucker who was coming to Reggie's aid, and doing all right, doing pretty damn good for a lawyer wearing a suit and tie, actually holding his own in the fracas for a split second or two.

Melissa Sue Pauley's cameraman caught not only Walker's valiant struggle with Reggie, but the subsequent beatings both he and Steven took when the rest of the truckers jumped into the fracas while the rest of the protestors cringed back. It was violent, gruesome footage and the cameraman never flinched. Not even when Melissa Sue Pauley, in an extraordinary attempt to stop what appeared to be a run of violence that could easily end in hot-blooded murder, shouted, "Stop! For the love of God, stop! *Stop! You're on live camera!*" Not even when Amy threw herself between the sheriff and Reggie and began striking at the huge trucker with her fists.

It was Amy's rash action that broke Reggie's concentration long enough for Clyde to shout, "You idiots, that's a cop Reggie's trying to kill! Stop him, before he gets us all thrown in jail for life!"

It was a command that Steven never heard until he watched the tape because by that point in time both he and the sheriff were beyond hearing anything at all.

BY THE TIME MOLLY ARRIVED at the New Millennium access road, having chafed and champed during the entire commuter flight, fidgeted impatiently while the car-rental agency finished the paperwork and handed her the keys, and driven like a madwoman from Bozeman to Moose Horn, the confrontation was over. Most of the protesters had dispersed and the media had departed with their high-tech equipment in a frenzied rush to get their footage on the evening news. For a moment she hoped that nothing really bad had happened, but then she caught a glimpse of the yellow police tape cordoning off the road, and Steven's Jeep parked higher up, beyond the police cars and the roadblock. Her breath caught in her throat. She told herself that he was all right. Steven was a peaceful man. He wouldn't have gotten involved in any violence, he was just waiting for her, that's all. She parked her rental car behind the banner of yellow tape and hurried toward the nearest uniformed officer, who stood on the outskirts, scribbling notes in his log.

"What happened here?" she said. "Was anyone hurt?"

The officer looked at her from beneath the wide brim of his hat. "I'm sorry, ma'am," the officer said with a disapproving pause, "but this area is off-limits to the public."

"A friend of mine, Steven Young Bear, is the attorney representing the people who blocked the road," she said. "His Jeep is parked up above. Can you tell me what happened?"

The officer rested his pen. "Are you Molly Ferguson?" he asked, and at her nod continued. "There was a fight between some construction workers and locals who tried to block the road. Sheriff Walker was taken by ambulance to Bozeman about half an hour ago, but your friend's still here. He's waiting for you in his vehicle." He nodded to the cluster of vehicles in the road ahead. Molly thanked the officer and started away. "Ma'am?" She glanced back. "According to the EMTs, your friend refused medical treatment, but in their opinion he belongs in a hospital. Maybe you could take him to get checked out."

She was half running through the maze of vehicles, heart in her throat, when she finally reached his Jeep. The driver's side door was open and Steven was sitting inside, head tipped back against the seat, eyes closed, holding a thick wad of very bloody gauze bandages to the side of his face. He didn't see or hear her approach. She stopped beside the open door and then gently laid her hand on his shoulder. "Oh, Steven, dear God in heaven, what have they done to you?"

His eyes opened. "Please don't faint on me," he said. "I need you to get me out of here."

"Don't worry." Molly's voice wavered, shocked by how badly he looked. "I only faint at the sight of my own blood. I'm parked at least five hundred feet down the road, and that's too far for you to walk in your condition. Wait here. I'll get some help."

"No. I'm all right, this looks worse than it is. But my Jeep's parked in, and will be for hours at the rate things are going."

"You're *not* all right. You should be in the emergency room right now. I'll have the officer I spoke to radio for an ambulance." Molly started to turn away but Steven's hand reached out and grasped her arm.

"Molly, I'm fine." As if to prove this to her, he levered himself out of the Jeep and stood. "Just a few cuts and bruises," he said. "Nothing serious. Besides, if I'd gone for a ride in the ambulance, I wouldn't have gotten to see you."

"Of course you would have," she said, slipping her hand around his upper arm to steady him as they began walking back to her car. "Do you honestly think I couldn't find the hospital in Bozeman?"

Five hundred feet passed slowly in Steven's tucked-over limp, but finally she was helping him into the passenger seat of the rental car. Her hands were shaking as she fumbled with the ignition key, turned the car around on the gravel road and started for the hospital as fast as she dared to drive, hoping he didn't die on the way. "For God's sake, what happened?" she asked, dismayed to hear her voice was shaking as badly as her hands.

"Amy and her group blocked the road, just like you said. One trucker was stopped coming up the mountain and apparently he radioed to the other truckers what was going on. They all converged just about the time the sheriff and the media showed up. Everyone was pretty hot under the collar, and when the sheriff tried to stop the dump trucks, there was some fighting."

"That's quite an understatement, from the looks of you. How badly was the sheriff hurt?"

"Don't know yet. They carted him off in an ambulance. None of the townspeople were injured, and I don't think any of the truckers were, either. I tried my best, but they were as big as their trucks. And that Reggie character…there was just no stopping him."

"Did you see Ken Manning?"

"No."

"Damn the man!" Molly blurted, gripping the steering wheel so tightly her hands cramped. "He could have stopped this, but I couldn't get hold of him. No one could."

"Amazing, what a lot of fuss one little legal document can cause."

She shot him a sidelong glance. "Yes, but is shutting down the access road for a week or two while the permits get straightened out worth all the pain and suffering? You're lucky you weren't beaten to death."

"It's the principle of the thing," he said. "Besides, the roadblock wasn't my idea. Amy thought it would be a good attention-getter."

"I hope she's satisfied."

"Subdued might be a better description."

"That cut on your face is going to need stitches, and you'll need X-rays, too. You could have suffered broken ribs, a fractured skull, internal injuries. They'll want to keep you overnight for observation—"

"All I need is the ice pack in my freezer, a few butterfly bandages from my first-aid kit, some aspirin, and a cold beer."

"I'm taking you to the hospital."

"I don't need a hospital. Take me home."

"Steven…"

"Home, please, Molly," he repeated in a voice that brooked no argument.

She bit her lower lip and drove.

"SO, TELL ME," Steven said as he sat back on the couch while Molly gently cleaned the cut on his cheek with a fresh gauze pad dipped in an antiseptic solution. "How did you come by such selective sensibilities? Fainting at the sight of blood should be an across-the-board reaction, regardless of whose blood it is." Her ministrations were deft and amazingly gentle, and it was nice, even in his misery, to have her bending so near.

"Just be grateful God made me so special," she murmured, concentrating on the task.

"Believe me, I am."

She drew back to survey her work. "Okay, the cut's clean and the bleeding's stopped, but it's a nasty gash and needs stitching. I don't stitch, Young Bear. I flunked sewing in grammar school."

He handed her the package of butterfly strips. "Just close it up with these and it'll be fine."

She sighed, took the package and removed several sterile strips. "What did you get hit with, anyway?"

"A big fist, wearing a big ring."

"Did he hit you twice?"

"After a while I lost count. Why?"

"You have another cut on your chin, but it's not as bad or as bloody." She dabbed at it with a fresh piece of gauze and then applied antibiotic ointment. "I never thought of you as being a fighter, Young Bear. You seem more like a peacekeeper to me."

"The sheriff thought he could arrest all of them single-handedly, but as it turned out he needed help. That Reggie character…"

"By now they're probably all in jail, where they deserve to stay for the rest of their lives for what they did to you. There. How does that feel?"

"I could get used to being fussed over," Steven said. "Thank you, and thanks for the ride home."

Molly regarded him somberly for a moment, then gave him a tender smile that warmed that lonely place deep inside of him. "You're welcome. I owed you that much, and a whole lot more. I'll get you that cold beer." She pushed off the couch as she spoke, gathering the first-aid supplies, and walked into the kitchen. He leaned his head back and closed his eyes, heard the refrigerator door open, heard her returning footsteps and opened his eyes again to accept the beer. "You probably haven't eaten since breakfast. What can I get you for supper?"

Steven twisted off the bottle cap and took a swallow of the cold brew, letting the bitterness wash away the sweet, coppery taste of blood. "More beer," he said. "And more aspirin."

"After what you've been through today, you need proper nourishment."

She returned to his kitchen and he heard cupboard doors opening and closing. Then he heard the freezer compartment open as she searched, no doubt, for a frozen dinner she could zap in the microwave. But she'd find no quick fixes there.

She then opened the lower compartment and he imagined her studying the contents of the refrigerator. After that, the cupboard doors opened and closed. "I have a confession to make," she called out after a long pause. "I flunked cooking in grammar school, too, and you don't seem to stock up on my kind of groceries. Easy, foolproof meals like canned soup and frozen dinners. How about scrambled eggs and toast?"

"Don't worry about it. I'm not hungry."

She fixed him scrambled eggs and toast anyway, setting the plate on the coffee table and dropping down beside him, bracing her elbow on the back of the couch and leaning her head into her hand. "Go ahead, the eggs are edible and I scraped most of the charcoal off the toast."

Steven did his best, but after a few mouthfuls he retreated to his beer. "It's good, thanks," he said. "I just don't feel much like eating."

Molly studied him gravely and nodded her understanding. "I'm sorry this happened."

"It's going to complicate things," Steven said. "Charges will be filed, arrests will be made. All that bad publicity for New Millennium isn't going to help your presentation at the next public hearing."

"Probably not, but right now all I care about is that you're all right." Her expression suddenly changed. "Are we still on for Saturday?"

He took another sip of beer while he considered. "I won't be as pretty, but if you're still game…"

A faint smile chased the shadows from her face. "I'm game. Will there be horseback riding?"

"Not for me, thanks, but there are plenty of horses to ride."

"I'd rather just hang out with you, if you wouldn't mind too much."

He reached out a hand and smoothed a stray curl of hair back from her face. "I'd like that," he said. "Now you'd better get going. The last commuter plane leaves at seven, and my guess is everyone at Taintor, Skelton and Goldstein is waiting at the office with bated breath to hear your report."

"You shouldn't be alone," Molly said, her forehead furrowing with concern. "You could be more seriously injured than you realize."

"Get going, Ferguson. Don't get me wrong, I'd love to have you stay, but I won't be responsible for you being fired from your job because you played nurse to the nefarious Young Bear."

"But…"

"Go. I'll be fine."

She sighed her disapproval, bent toward him and brushed her lips ever so tenderly across his own, the lightest of kisses, and then rose. "If you so much as feel the slightest bit dizzy or nauseous, promise me you'll call an ambulance. And promise me you'll call your sister right away and tell her what happened, so she'll know enough to worry about you. Promise." She waited for his assenting nod before gathering her jacket and purse and then, with one last anxious glance over her shoulder, she departed. He heard the car door slam, the engine start, the crunch of tires on gravel and then nothing but silence. Molly was gone. He sat in the lonely void that her absence created and touched his fingers to his mouth, pondering the miracle of her kiss.

CHAPTER SEVEN

THURSDAY MORNING DAWNED ON waves of agonies that brought an involuntary groan from him as he struggled out of bed. The night had passed slowly, sleeplessly; a long-suffocating darkness filled with dizziness, nausea and unimaginable pain. He sat on the edge of the mattress, waiting for the worst to pass. He was still sitting there, bent over, when his phone rang. "Are you all right?" Molly said.

"I'm fine. Stop worrying," he replied, wishing desperately that she'd never left, that she was with him now, helping him stave off the grim reaper.

"Did you call your sister?"

"Yes," he lied.

"I don't believe you're fine, and I don't believe you called your sister," Molly said. He could picture her scowling with disapproval as she spoke. "I just phoned the hospital. The sheriff's kidneys were bruised so badly the doctors were afraid they might shut down, and he has some fractured ribs and a broken nose. They thought his spleen might have been ruptured and they prepped him for surgery, but his condition has stabilized. They're monitoring him in intensive care, which, incidentally, is where you should be right now."

"Intensive care is for really sick people."

"Do you feel dizzy? Are you nauseous? Is there blood in your urine? Can you take a deep breath without—"

"Dr. Ferguson, I presume?"

"Try to eat something, even if you don't feel like it," she said. "And Steven? Stay in bed until Saturday and drink lots of fluids. I'll call you this afternoon to make sure you're following orders."

He was still sitting on the edge of the bed when the phone rang again. It was Amy Littlefield, and her voice was choked with remorse. "You were right, Mr. Young Bear. Yesterday was so violent. I've never seen anything like that before. It was on the news last night, and on the front page of the newspaper this morning." There was a long pause, and then she asked timidly, "Are you all right?"

"Fine," Steven said.

"I mean, the sheriff is still in the hospital," she blurted out. "I went to see him. I could only peek through the window in the nurses' station. He looks just awful."

I believe it, Steven thought, feeling the sheriff's

pain in every cell of his own battered body. Poor brave stupid bastard.

"Those men were vicious with you. I thought they meant to kill you."

So did I, Steven thought.

Amy had obviously spent a bad night thinking about things, probably as bad a night as he had, though for different reasons. "I don't know what to say to you except I'm sorry. It was all my fault."

"You were doing what you thought was the right thing," Steven said.

"But you told me it was the wrong thing to do, and I did it anyway."

"The news footage was great, though," Steven said with a wry grin that made him wince. "I doubt anything could've gotten Madison Mountain and the plight of our national forest on the table as quickly and dramatically. Don't beat yourself up."

The third call was from his sister. "Molly just phoned. She told me what happened yesterday," Pony said, her voice terse. "My God, Steven."

"Are we still invited to your barbecue?"

"You could have been killed. Are you all right?"

"I'm fine. I'd be on my way to work if I had my Jeep, but it's up on Madison Mountain."

"You would be working if you were dying. It's a good thing your Jeep is on the mountain. You should be in the hospital. Caleb and I are coming to see you. He wants to help in any way he can, and I want to make sure you really are okay."

"Look, Pony, don't make a big deal out of this. Tell Caleb I'll talk to him on Saturday. Right now I'm trying to figure out how to get my Jeep back. Molly drove me here last night before going back to Helena."

"If you are so okay, why did she have to drive you home, and why did she just call me? Steven, we are worried about you. I love you, and I know how stubborn you are…."

"I'm fine," he repeated, "and everything's going to be okay. I'll see you on Saturday, okay?"

She paused. "You will see us in an hour, and we'll take you to get your Jeep."

Steven felt a pang of tender gratitude. "I'd appreciate that."

It took him nearly an hour just to get dressed, but he was ready when his sister and her fiancé arrived, and the handful of aspirin he'd swallowed with his coffee had made it a little easier to move. By nine he'd retrieved his Jeep and was at his office, where the phone was ringing off the hook. He spent the entire morning fielding calls from journalists and reporters, from well-wishers and sympathizers, and from a hostile handful who told him in no uncertain terms where he could go and what he'd find when he got there. By noontime he was beginning to wish he'd taken all that well-intentioned advice and stayed home in bed.

MOLLY WAS SITTING at her desk, working on a binder for a new mine-site claim and wondering for the millionth time how Steven was, and how he could possibly be anything but in critical condition after the beating he'd received at the hands of those brutish truckers. She'd watched the graphic footage on the late news and sat in shocked stillness, her blood running cold, her mind a blank. She'd never seen anything like that before. It had shaken her badly, and now she couldn't help but question why she was sitting here in this office when she should be with Steven, making sure he was all right. She should never have left him alone yesterday. She should have driven him to the hospital no matter how he protested. She was reaching for her phone to call him for the second time that morning when Brad's secretary poked her head around the door.

"Sorry to bother you, Molly, but have you seen Brad? He has a call from the CEO of Condor International but I can't locate either Mr. Skelton or Brad, and I really don't want to keep Mr. Dehaviland waiting...."

Molly didn't hesitate. "Put the call through to me, please. Perhaps I can answer his questions."

Within seconds she was speaking to Gregory Dehaviland, chief executive officer of one of the biggest oil-and-mining conglomerates in the world. His voice was smooth and professional, and he wasted no time getting to the point of his call. "I watched the evening news last night, and I understand what's transpired here," he said after Molly had explained that Brad was out of the office and that she was just his assistant, "but what I don't understand is why New Millennium's permitting process was flawed. Why in hell are we building an access road to a proposed mine site when we don't have the proper paperwork in place?"

"Mr. Dehaviland, we're looking into this as well. It would appear that these permits, once they're in the works, are considered to be valid even though they have yet to be approved. Standard procedure seems to be to move ahead once the paperwork is submitted to the proper authorities."

"*Whose* standard procedure are you referring to?" The man's voice was clipped and acerbic.

Molly paused. "I admit I'm very new to these practices and I can't answer that question. However, in this instance, standard procedures obviously didn't work. The citizens of Moose Horn are opposed to the proposed New Millennium mine and have engaged the services of an environmental attorney to fight it, and he—"

"That would be Steven Young Bear, based out of Bozeman?"

"Yes, sir."

"Obviously he's caught us red-handed, breaking the law. I wasn't the only one watching the news last night. This incident has gone national."

"Yes, sir."

"I want an explanation," Dehaviland commanded. "Bending the law as 'standard procedure' is not a means to an end. Bending the law is akin to breaking it in my book."

"Yes, sir."

"We don't need to be bending *or* breaking the law for any reason whatsoever. All permitting processes should be followed to the letter, *always*."

"Yes, sir. Perhaps you should speak with Ken Manning. He's in charge of the New Millennium proposal."

"Ken Manning acts on the legal counsel of Taintor, Skelton and Goldstein," Dehaviland countered. "That's his job. *Your* job is to do the proper groundwork and make sure he gets the right advice. We pay your firm a lot of money to do that."

"Then perhaps you should speak with Mr. Skelton himself," Molly said, her heart trip-hammering. "I'm not sure he's in his office but I could transfer your call if you like, and you could leave a message on his voice mail."

"Please do so."

Afterward, she sat with her head in her hands, a myriad of emotions jumbling her thoughts. Dehaviland sounded like the kind of man who abided by the law and was sensitive to public relations, which was a good thing, as far as she was concerned. But what he had just intimated was that she might be in the employ of a firm that operated by an entirely different set of standards. That was a bad thing, and there were all kinds of bad implications wrapped up in it. She wished she'd had the nerve to ask Dehaviland about the Soldier Mountain uranium mine. She wondered what he knew about that lawsuit, and if he knew why the files were sealed.

She tried Ken Manning's office number and got his answering machine. She tried Steven's home phone and got his answering machine. She tried his office and the line was busy. Tried it again five minutes later and it was still busy. Tried it every five minutes until he finally answered.

"Young Bear."

"Ferguson," she said, relief flooding through her at the sound of his voice. "You're a hard man to get hold of, but I take it you're still alive, even though you didn't follow my advice about staying home and taking care of yourself. How are you feeling?"

"Like six truckers the size of Madison Mountain beat the hell out of me yesterday," he said. "Other than that, pretty good. I just got off the phone with Gregory Dehaviland. He's the CEO of Condor International and he called me personally to apologize for the mess your firm has made of things." Molly heard the undercurrent of humor in his deep voice. "So I told him that the only honest and intelligent attorney Taintor, Skelton and Goldstein had working for them was a redhead by the name of Molly Ferguson, and the rest of them spoke with forked tongues and walked a crooked path."

"You didn't." Molly felt a flush of heat in her face.

"It's the truth."

"What did he say?"

"He said he'd bear that in mind."

Molly pressed the phone to her ear as if by doing so she could bring herself nearer to him. "Well, I just called to make sure you were okay. You should be in the hospital, Steven, not at work. They aren't releasing the sheriff until tomorrow or the next day. That should give you an idea how badly you're hurt."

"That should give you an idea of just how tough I am," Steven replied. "Besides, I don't have time to be lying around in a hospital bed. I have a lot of work to do before Saturday rolls around."

Molly heard a tap at her door and Brad stepped

into her office. "Yes, that's right," she said briskly into the phone. "I understand that he's a busy man, but my client needs that paperwork right away."

"See you Saturday?" Steven said, without missing a beat.

"I'll be waiting impatiently." Molly hung up the phone and raised an eyebrow at Brad. "Where have you been?"

"Meeting with Ken," Brad said. "Listen, Molly, we need to talk. The shit's about to hit the fan. Bottom line, if we lose Condor International as a client because of this road-permitting business, we'll lose our jobs, and that comes straight from Skelton."

Molly stood, the blood draining from her face. Her fingers rested on her desktop and she felt a sudden wave of dizziness. "When you say *we,* to whom are you referring?"

Brad ran his fingers through his hair in a frustrated gesture. "You and me, baby," he said. "You and me."

BEFORE HE WENT HOME that evening, Steven dropped by the hospital to visit Conrad Walker. The sheriff was in a private room and looking none too pleased to be there, but when Steven appeared, his swollen, battered countenance brightened to the extent that it possibly could.

"You're a lawyer," he said, speaking with difficulty. "Can I sue New Millennium for disfigurement and suffering?"

Steven laughed and groaned simultaneously as the pain racked him. "How much do you figure it's worth?"

"A couple billion, easy. That outfit should be good for it."

"I'd have to get a percentage of that. Ten percent, maybe twenty."

"Fifty," Walker said. "You took at least half the pain and suffering. Probably more, by the looks of you. Thanks for jumping in, but you should've run for it, just like the news lady said."

"Next time I will. I've learned my lesson."

"Those bastards that did this to us are in jail," Walker said with obvious satisfaction. "They put 'em in the slammer where they deserve to stay for a very long time."

"Sorry to be the bearer of bad news, but their bail was posted this afternoon and they walked."

"Even Reggie?"

"Turns out Reggie is kind of like their mascot. He's mildly autistic, and is on medication for attention-deficit disorder. Clyde happens to be his brother, and when Reggie saw you threatening Clyde, he went berserk. When the other truckers saw us supposedly beating up on Reggie, *they* went berserk."

"They thought we were beating up *Reggie?* A Goliath who could single-handedly whip four heavyweight prizefighters?" There was no humor in Sheriff Walker's voice.

"They'll be arraigned sometime next week. Meanwhile the access road's now officially closed, per instructions of Condor International's CEO."

Walker brooded for a moment. "They just turned them loose? What would they have done to Reggie if I'd died?" he said.

"The bail would have been set a little higher, they'd have closed the road just the same, and maybe put up a nice memorial plaque for you when they reopened it." Steven handed him a paper bag containing a book he'd brought. "Thought you might like some reading material, since it sounds like you're going to be down-and-out for a while," he said.

He heard Walker opening the bag as he left the room and was halfway to the nurses' station when he heard him call out, "Damn you, Young Bear," and laughed again in spite of the pain. The book he'd given Walker to read was entitled *The Standard Police Procedural for Non-Violent Negotiations.*

MOLLY SIPPED her glass of wine slowly, looking around the candlelit dining room. The restaurant was busy for a Thursday night. She would have preferred a quieter atmosphere but Dani had suggested meeting here because the recent reviews had been very good. The cuisine was French and the menu was indecipherable but Molly didn't give a damn. She wasn't in the least bit hungry, and when Dani arrived and was shown to the table, she looked into her friend's concerned face and to her absolute mortification she felt her eyes flood with tears. "Damn, I'm sorry," she said, fumbling for a tissue in her purse as her friend came around the table to comfort her.

"What is it, Molly? Is Steven all right?"

She shook her head, unable to speak for a moment as she struggled for control. She wiped her eyes, drew a shaky breath, gave her friend a wan smile. "He's as fine as he can be, considering what he's gone through. It's just been a long and awful day."

Dani took her own seat and leaned across the table. "Talk to me."

Molly crumpled the tissue in her hand and glanced self-consciously at the other tables, but nobody was paying the slightest attention. "You know what happened yesterday."

Dani nodded grimly. "The whole nation knows what happened on Madison Mountain yesterday."

"Well, it looks like I might lose my job over it." Her voice trembled and she cleared her throat and took another sip of wine.

"How is that possible?" Dani said, indignant. "You weren't responsible for the citizens blocking the road, or the truckers wigging out on them."

"No, but the firm was responsible for giving the green light to begin building the access road before all the permits were approved. I wasn't aware of it, but apparently this sort of juggling happens a lot."

The server approached the table and Dani gave her drink order and accepted the menu. "Only this time someone found out," she said wryly.

"Steven."

"Of course. That's easy beans for him to dig up that information, and damned good ammunition for his fight."

Molly nodded as she dabbed her eyes. "Great ammunition, what with that spectacular media coverage showing him being beaten to a pulp by a mob of redneck truckers. And now Skelton needs a scapegoat to thwart any liability by the firm, so he's throwing Brad and I to the wolves."

"Did Brad know about the permitting?"

"Yes, but when I asked him about it he acted like it was no big deal. He was trained by Skelton, don't forget. Ken Manning was aware, as well. The way they look at it, everything was going to be approved any day, so why wait? Any fines that might be levied if they get caught jumping the gun are automatically built into the cost of doing business. They wanted to get the majority of the roadwork completed before winter and were willing to take the risks. According to Brad, this kind of stuff goes on all the time."

"I'm sure it does."

"Dani, I spoke with Dehaviland himself this morning."

Dani's eyes widened. "The big cheese at Condor International? Wow."

"I honestly believe he had no idea all this was happening."

"Not surprising. Think about all the stuff that man must have on his plate. He counts on his upper-management teams to keep things running smoothly, and obviously New Millennium fell on its face."

"As did my law firm," Molly added miserably, reaching for her glass of wine again. "I should have been paying more attention. I should have known about the permitting glitch."

"This is your first year out of law school and you're still apprenticing. I highly doubt that's the sort of information that's handed out freely. You assumed everything was by the book and aboveboard, and why shouldn't you?" The server returned with Dani's drink and raised his eyebrows questioningly. "Could you give us a few more minutes?" Dani said, and he bowed away politely. "Okay, so Taintor, Skelton and Goldstein, with Manning's wholehearted cooperation, screwed up and Steven drew the nation's attention to the situation, which resulted in a violent confrontation, and an embarrassed Dehaviland is now asking for an accounting. Skelton's blaming the incident on you and Brad, and he's going to make the two of you his official scapegoats. Have I got this straight?"

Molly nodded.

"There's only one thing you can do," Dani said flatly. "Tell them sayonara and thanks for the memories."

"Resign?" Molly stared, glass of wine in hand. She shook her head. "I can't do that."

"Why not?"

"I need this job to further my career, I need the money to pay my bills, and I've done nothing wrong."

"No, you haven't, but I think your precious law firm is about to be dragged through the mud by Young Bear. Resign before that happens, and before they can sacrifice you."

Molly set her glass down. "And then what would I do? Apply for a job as a supermarket cashier?"

Dani shrugged. "You're a survivor. There are other positions in other law firms. You could sell your fancy car, get a cheaper apartment, and cut your cost of living in half. You'll be fine."

Molly dropped her eyes to her empty glass of wine. "Brad says if we can somehow smooth this over with the media and with Dehaviland, we'll be okay."

"*Brad* says? Molly, you told me not that long ago you thought Brad was a dweeb."

"He is, but he's fairly smart." Molly rubbed at the crushing band of tension gathering between her eyes. "I'm sorry about what happened yesterday, but I don't feel as if I should be blamed for it, and I don't feel like resigning. Resigning would only make me look guilty. I feel like fighting back tooth and nail."

"That's your Irish ancestry speaking, Molly." The server reappeared, tall, thin and solemn. Dani glanced up at him and then back down at her menu. "Oh, dear God," she murmured. "The entire menu's in French."

Molly sighed. "You're French, Dani Jardine. Your own ancestry should be speaking to you right about now. As for me," she said to the waiter, raising her empty wineglass, "*Muchas* more *vino, por favor, mon ami.*"

THE SECOND MORNING was much easier than the first. Steven took a very long, very hot shower and was drinking his second cup of coffee when Amy Littlefield knocked at his door. He invited her in.

"Coffee?"

She shook her head. "No, thanks." She was agitated and paced around the living room, hands shoved in her jeans pockets while Steven patiently waited for her to reveal the reason for her visit. At length she stopped and pulled out an envelope, handing it to him. "I brought you some money. Not much, I'm afraid, but it's all we could scrape together. We're still planning on the bake sale and raffle but we're hoping you'll stand with us in spite of what happened, and in spite of the fact that most of us have low-paying seasonal jobs and next to nothing in our savings accounts."

Steven took the envelope and set it on the counter. "Orange juice?"

Amy shook her head. "We're holding a special town meeting Monday night to discuss implementing the emergency zoning plan that you suggested. It's at the town office at seven. We thought we'd better talk about the plan before the public meeting on Tuesday."

Steven nodded. "All right. I'll be there."

"Sheriff Walker's being released from the hospital this morning."

He nodded again. "I saw him yesterday."

"I'm picking him up," Amy said, her cheeks

coloring faintly. "I visited him yesterday, too, and it turns out that he has no immediate family in the area, so I offered to give him a ride home."

"That was nice of you."

"Well, after what happened…" She paced to the window and looked out. "I still can't believe they let those men out of jail when they so brutally attacked an officer of the law," she said. "And you, too," she added quickly. "I mean, they might have killed you both."

"But they didn't, and Condor International pulls some powerful strings," Steven said. "They posted the bail. They're responsible for their employees' behavior and whereabouts until their court appearance. Tea?"

"No, thanks. I have to be going. I told Sheriff Walker I'd pick him up at 8:00 a.m. sharp. He said he didn't want to spend one minute more than he had to in that place, and I don't blame him. Oh, and by the way, the public meeting on Tuesday's been relocated to Bozeman's town hall. There's not enough room in all of Moose Horn for the crowd that's expected to attend."

After she had left, Steven finished his coffee and on the way to put his cup in the sink, the envelope he'd left on the counter caught his eye. He opened it, counting the money within. One hundred and eighty-six dollars wasn't exactly what a campaign like theirs needed in order to do proper battle with New Millennium Mining, but what the hell. It was a start.

FRIDAY MORNING, Molly dressed very conservatively and with a sense of impending doom. She left her apartment after another sleepless night pondering her limited options and drove down the familiar streets. She tried to meditate and deep breathe her way to calmness, but by the time she reached the venerable brick building that housed the law firm of Taintor, Skelton and Goldstein, she was a nervous wreck. She hadn't been in her office for more than thirty minutes when Brad knocked and entered, looking as haggard as she felt.

"You have to somehow convince Young Bear to back down from this fight," he said without preamble. "I think that's the only way for us to save our jobs."

Molly shook her head. "There's no way I could ever do such a thing."

Brad leaned his palms on her desk and stared her aggressively in the eye. "Think about it. You saw what happened to him just two days ago. There's a lot riding on the success of this mining proposal. A lot of jobs, a lot of money. If Young Bear spearheads the fight to stop the project, he stands to gain a lot of enemies. Things could get even worse for him."

Molly felt her heart skip a beat. "Is that a threat?"

"That's a reality check. You like the guy, right, or am I way off base here?"

"My personal feelings are my private business, and they have nothing to do with my job performance," Molly replied stiffly.

"You're wrong about that," Brad said. "They have everything to do with it. I'm warning you, Molly. This could get really ugly, really fast, but you could stop it. You could keep a lot of people from getting hurt. Tell Young Bear that if he keeps pushing, and if he grandstands at that public hearing on Tuesday and drags this firm through the mud, you'll lose your job."

"Is *that* a threat, too?"

"Another reality check. Things are kind of shaky for you right now, if you get my drift."

"Even if I could convince him to quit, the people of Moose Horn would find help somewhere else," Molly said. "They won't give up."

Brad shook his head. "Maybe not, but Young Bear's the only lawyer they'll ever find who gives his time and expertise away and expects nothing in return. Nobody else will represent their interests without a big retainer, and without legal representation, no one will pay the slightest attention to them. Talk to him, Molly, or we both stand to lose our jobs. Skelton will kick our sorry asses right out the door, and we'll be standing in the unemployment line, make no mistake about that."

He spun on his heel and left before she could reply, and she sank back into her chair. Her heart was pounding and her mouth was dry. She thought about Dani's advice and dropped her head in her hands with a soft moan. Should she resign? The public hearing was only four days away. In four days time she might already be fired, her name and reputation permanently ruined in the most important legal circles. Dani was right. She should spend the morning working on her resignation. But she'd done nothing wrong.

She looked around her office, her own private space in a prestigious law firm with its cherry desk and matching chair, the plush Berber carpet and tall cherry bookshelves filled with leather-bound volumes. Her pictures hung on the walls along with her framed diploma, and family photos lined her desktop. It was all so pleasantly personalized and comfortably professional. If her parents could see where she worked, they'd be proud of their only daughter—wouldn't they? She gazed at a picture of her parents, her mother's stern, matriarchal face showing the faintest trace of a smile, as if she were trying to appear solemn for the photograph but someone, her father perhaps, had just whispered something outrageous in her ear. Her father, mustached and solemn, with that ever-present glint of mischievous humor in his eyes.

What *would* her mother and father think about this awful mess she'd gotten herself into? Molly chewed on a fingernail and frowned. A lump formed in her throat as a wave of homesickness overwhelmed her. How she missed the wise counsel of her parents! But as much as she wanted to pick up the phone, she knew her mother would tell her to quit her job and come home, her father would tell her he was on his way to help her move back East…and she couldn't do that. She couldn't run back home at the first sign of trouble she encountered. No, somehow she was going to have to work through this dilemma on her own.

Instead of calling home, Molly returned several phone calls she'd missed and worked halfheartedly on the papers she'd begun earlier, but the restlessness inside of her increased by the moment until finally she pushed away from her desk and paced the room. There was something she didn't understand about Skelton's reticence to discuss the Soldier Mountain mine and the lawsuit Steven had brought against it for polluting the river and ground water that provided the Rocky

Ridge Reservation with most of its water supply. There was something she didn't understand about why they felt it was so important to discourage Steven from representing the opposition to the New Millennium mine. Surely if they were doing everything aboveboard and by the book, nothing Steven could do would be enough to stop the Madison Mountain project.

It was so puzzling. On the one hand, Skelton pegged Steven as a two-bit podunk attorney, yet on the other, he clearly felt Steven was a big threat. Why? How could one attorney representing a handful of people with no financial backing possibly pose a threat to a powerful law firm like Taintor, Skelton and Goldstein representing a huge corporation like Condor International? She couldn't help but feel that if she could access the sealed files at the federal courthouse, she would find the answers. Perhaps she could convince Steven to tell her, but how? He was as reluctant to discuss the Soldier Mountain lawsuit as Skelton had been.

Molly paced and brooded and glanced at the clock on her desk. Somehow lunchtime had come and gone, but no matter. She wasn't hungry. She had tons of work to do before the weekend and hadn't even made a dent in it. She thought about Dani's advice. She thought about Brad's warning and Steven's safety and the accidental drowning death of Steven's legal assistant, Mary Pretty Shield, during the Soldier Mountain lawsuit.

"What to do…" she murmured aloud, and a tap on her door made her jump. "Yes?"

Mr. Skelton entered. He looked more somber and self-important than usual. "Would you join us for a late lunch, Molly? Ken Manning's here to speak with Brad, and we thought the four of us should talk before we give our statement to the press."

"What statement?"

"We've had so many calls from the media that we decided to hold a brief press conference right here in our boardroom at 4:00 p.m., and it would be most advantageous for all those who will be present to discuss the New Millennium permitting procedures in advance. That's what they'll be asking us about."

Molly drew a deep breath. The last thing in the world she wanted to do was have lunch with Ken Manning, but Mr. Skelton was right. The press and the public needed and deserved some answers, and the firm needed to get to the bottom of what went wrong with the permitting process. There had to be some perfectly logical explanation to this awful mess. Brad was experienced. He knew what he was doing. He wouldn't have deliberately jeopardized the project by ignoring important legal protocol. Could *she* be fired for Brad's indiscretions? She had a feeling she was about to find out.

"Of course, Mr. Skelton," she nodded. "I'd be glad to."

IT WASN'T OVERLY LATE when Steven's phone rang, but he was already in bed, trying an ice pack on his ribs to see if it eased the pain of breathing and brought sleep to him any easier. So far nothing he'd tried had worked. "Young Bear," he said.

"Ferguson," came the voice he'd grown so hopelessly addicted to.

"Tomorrow's Saturday," he said.

"The day I've been waiting for all week," she said, sounding both distracted and exhausted.

"If you meet me here, we can go together in my Jeep," he said, shifting the ice pack.

"Fine," she said. "I'll be there by noon or a little after. Are you okay?"

"Better and better, but if you want to ride wild horses up into the mountains tomorrow, you're on your own."

"I've never aspired to ride wild horses. All I want tomorrow is to be with you."

There was a forlorn drift to her words that clutched at him. "What's wrong?"

"Nothing. I just called to find out how you were feeling, and make sure we were still on for tomorrow."

"You sound kind of down."

"Oh, Steven," she said, her voice changing, breaking.

He lay on his bed, ice pack held to his aching ribs, and felt a pain far worse than anything the truckers had bestowed upon him. "Did something happen at work?"

"Politics happened at work," she said. Did he imagine the tremor in her voice? He said nothing, waiting for her to elaborate, but she didn't. "I guess I'll see you around noon, then," she said softly. "Good night, Steven."

Even if the ice pack had worked, he wouldn't have slept. He lay awake staring into the darkness and wondering what abyss Molly had stared into that day to have cast such a pall on that indomitable spirit of hers. He could only hope it had nothing to do with the New Millennium mine proposal and Wednesday's confrontation on the access road, but he had a strong hunch that it did.

CHAPTER EIGHT

STEVEN'S HUNCH was verified the next morning when he walked out to his mailbox to retrieve the newspaper. There it was, plastered on the front page of the *Bozeman Sentinel.* Law Firm Representing New Millennium Mine Admits to Jumping Gun on Road Permitting. He scanned the article as he walked back down the gravel drive and read it a second time more carefully while drinking his second cup of coffee. He read it a third time because he really couldn't believe what he was reading, couldn't believe that Molly Ferguson was being named as the inexperienced attorney whose misinterpretation of the permitting process had led to the ugly confrontation on the access road. Couldn't believe she was actually quoted as saying, "I want to stress that in no way did my actions represent the law firm of Taintor, Skelton and Goldstein. I accept full responsibility, and want to apologize to everyone involved."

The article then went on to quote Skelton describing Molly as a good attorney but "young and impulsive, and obviously needing much closer supervision until she fully understands the complex and critical process of mine permitting." And Ken Manning: "It's extremely unfortunate that Ms. Ferguson's lack of judgment caused such a major conflict, but I'm sure she's learned a valuable lesson. Needless to say, she's been removed from the legal staff representing the interests of my company until all the permits are properly in place."

Steven threw the paper aside and pushed out of his chair with a surge of anger. "God, Molly, what have they done to you?" He took another handful of aspirin and a long hot shower, dressed in blue jeans and a red-and-black plaid flannel shirt, and padded barefoot into the living room with the newspaper to read the article yet again. By the time Molly arrived in her fancy red Mercedes he had practically memorized every infuriating word. He met her at the door and stared for a moment, the newspaper headline momentarily forgotten. "You look great," he said.

She was wearing a black flared skirt with silver conchas, a white pleated blouse with an embroidered vest of a dark brown-and-green tapestry, and a pair of expensive hand-tooled cowboy boots. Her hair was pulled back into a French braid and she looked like a very beautiful red-haired cow-girl standing before him. She stared up at him, eyes wide and face pale enough to show all her freckles. She said nothing, just stood there until he reached a hand and drew her inside. He could feel her hand trembling in his as he guided her into the living room. Her eyes fell on the newspaper and then lifted to his face. "Please, Steven, let's not talk about it," she said.

He remained silent for a few moments longer, then nodded. "Have you had any lunch?"

She shook her head. "I'm not hungry."

"You'd better work up some kind of appetite by the time we get to the Bow and Arrow," Steven warned with a faint smile. "There's a woman who lives there, a fat old Mexican woman named Ramalda who cooks and cleans and grumbles a lot in Spanish. She gets really upset if people don't eat her cooking. She thinks they must be sick, so she tries to make them better by cooking more and more things for them. You're so thin to begin with that if you don't eat everything she puts in front of you, she might bundle you off to bed and keep you there until spring, which probably wouldn't be the worst thing that ever happened to you."

Molly gazed at him as if he'd just related the saddest story she'd ever heard, and then she dropped her face into her hands and burst into tears. After a shocked pause Steven reached for her and pulled her into his embrace.

"I'm sorry," she sobbed while his arms tightened around her protectively.

"Don't be sorry. It'll be all right," he soothed.

"No, it won't. It'll never be all right again. Oh, Steven." She drew a deep, shuddering breath and leaned her forehead against his chest. Drew another breath, turned her head and rested her wet cheek against the soft flannel of his shirt, eyes closed, lashes dark against pale cheeks. She was still shaking like an aspen leaf in a steady breeze. Steven stroked the back of her head. They stood like that long enough for him to reflect that being so close to a woman had never felt so right as it did with Molly. In spite of the fact that she was so distraught, he was sublimely happy to be holding her in his arms. Finally her trembling subsided, and she pushed away from him, raised her eyes to his and gave him the sweetest little beginnings of a smile. "Thank you," she said.

He kissed her then. It would have been impossible for him not to. He lowered his head and kissed her very gently, very tenderly. Her lips parted beneath his, and she opened herself to him and kissed him back. He was unprepared for the response, unprepared for the transition from sweet to questing, from needing to demanding. Unprepared for the fire that swept through him, ignited by the heat of her kiss and the feel of her body moving against his. He was totally and completely unprepared for the way he lost all control in the presence of this extraordinary woman.

When at last they broke apart, it was a move initiated by him, because to have gone any further would have been to go way beyond the point of safe return, and he knew what Molly needed now was safety more than anything else he could offer her. She was too vulnerable right now, too much a hostage of her turbulent emotions. He kissed her forehead, ran his thumb along her lower lip, and brushed a stray lock of hair behind her ear.

"We'd better go," he said.

"I know."

"Because if we stay here any longer, we might not go at all."

"I know," she repeated.

"But we can come back."

"Yes," she breathed, reaching on tiptoe to kiss him again. Her hazel eyes brimmed with tears. "Thank you so much for being here for me."

He closed his hand around hers and brought it against his chest. "What they did to you yesterday was unforgivable," he said, and then, reading the unspoken rebuke mingling with the fierce hurt, he kissed her one final time. "I'll speak no more about it, I promise. But it was unforgivable."

STEVEN DROVE HIS JEEP toward the Bow and Arrow, cruising the quiet roadways in the bright blue and gold of a fine September afternoon. Molly sat quietly in the passenger seat, eyes drowsy with fatigue, looking like she hadn't gotten much sleep in the past few nights. Even his stolen glances were enough to kick his heart into high gear, remembering what had almost happened between them just a short time ago. Her kisses had been a mingling of honey and habanero chili peppers. Like icy spring water in the midst of a desert, and like the scorching desert itself. Her kisses had brought something long dormant within his heart to life, reawakened him to the universe, connected him once again to all living things.

He was so lost in his silent reverie that he nearly forgot his promise to Pony to stop at Luther Makes Elk's shack in the foothills and get a definite answer from the old man about his sister's upcoming wedding ceremony. Steven glanced at Molly. Her eyes were completely closed now, head back against the rest. He cleared his throat and spoke softly. "Sleeping?"

"Dreaming," she replied, eyes still closed.

"Good dream?"

"Wonderful," she murmured. "We're climbing a mountain together, the same mountain you climbed on your vision quest. Brave Heart. You're holding my hand, helping me up a steep section of the trail."

He was startled that she remembered the mountain's name. "Are we near the top?"

Her lips curved in that small sweet smile. "I think so," she said. "I think we're almost there. I see an owl sitting in a tree, watching us. It must be night."

Steven's eyes narrowed on the road. "You see an owl in your dream?"

She tilted her head to look at him. "It's not a real dream. It's just a wishful dream, and the owl just flew away."

"How do you know wishful dreams aren't real?" He had to ask because, after all, an owl flying through one's consciousness was an omen of death.

She sighed. "I think they can become real. I mean, when I was young I dreamt about becoming a lawyer, and those were wishful, waking dreams. I wanted to change the world for the better. I wanted to influence the universe. I wanted to make my parents proud of me." Her laugh was small, bitter. "And look at me now. I've made the front page of a newspaper I can only hope to God my parents never see."

"Go back to the mountain," Steven said. "*Cante Tinza*. Where are we now?"

"Brave Heart," she echoed softly, her thick eyelashes brushing her cheeks. "All right. We're almost to the top…." Her eyes fluttered open, her gaze was beseeching. "Can we go there, Steven? Just the two of us? Can we climb it together?"

He glanced at her and then back at the winding road. "When?"

"Soon. Maybe we could camp there, make a little fire, count the stars in the sky while we wait for the dawn. Maybe the spirits will come and speak to both of us and tell us all the secrets of the universe."

He drew a deep breath, his heart thundering in his chest like a war drum. They were approaching the turnoff to the reservation. "You tell me when you want to go, I'll have everything packed and ready," he said, slowing for the turn.

"Are we almost there?" she asked, confused.

"Not really," he said. "I have to make a brief stop at my grandfather's place to ask him if he'll marry my sister."

Molly sat up straighter and looked at him. "Is he a priest?"

"A holy man, the Indian equivalent. Pony wants to do the seven sacred steps for her wedding, but Luther Makes Elk, my adopted grandfather, has never wed a full-blood to a white man. I'm not sure he will."

"What if he says no?"

Steven's laugh surprised them both. "Then we'll have to climb *Cante Tinza* tonight and hope for a good vision, because if Luther Makes Elk says no, I don't dare go to Pony's barbecue."

THE OLD MAN WAS SITTING OUT in the sunlight outside the door of his shack. He had a blanket draped over his legs and was bundled in a faded wool peacoat to turn the crisp autumn wind. A black wide-brimmed hat was pulled low over his brow.

"Good to see you," Luther said as Steven and Molly approached. He studied Steven's battered face and then nodded to indicate Molly. "I guess you didn't go on that vision quest, but red was the right color."

"Grandfather, this is Molly Ferguson, a friend of mine. We're on our way to Pony's for a barbecue. Pony wanted you to come with us."

Luther shook his head. "I just ate, and my bones are tired. I think I'll have a nap, maybe. Maybe you should, too. The world you live in moves too fast. Keep the sacred bundle I gave you, and go on your vision quest soon, before it's too late."

"Pony's wedding ceremony is in two weeks, the first Saturday in October."

"I know," Luther said. A rusty pickup drove past, lifting a cloud of dust. "I made some food, a pretty good stew. This time, I know what's in it. The pot's on the stove. It would probably be better if it had more time to age. A stew always tastes better the second or third day. Some stews need a week. You should eat some of that stew. It's powerful medicine and you could use some." Luther reached into the pocket of his coat and drew forth several feathers bound in a strip of rawhide. "I saved some of the owl's feathers for you," he said, extending the offering toward Steven. "The feathers are blessed, but I didn't bless the stew. I wasn't sure if it was going to be good or not." He paused and looked up at Steven. "You sure you don't want some?"

"Grandfather, we should be going. About Pony's wedding…"

"Wait. Before you go, I better give you something." Luther pushed off the bench and in his bent, shuffling gait he entered his little shack. He switched on the single bulb that hung from the ceiling and rummaged among a pile of clothing heaped on his narrow bed. He pulled out a long object wrapped in oiled canvas and laid it upon the battered metal table in the center of the room as Molly and Steven watched.

"This rifle is older than me, even," he said as

he unrolled the object from the protective cover. "It was at the battle of Little Big Horn. My great-grandfather was a scout for one of the bluecoats. He gave it to my grandfather, who used it to prop open the cabin door on hot days, because back then, there was nothing left on the rez to shoot." He held the heavy rifle out to Steven. "Take it."

Steven took a step backward and shook his head. "I don't need a gun."

"Not today, maybe. But sometimes, a gun comes in handy. I kept it clean. Look, no mouse nests in the barrel."

"There's been enough violence."

Luther Makes Elk nodded his agreement. "That's so. Now take Red Hair and go, so I can have my nap." He gestured with the rifle, and Steven took it from him reluctantly. The heaviness of the old weapon surprised him. The cold steel carried the weight of deaths that spanned three centuries. "Take this, too," Luther said, handing him a small pouch tied with a leather thong. "There's a bullet for the rifle, and some big medicine. Better keep it close to you." He gestured again. "Now go," Luther said, "and tell your sister I'll marry her to that white man, but only because his heart is good. Otherwise, I would never do such a thing."

Steven began walking to the Jeep but Molly paused behind him and he heard her say, very gravely, "Goodbye, Luther Makes Elk. It was a great honor to meet you."

FOR A WHILE AFTER THEY LEFT Luther's shack they drove in silence, long enough to restore the time-line and reaffirm contact with their modern lives. When they reached the main road Molly swiveled in her seat, drew her knees up, and said, "Wow. He's your grandfather?"

"I got him out of jail once, and he adopted me," Steven explained, eyes on the road. "We're not blood relatives. Most white people think Luther's just a crazy old man."

Molly studied his profile and thought that she could look at Steven like this forever, in quiet contemplation of a man she truly believed she couldn't live without, yet didn't begin to understand. "Well, I think he's wonderful," she said.

Steven glanced at her briefly but made no reply. His silence got her dander up.

"He's going to marry your sister to a white man," Molly said, "in spite of the fact that it goes against everything he believes in. And he gave you that old rifle he obviously holds so dear, and he made a stew for you out of an owl, which must have powerful medicine to protect you. I think he's wonderful, and I think you should have eaten some of the stew."

"You've never tasted his cooking."

Molly sighed. "Steven, it was rude not to have eaten any. You should have at least taken one spoonful."

Steven cast her an unfathomable look. "Luther's owl flew through your dream."

"Yes," she said impatiently. "Don't you see? That's precisely why you should've eaten the stew."

"You're Catholic, aren't you?"

Molly sighed. "My father's Catholic, my mother's Protestant, and I don't know what that makes me. Right now, I'm confused about life in general and my job in particular, but if you're asking what religion I subscribe to, the jury's still out."

"Maybe that's why Luther liked you," Steven said.

Molly brightened. "He did? How could you tell?"

"If he didn't like you, he wouldn't have acknowledged your presence. He called you Red Hair, which means you have a place."

"A place where?" Molly asked, awed because the old holy man had both intimidated and intrigued her.

Steven's somber countenance never changed. "That remains to be seen," he said.

Molly sighed. "Along with a whole bunch of other things," she said. "Tell me about the Bow and Arrow, and the school you helped Pony start."

"The Bow and Arrow was settled back in the mid-1800s by a man by the name of John Weaver, who drove a herd of longhorns up from Texas," Steven began.

"Steven?" Molly interrupted, sitting up straight, a lurch of adrenaline souring her stomach as the guilt she'd been suppressing flooded back into her consciousness. "I was supposed to try and persuade you to drop the fight against the New Millennium mine."

The Jeep's wheels whined on the asphalt and Steven kept his eyes to the front. Several minutes passed before he continued in the same deep, calm voice. "John Weaver was Jessie Weaver's great-grandfather. He married a Crow Indian woman who was given to him in thanks for giving the tribe some of his beef cows to help them through a bad winter." He paused for a moment before glancing at her. "So, are you going to try to make me see that the mine will be a good thing?"

She shook her head. "No. I said that I had no intentions of asking you to." She gazed out at the flanks of the mountains, bright gold with the color of fall aspen, and felt her cheeks burn with shame that she hadn't told him this as soon as she'd arrived at his house. "Brad said the fight could get really nasty. He said more people could be hurt."

"And a giant meteor could collide with the earth

next week and wipe out all of civilization. Should we stop living because that might happen? Molly, the law is the law, and most people abide by it. What I'm doing needs to be done. If the mining companies won't follow due process, someone needs to be watching them."

"But it doesn't have to be you," Molly said passionately, turning in her seat to face him. "You shouldn't be the one getting beaten up for being the watchdog. The mine is in a national forest, and that makes policing it the federal government's job. It's not up to you to enforce the laws."

"In a perfect world I might see things your way."

"Okay then, what about Gregory Dehaviland. He's only been CEO of Condor International for less than a year, and I think there's potential for great things to come from his leadership. He talked to us both to get the real scoop as to what happened on the access road. You have to admit, that's an extraordinary thing for a man in his position to do."

"Yes," Steven said.

"He has the power to change things for the better. I believe he wants to do the right thing, and I also believe he's going to make sure his subsidiaries are toeing all the proper lines."

"I hope you're right," Steven said, "but either way, I'm not going to back down. Establishing an open pit mine in the middle of a national forest that borders on the Yellowstone ecosystem is wrong, and the laws need to be changed to prohibit all mining claims on federal lands. Those laws were created in 1872 to promote westward expansion. We no longer have to offer land giveaways in order to settle the West. The West is settled, Molly, and has been for well over a hundred years. The savage Indians have been subdued and put on reservations. We need to protect what little wilderness remains, not continue to exploit it."

Silence filled the Jeep. Molly could think of no good reply, so she folded her hands together in her lap and gazed out at the high beauty that surrounded them. "I still think you should've had some of your grandfather's owl stew," she said.

CHAPTER NINE

THEY ARRIVED at the Bow and Arrow just shy of three, and Steven was surprised that there seemed to be no one around. He narrated their approach to Molly as they drew near. "That cabin on the bend of the creek to your right is the original homestead, built by John Weaver in the mid-1800s. Caleb and Pony live there now. They prefer it to the main house. The ranch house was built above the cabin on the knoll just ahead. That's where the boys and Ramalda live. They're planning a new, separate building for the school itself, but construction of that won't begin until spring, and it will be where the original bunkhouse used to be, on that flat piece of land between the ranch house and the pole barn."

Molly looked this way and that, taking it all in, rolling her window down and leaning out. "Horses," she exclaimed with obvious delight. "And dogs, and *puppies!* And there, by the barn, isn't that a buffalo?"

"Absa," Steven replied, catching sight of the young buffalo. "Her leg was broken shortly after she was born and she had to be hand raised. One of the boys, Roon, adopted her and she follows him around like the dog she thinks she is."

"She's a pretty big dog," Molly laughed. She was out of the Jeep practically before it stopped rolling, kneeling down to pat the two fat little pups that bounded down the porch steps of the ranch house and cavorted about her feet. "Oh, they're adorable, Steven. Look at them." She swept one of the wriggling pups into her arms and it began licking her face. Within moments she had paw prints on her pretty blouse, several unruly curls had escaped her braid, and she looked thoroughly, beautifully happy. All vestiges of her previous torment had miraculously disappeared.

Steven watched her and felt an easing inside of himself. It was this place. The Bow and Arrow had the power to transport people beyond their immediate troubles. He'd felt that same magic himself a time or two before. He'd stood in awe and looked around him at the towering wall of the Beartooth Mountains, at the old ranch buildings near the bend of the creek and the slow curl of wood smoke from weathered fieldstone chimneys. It was a nurturing and timeless place that somehow made sense out of every dawn and sunset, and every moon that ever gave name to a season.

"Those are Blue's pups," he said. "Blue belongs

to Jessie and Guthrie. She's the cow dog that keeps everyone in line."

"Well, puppies like to cuddle, and that makes them just about perfect in my book," Molly said beaming, and he couldn't help the twinge of jealousy he felt toward the pup she cradled so lovingly in her arms.

At that moment the screen door banged open and Ramalda waddled onto the porch. She was holding a big wooden spoon in one fat fist and wearing her infamous scowl, which she fixed first on Molly and then on Steven. "You are hungry," she accused.

Steven glanced around at the absence of vehicles and other people. "Ramalda, my apologies," he said. "Pony invited me to a barbecue, but I must have mistaken the day or the time. This is Molly Ferguson, my friend from Helena, and she hasn't eaten all day. She's too thin, and needs good cooking like yours."

Ramalda's stern features softened as she fixed her gaze on Molly. "You need to eat much," she agreed. "You too thin. But first, there is big problem down in the barn."

Steven glanced down toward the pole barn. "Is that where everyone is?"

"*Si*. Yes." Ramalda nodded, her scowl deepening. "It is always something. This time, a sick horse. They are down there. You go get them, tell them it is time to eat or they get sick, too."

"All right. We'll round them up." He caught Molly's hand in his and started down the slope. She was still holding one puppy while the other gamboled at her heels, and he heard her soft laugh as she fell into stride with him.

"She's intimidating," Molly confided, "but I'm guessing she's a big softie at heart."

"As well as a great cook," Steven said. "She practically raised Jessie and Guthrie." He stopped so suddenly that she stumbled into him.

"Steven? What is it?"

His eyes had caught the glimmer of sunlight on metal out behind the barn, metal where there shouldn't be metal, only grass and dirt and curlews and horses and Absa, waiting on Roon. He stood in silence for a moment, processing the sight. "There's a party here today, all right," he said, eyes narrowing, "but for some reason everyone's parked out behind the barn."

Molly shifted the puppy in her arms. "That's not where they normally park?"

"No. Everyone parks just below the ranch house, where we did."

"Maybe there isn't enough room there for all the people who're coming to the party," she offered. She looked happy and content, the color in her cheeks bringing out the clear shine of her eyes. "Come on, let's go see what's going on in the barn. I want to meet that buffalo, too." She abruptly abandoned him, continuing on at a brisk walk, still holding the one pup, who showed no desire to leave the cradle of her arms, the other one following behind her.

Steven hesitated only briefly before realizing that his trepidation was foolish, and he followed because there was no other place he wanted to be than with her. Thus they walked together into the dimness of the barn, and it was Molly who was astounded by the sheer number of people gathered there, awaiting their arrival to spring this surprise party on Steven. But it was Steven and Molly together who shared the enormity of the moment, who leaned into each other when all those voices shouted *"Surprise!"* and when the barn full of faces moved toward them, beaming and smiling and full of the celebratory essence of the word *party!*

Molly looked at him, eyes shining and face alight. Still holding the puppy in her arms, she stood on tiptoe and kissed him lightly on the cheek before the first of the well-wishers reached them, and somehow, in that sweet, simple gesture, she made all the embarrassing fuss and fanfare bearable.

MOLLY WAS DAZZLED, entranced, swept away by her introduction to the Bow and Arrow. If not for the welcoming committee of two cuddly puppies and the scowling but soft-hearted Ramalda, it would have been for the sheer magnificence of the historic mountain ranch, the safe feeling of home she had experienced upon simply alighting here, and the unexpected presence of fifty people surprising them in the barn with a tribute and accolade to Steven that had brought tears to her eyes and had made her stand on tiptoe to kiss him with love and pride and something she couldn't even begin to identify because it was way beyond any emotion she'd ever felt before.

She was standing by the door, watching Steven be inundated by well-wishers, when Pony touched her arm and smiled in greeting. "I was afraid the two of you weren't coming. Steven hates parties. His birthday is next week, but we wanted to surprise him."

"You certainly did. He's so deserving of this," Molly said, her voice choked with emotion. "I think it's wonderful and it's just what he needs. What can I do to help?"

"Everything is pretty much done. We were just waiting for you to arrive. Come on, let me introduce you around."

"Wait," Molly said, indicating the puppy who

lolled contentedly in her arms. "First introduction. Who's this?"

"That's Bonnie. Tessa is the one gnawing on your fancy boots. Tess belongs to Caleb, but Bonnie is as yet unclaimed, along with her brother Bandit, who's probably in the kitchen keeping an eye on Ramalda. He has already figured out that the best place to be is close to the cook."

Molly shook hands first with Pony's husband-to-be, Caleb McCutcheon, a handsome, athletic man with sandy hair and mustache, and keen blue eyes. Then Badger, a crusty old wrangler who took her hand and kissed it with a gentleness that made her smile and blush like a schoolgirl. Badger's friend Charlie promptly shouldered the old cowboy aside and removed his hat. "A pleasure," he said, matching his friend's gallantry with a stiff bow from the waist that nearly did his arthritic body in.

She met Jessie Weaver and Guthrie Sloane. "Steven's told me so much about you and the Bow and Arrow." Molly smiled. "I'm so glad to finally meet you and see this beautiful place." The two of them looked so happy and content that it reaffirmed Molly's belief that true love wasn't just a myth perpetuated by fairy tales.

She met the five teenage boys Pony was fostering: Jimmy, Dan, Martin, Joe and Roon, all full-blooded Crow. She greeted Bernie Portis, Guthrie's cheerful and organized sister who was catering the barbecue, and the rest of her family, and so many others that the names and faces quickly became a scrambled blur. "There," Pony said, as they trailed the group from the pole barn to the ranch house. "You have just met the entire population of Katy Junction."

"Except for the buffalo," Molly reminded her.

Pony paused and called to Roon. "Where is Absa?"

Molly then followed the boys to the corral, where she set down the puppy and, skirt be damned, scrambled up and straddled the fence rails to watch the horses milling about while Roon fetched Absa. Steven came up to stand beside her, resting his forearms on the top rail. She glanced down at him and smiled. "Neat placc."

"Neat place." He nodded.

The buffalo followed Roon from behind the barn like a dog. She allowed the boys to fuss over her while Molly climbed down from the fence and held her hand out cautiously. Absa gave it a brief sniff and appeared unimpressed, and Molly thought the buffalo calf was the oddest-looking creature she'd ever seen. "She's kind of cute, in a prehistoric sort of way."

Roon regarded Absa somberly. "She's beautiful," he corrected.

"She's a buffalo who thinks she's a dog," Jimmy explained. "But she's just a calf still."

"A three-hundred-pound calf," Caleb McCutcheon said, joining the group. "She tried to come into the kitchen yesterday. Ramalda wasn't amused."

"I can't imagine who taught that critter to come inside in the first place," Badger groused, staring pointedly at Roon.

"That would be me," Guthrie admitted. "The day Caleb took Pony and the boys to the Fourth of July celebration in Livingston, I was working on the books, and it just seemed easier to let Absa come inside with me where I could keep an eye on her."

"Well, now, I wouldn't be too critical of that behavior," Charlie interjected on Guthrie's behalf. "I mind the times when Badger and me babysat our fair share of orphaned beef calves in the old bunkhouse."

"Just like Mother Roon," Martin teased. "Absa thinks Roon's her mother, so he sleeps in the barn with her, to keep her company."

"Absa was hurt when she was very young," Roon explained to Molly. "Her leg was broken and she couldn't nurse from her own mother, so we had to bring her back to the ranch and bottle-feed her. That's why she's so tame. The other buffalo are wild, the way buffalo are supposed to be. The herd is up near Piney Creek now, nearly a hundred head."

"A whole herd of them must be something to see," Molly said.

"I could take you up there," Roon offered. "Do you ride?"

"Hold your horses," Steven said. "We have a barbecue to attend, and people to mingle with, and lots of food to eat."

"Yes, but we could eat really fast," Dan said, "and then go see the buffalo, all of us together. It would be fun."

Molly looked hopefully at Steven. "Could we?"

"Leave me out of this conversation," he said. "I don't ride."

"You rode a horse once," Jessie reminded him. "Remember? It was the day we showed Caleb the ranch."

"I'll never forget. I couldn't walk for a week afterward," Steven said with a wry grin. "Let's eat first, and talk horses later."

"Okay," Molly promptly agreed because she was suddenly ravenous. "But it *would* be fun to see the buffalo herd."

PICNIC TABLES HAD BEEN set up behind the ranch house around the big stone barbecue pit itself, and the sweet tang of mesquite coals flavored the crisp September air. Earthenware bowls containing several different salads anchored the red-and-white checked oilcloth coverings at each table. A big cast-iron pot of spiced beans steamed from a pot hook suspended over the fire, and in the old-fashioned kitchen, Ramalda, wearing a bright blue bandanna over her white hair, was baking pan after pan of biscuits so light that even after eating them for decades they could still bring a reverent expression to Badger's bewhiskered face. Ramalda caught him secreting some into his hat and spoke several rapid-fire sentences in Spanish while brandishing a wooden spoon in a threatening fashion.

"Quality control, old gal," Badger said, sidling out of range and winking at Molly as he did. "Someone's got to make sure your biscuits are edible."

Molly placed a basket of the piping-hot biscuits on each picnic table next to the butter crocks. She helped Bernie baste the ribs with sauce as they browned slowly over the coals, and absorbed the babble of conversations, the laughter, the interaction of the partyers as if it were a precious elixir. She hadn't realized how much she missed the big family atmosphere back home. When Steven found her and handed her a glass of wine, she had to restrain herself from throwing her arms around him in blissful gratitude. "This is so much fun," she said.

"I just hope you're hungry," he said as they found a table to sit at. "Remember what I told you about Ramalda."

Pony and Caleb and the boys shared their table, and in between jumping up to help Bernie and Ramalda replenish the heaping platters, Molly ate more than she'd eaten in a long time. The food was delicious, and true to Steven's prediction, Ramalda fully expected every last bit of it to be devoured. Molly had no trouble cleaning her plate several times, nor did anyone else.

During the course of multiple lively conversations, the subject of her occupation came up.

"I'm an attorney," she responded over her shoulder to the gentleman who'd asked.

"Oh?" he said. "Do you work with Steven?"

"Well, no, not exactly," she said, blushing as Steven caught her eye.

Pony waited until the meal was nearly over before she asked her brother, "Did you stop to see Luther Makes Elk on your way here?"

"As a matter of fact, we did," Steven replied after a lengthy pause, leaning his elbows on the table and turning his bottle of beer between his palms. "That's why we were a little late getting here. He gave me an old rifle. He said it was at the battle of Little Big Horn."

Caleb perked up. "No kidding? Was it by any chance a Winchester?"

"I don't know much about guns. He said his great-grandfather was a scout for the bluecoats."

"Did he mention which officer?" Caleb leaned over the table, his expression intent.

"Never mind all this talk of guns," Pony interrupted. "What did Luther say about our wedding?"

Steven shook his head. "Well, Pony, it's like this," he began slowly.

"Steven," Molly said, her disapproval mirroring Pony's. "This is not a joking matter."

Steven glanced between the two of them and relented. "He said yes."

"Yes? He said *yes?*" Pony came off the bench with a cry of delight. "He said yes!" She flung her arms around Caleb from behind. "We are doing the seven sacred steps."

"That's great, that's good news." Caleb patted her arm. "Do you have the rifle with you?" he said to Steven.

"Caleb," Pony protested.

He swiveled on the bench seat to look up at his bride-to-be. "It's not every day a person gets close to a weapon that was at the battle of Little Big

Horn, and I think everyone here should see it. It's an important piece of history."

Pony sighed. "It is a depressing piece of history."

"What do you mean, depressing?" Steven teased his sister. "We Indians won the battle, didn't we?"

"You'd better show it to him." Pony frowned. "He won't rest until you do." And then to Molly she said, "Caleb collects old guns."

"It could be worse," Molly responded with a philosophical shrug. "One of my uncles collects old farm tractors."

STEVEN FETCHED THE RIFLE from the Jeep and carried it to the picnic table, still wrapped in the oilcloth Luther had presented it in. He laid the long bundle on the table in front of Caleb and let him unwind the shroud, an act he performed with a kind of reverence while the other guests rose from their tables and gathered around to watch.

"Was the gun a birthday present?" Bernie asked.

"No. Luther didn't know this was a birthday party," Steven said. Then he gave his sister a suspicious glance. "Or did he?"

Pony shook her head. "I haven't seen Luther in ages."

Caleb had the rifle in his hands. "By God," he marveled. "It's a Winchester 66. This rifle could

very well have been at Little Big Horn. I can research it, all I need to do is write down the serial
number and call up an old friend."

"Really?" Molly said. "How does that work?"

"If it's an army-issue weapon, the tracking system works pretty good. All soldiers were given a
rifle, of course, and a record was kept of its serial
number and who it was issued to. At the end of a
soldier's enlistment he returned the rifle. Obviously,
this one was never returned to the quartermaster, but
most of those old army records still exist. I should
be able to find out who it belonged to."

"Wow," Molly said. "That's kind of neat."

"Maybe it belonged to General George Arm-
strong Custer," Badger said, smoothing his mustache. "That would really be something."

Caleb laughed. "I guess to hell it would. That
would make it a pretty valuable birthday gift."

"How valuable?" Pony asked.

"It would depend on who wanted to buy it and
what they were willing to pay, I guess," Caleb replied. He handed the rifle to Steven, who handed
it to Guthrie, who handed it to Badger, who
handed it to Charlie. By the time it returned to the
table everyone had examined it, and Molly was
still wiping the cold, greasy feel of it from her
hands. "Well, seeing that gun was a real treat,"
Caleb said, wrapping the oilcloth around it once

again. "Almost as good as doing the seven sacred steps will be," he teased his future wife.

Once the rifle was put away, the festivities began with the presentation of a multitude of mostly humorous birthday gifts to Steven, including a deluxe first-aid kit and a box full of things like linaments for sore muscles and extra-strength aspirin. After the joke gifts, he was given a new leather briefcase and an engraved wall plaque lauding his involvement with the creation of the school, which he accepted from Pony along with a hug and a kiss. "Thank you for making our school a reality," she said.

Steven read the plaque and then looked at his sister. "Pony seems to think this wouldn't have happened without me, but this is a shared vision both she and Caleb brought to life. Without the two of them, there wouldn't be a School of Native American Studies at the Bow and Arrow. All I did was file the legal papers. They did the real work, and they deserve all the credit."

Caleb stood beside Steven and raised his bottle of beer. "All I have to say is, I don't know the first damn thing about how to legally create a school. This man here stepped right in and guided us through the entire complicated process, and let me tell you, it was a complicated process. I don't know when I've ever had to jump through so many hoops. He even made a special trip out here when the official papers arrived at his office because he knew a phone call wouldn't have sufficed. Steven Young Bear is without a doubt the hardest man to read that I've ever known, but on that day he was as revved up as we were. I'd like to propose a heartfelt toast to a great man and a dedicated attorney who was instrumental in making Pony's dream come true."

"Hear, hear," Badger said, lifting his own bottle. "Now for the love of bald-headed consumption, let the partying begin."

THE SOUND SYSTEM was pretty good, for a jury-rigged setup put together by Bernie and Pony, both of whom admitted to knowing nothing about woofers and tweeters and generators and nonstop auto CD programming. The area for dancing was ringed by the picnic tables and freshly mown, and as soon as the generator was fired up and country music filled the valley, folks just naturally jumped up to dance.

"I promised I'd teach you the two-step, and I'm a man of my word," Steven said at Molly's elbow as they stood on the sidelines and watched the fun.

Molly felt a momentary qualm. "There's something you should know before you even try," she said, her fingers twisting the stem of the wineglass in her hand. "I have two left feet."

"Says who?"

"My mother insisted that we all learn the social graces at a young age, so we had to take lessons in ballroom dancing, as if we'd be doing a lot of that throughout our lives. It was horrible, and I had to dance with one of my brothers, which made things even worse. I think the whole experience soured me on dancing for life."

"Ballroom dancing is about as far from the Texas two-step as you can get," Steven said, gesturing. "Look at them. They're all having fun, even Badger, and he has to be as old as Luther."

"Does Badger live here, on the ranch?"

"Most of the time. He and Charlie sort of came with the place when Caleb bought it. They were hired on by Jessie Weaver's father back in the late fifties, which was about the time Ramalda came, too."

"Talk about long-term employees," Molly said, dutifully impressed.

"They're more like family. There were plenty of hard times when no paychecks changed hands, but they're a loyal bunch." Steven took the wineglass from her hand and set it on the picnic table. "The sun's setting, Red Hair," he said. "It's time to dance."

Before she could voice another protest, his hand closed on hers and the next thing she knew she was in his arms and she'd forgotten all about not being able to dance, not even liking to dance, and thinking she had two left feet. She was a little giddy from two glasses of wine and she melted into the solid strength of him, letting go of any attempt to make sense of the steps and the moves. She simply closed her eyes and enjoyed the sensation of being close to a man she was falling more deeply in love with by the moment.

Another song followed the first, and another after that, and only when they both felt the fatigue of the long days and the sleepless nights did they take a break. Steven brought her another glass of wine and they walked away from the noise of the party, down past the ranch house and the pole barn to where the creek sparkled like molten gold in the sun's last rays. They sat down side by side, shoulders touching, and Molly leaned into him gratefully. She felt as if a hollow place inside of her were slowly filling with a depth of peace like she'd never known, and she needed to sit in quiet abeyance and experience every precious moment until she was full and the flow, like the swinging shift of a flood tide, eased within her. "Thank you, Steven."

"For what?"

"For asking me here. I don't know when I've ever had such a good time with such wonderful people in such a beautiful setting. If I stay here much longer I might begin to understand why you want to protect all this," she said, indicating the purple mountains that drew a rugged line against the western horizon.

"Then maybe I should tie you up and keep you here."

"You wouldn't need to tie me up," Molly murmured. "Just build me a little cottage on the bank of this river, and let me adopt Bonnie and Bandit."

"Bonnie and Bandit?"

"The two as yet unclaimed puppies. And of course, I'd want a horse or two."

"Of course," he said. "How about a buffalo?"

"Hmmm. I'll have to think about that one. Absa's cute, but my hunch is she's going to get a whole lot bigger." Molly took a sip of wine. "I really would like to ride up and see the herd."

"The boys looked pretty disappointed when you kept on dancing. I think they probably had the horses saddled and ready to go before we were done eating," Steven said.

"Really?" Molly lifted her head off his shoulder to look at him.

"I'm sure they'll take a rain check. It'll be dark soon, and we have to get on the road."

She sighed. "I don't want this day to end."

"There'll be other days as good."

"How can you be so sure?"

"There's going to be a wedding here in a few weeks and it just so happens that I'm giving the bride away. I need a date. Want to come?"

"Oh, Steven." Molly leaned toward him and tenderly kissed his bruised cheek. "If I ever find paradise, it will be a place just like this. Yes, I'll come. I'd love to come to your sister's wedding."

"BUT YOU CAN'T LEAVE," Pony protested when they walked back up to the ranch house to say their goodbyes. "This party is for you."

"We have a long drive ahead of us," Steven said.

"Exactly why you should spend the night," Caleb pitched in, coming to stand beside Pony and drape an arm over her shoulders. "Besides, the boys are anxious to show Molly the buffalo herd. We could all ride up to Piney Creek after breakfast tomorrow. You'll be on the road after lunch and get home well before dark. That's a much better plan, don't you agree?"

"I think it sounds wonderful," Molly said, "but I don't have anything with me for spending the night, and no clothes fit for a horseback ride tomorrow."

"That's not a problem," Pony said. "I can get you everything you need. Please say you will stay."

Molly turned her pleading gaze on Steven. "Could we, Steven?" she said.

He reached for her hand. "All right," he relented. "But I'm not riding tomorrow."

"I promise I won't ask you to, just as long as you promise to dance one more dance with me tonight," Molly said.

And so they danced until the stars shone down out of that wide, dark sky and most of the guests had departed and Ramalda had made it perfectly clear, in a jumbled mix of broken English and rapid-fire Spanish, that it was late, too late for the boys, too late for Mr. Steven who was injured and needed his rest, and too late for her, for she had worked hard all day, cooking this most delicious feast. Steven became aware of this diatribe only when Pony turned down the volume on the sound system and they heard Badger saying, "Dang it, old woman, have you forgot what it's like to be young? Lookit that full moon rising. Now, ain't that worth losing a little sleep over? Love keeps its own time. Always has. Leave 'em be."

They turned to look at the moon and Steven felt Molly's arms tighten around him. "It's so beautiful," she murmured, resting her cheek against his chest. He felt her shiver a little and pulled her closer.

"It's getting cold," he said, "and Ramalda's right. It's late and you've had a long day."

"Is that your way of telling me you're tired?" she said with a smile in her voice.

"It's my way of keeping the peace with Ramalda," he said. "It must be midnight or later, and she gets up at 4:00 a.m."

"But why?" Molly murmured in protest.

"Because that's what time the day begins when you live on the Bow and Arrow."

"Does that mean *we're* getting up at 4:00 a.m.?"

"Don't you want to see the buffalo?"

"Will they be awake that early?" she said with a soft laugh. "Oh, Steven, thank you for letting us stay. Thank you, thank you."

She pulled away from him then, to help Pony with the final cleanup of Ramalda's kitchen, to say goodbye to Bernie and Guthrie and Jessie, to accept the somber bow and the kiss on the cheek from both Badger and Charlie as they departed to overnight on the ranch in parts unknown, and to follow Pony down the back hallway to the guest room where she'd be sleeping. Steven trailed along behind, curious. It was a small room with rose-printed wallpaper, a small bed, bureau and desk, with a braided rug on the floor. "It's lovely," Molly said. "Thank you."

"You'll be sharing the bathroom with the boys," Pony said. "Let me know if they're a problem. You will find a new toothbrush in the cabinet above the sink."

"I'll be fine. Thank you so much. The party was great. Tonight's been just perfect."

Pony smiled. "Steven will be sleeping in the living room on the couch. If he gives you any trouble, just call out and Ramalda will see to him."

Molly's soft laugh brought the heat to Steven's face. He followed his sister back out into the kitchen and waited while she added a few sticks of wood to the stove and shut the dampers down. She met his gaze then and the faintest of smiles warmed her expression before she dropped her eyes and turned toward the door. She opened it and started out onto the porch, then paused and glanced back. "I left blankets and pillows on the couch in the living room." She paused again and the silence stretched out while he patiently waited. "I like her," she concluded. "I am glad you both stayed."

He nodded. "I'm glad you asked us to."

CHAPTER TEN

MOLLY AWOKE in the little bedroom with the cabbage-rose wallpaper and the 1930s vintage furnishings. It was early, dark early, and she opened her eyes slowly, roused by the fragrant aroma of coffee. She stretched and yawned and felt that same warm, peaceful feeling fill her that had filled her the night before, and thought that she could live like this forever as long as Steven was near.

Steven…

Her smile widened as she remembered how she'd crept into the living room after Pony left, while the ranch house slept and the moon rose ever higher to cast its celestial light through the old, rippled panes of glass. She'd been able to see plainly enough to walk in the unfamiliar darkness to the place where he slept. Or, as it had turned out, didn't sleep. When she'd entered the living room, her eyes searching for his form on the sofa, she was startled to see that it was empty, that the room was empty, and that the door leading out onto the porch was ajar. She'd found him sitting on a bench in the chill of the earliest of morning hours, gazing out across the moonlit distance.

"Steven?" she had whispered, and he had turned his head and held out his hand to her. She had joined him, clad only in the oversize T-shirt that Pony had given her as a nightgown. It floated to her knees in a baggy, shapeless cotton tent and once upon a time she would have died before being seen like that by a man she cared about, but that had been another time. With Steven she'd never given it a thought, just let him pull her down next to him and wrap her in his warmth.

The sound of a horse whinnying and a boy's voice shouting roused her from her reverie. Molly got up and was startled to see that neatly folded on the chair by the door was an entire outfit suitable for a long ride up into the September mountains of Montana, obviously delivered while she slept. She dressed hastily after the prerequisite scrub up in the bathroom, which, due to the apparent lateness of the hour, she had all to herself. When she entered the warm kitchen, Ramalda was washing dishes at the sink while firewood snapped in the cookstove and a pot of coffee steamed enticingly.

"Good morning, Ramalda," she said. "I'm sorry I'm late…,"

"Breakfast long over," Ramalda said, swinging

her formidable bulk about and giving Molly her darkest scowl.

"Yes, I'm sorry I overslept, but I ate too much yesterday. Your food was so delicious I couldn't get enough, and eating so much of it made me very sleepy, and so this morning I overslept."

Ramalda's face softened. "Yes," she said. "So. He sleeps still." She nodded toward the living room. "He ate too much, too, *si?* My food is very good."

"Your food is wonderful. I'll bring him coffee," Molly offered, and Ramalda poured two cups from the pot that was pushed to the back of the woodstove. Molly carried both into the living room and paused when she saw that Steven was, indeed, sound asleep, lying on the couch on his back, fingers laced across his stomach. No blanket, fully clothed. The murky light made the cuts and bruises on his face look even worse. She sat on the very edge of the couch and he opened his eyes and moaned.

"It's too early for it to be morning," he said.

"We're on cowboy time now, Young Bear, remember?"

"I'm an Indian. I don't subscribe to that foolishness."

"You still have time to change your mind about the horseback ride." She smiled.

"Never," he said. "And don't say I didn't warn

you. It's a hard ride up that mountain. Monday morning you'll be on your hands and knees."

"Never," Molly echoed, chin lifting. "I brought you a cup of coffee." She set the steaming mug on the table beside the couch. "I'll see you around lunchtime. Try to sit out in the sunshine today. It will help heal your bruises."

"Really?"

"Really. It's a good thing to know if you should ever happen to get beat up." She leaned over, kissed Steven very gently, and rose to her feet. "They're waiting for me. I'll see you later."

She carried her coffee with her to the pole barn, sipping it along the way and admiring the clear yellow band of light that defined the mountain peaks to the east. It was cold, and she was glad for the warm clothing, especially the sheepskin jacket and the fleece-lined leather gloves. She could hear the murmur of voices as she drew near the barn. The boys were in a huddle around one of the horses in the corral and several other horses were all saddled and ready to go.

"No, stupid," she heard one of them say. "Red Hair's legs are long. Lengthen the stirrup straps a little."

The huddle immediately dispersed when they heard her approaching footsteps and the boys lined out, facing her, five pairs of somber eyes no doubt measuring her worth as a cowgirl. "Good morning," she greeted, leaning against the fence. "Sorry I'm late."

"Oh, you ain't late." The reply came from inside the barn as Badger emerged, leading a horse. "We're just trying to scare up enough saddles so's none of us has to ride bareback. Roon could ride thataway, but I sure as hell cain't."

"Nor I," Molly said. "I need that thing on the front of the saddle to hang on to."

"It's called a saddle horn," one of the boys volunteered. "And this is your horse. His name is Amos."

Molly crawled between the fence rails and approached the little brown gelding that the boys had been surrounding. "Is Amos gentle?"

"He used to be my horse," Jimmy said, "until I rode better. I ride that dun over there now. His name's Comanche and he's a real cow horse. I hope to ride him in the rodeo in Livingston next Fourth of July. We're going to compete in the team penning."

"Really?" Molly let Amos take a deep sniff of her hand before stroking his velvety nose. "Hello, Amos. I've never ridden a horse before, so please be extra patient with me."

"All right, boys, crawl aboard them hay burners. Daylight's wastin' and we got us a herd of buffalo to hunt up," Badger said. He walked back inside the barn and reemerged with a five-gallon bucket, which he upended next to Amos's shoulder. "Step up on that and put your left foot in this stirrup," he said to Molly. "Throw your other leg over the saddle. There, that's good. Amos here's a good steady horse, fine for a first ride. Your stirrup leathers look a hair short. Slip your feet out of 'em and I'll fix 'em proper."

"I thought Pony and Caleb were planning to come along," Molly said while Badger fussed over her stirrups.

"Oh, they left half an hour ago, with Guthrie and Jess," he said. "They were planning to stop for coffee up by the holding pens, so more'n likely we'll catch 'em up there." He swung open the corral gate and the boys rode out first. As Molly passed him, the old cowboy spat a mouthful of tobacco juice, wiped his chin on the sleeve of his coat, and said, "Sure hope they brung along some of Ramalda's bear sign."

AFTER A MILE OR SO of steady climbing, during which Amos behaved himself like the truly gentle horse he was reputed to be, Molly began to relax and take note of her surroundings. The higher they climbed, the more spectacular the view. She drew great lungfuls of the cold, clean air and looked this way and that, and thought how romantic it was to be riding a horse into such a beautiful mountain morning. "The only thing missing is the man," she murmured into Amos's swiveling ears. If Steven had come, the day would have been perfect.

They rode until the trail flattened out in a big meadow that seemed to reach out to the very base of the mountains themselves. On the near side of the meadow was a series of big sturdy corrals and chutes built of pipe. "For the buffalo," Roon told her. "We can hold the herd here when we need to give them vaccinations or test the cows to see if they're pregnant. Pony designed the corrals. She knows a lot about buffalo, more than any of us. She learned from Pete Two Shirts. Pete manages the Crow's tribal herd."

Molly was relieved to hear from Badger that they would stop here to give the horses a breather and have some refreshment. The trail thus far had been demandingly steep, and already her thigh muscles were cramping from the effort of staying in the saddle. She looked forward to taking a break and having a second cup of coffee. It was high time for a rest.

As Badger had predicted, Pony and Caleb were at the corrals, along with Jessie and Guthrie. They were sitting on some bales of hay, enjoying the sunrise and sharing a Thermos of coffee. They broke out another Thermos and treated the boys to hot chocolate while dispensing Ramalda's strong cowboy brew to Badger and Molly, along with one of the most delicious doughnuts she'd ever eaten. She sat down next to Pony and took a big bite. Then another. Two more and the entire doughnut was gone. "Thank you! That was delicious."

"That was Ramalda's bear sign," Badger said.

Pony handed her another. "Bear sign is cowboy slang for doughnuts."

"Best bear sign I ever ate," Molly admitted, biting into the second. She took another sip of coffee and massaged a sore muscle in the calf of her leg. "How much farther is it to where the buffalo are?"

"Oh, hell," Badger snorted. "We ain't even got started yet. The trail gets pretty steep from here on out, soon as we cross the meadow."

"Steeper than what we've already climbed?" Molly asked with a lurch of anxiety, and the boys' laughter was answer enough.

"So, you couldn't talk Steven into coming," Pony said.

Molly finished off the second doughnut and tried to calculate how far across the meadow was and how high that pass that they had to ride through could possibly be. "No," she said. "And I'm beginning to understand why."

TWO HOURS LATER she was well beyond wishing she'd stayed behind and snuggled on the couch with Steven or just plain died outright in his arms. She'd long since dropped Amos's reins on his neck and was devoting all her energy to clinging with both hands to the saddle horn, murmuring repeated Hail Marys beneath her breath and promising God that if she ever survived this awful experience, she would never mention the words *horse* or *buffalo* again.

Ever.

Her death grip on the horn was so fierce that when Amos suddenly stopped and she lifted her head to look around, she couldn't loosen her fingers. "It's all right, Molly," she heard Pony say through her fog of exhaustion. "We're at the line camp on Piney Creek. The worst of the climb is over."

Molly nodded that she understood as Badger helped her out of the saddle. Her legs could barely support her and he assisted her to a bench in front of what appeared to be a very old, weather-beaten log cabin that she hadn't even noticed moments earlier.

"You ladies rest up," he said gallantly. "The boys and I'll hunt up the herd while you eat." Molly was certain she was the only lady who needed to rest, but she wasn't about to argue the point. She rubbed her hands against her thighs and looked around. In front of the cabin was what she assumed was Piney Creek, and beyond it a large, tree-dotted meadow rimmed with mountains that were flanked with the golden colors of fall. It was, she supposed, an idyllic western setting, but all she could think about was that horrifyingly steep trail they'd just ridden in on, nearly vertical in places, and how equally terrifying the ride back to the ranch was going to be.

She didn't have the strength to make it back to the Bow and Arrow. No way. Her legs were like rubber, and her hands... She held them up to examine them. They looked normal, but... "Here," Pony said at her elbow, startling her. "It's a ham sandwich and a cold soda. The food will help. You should have eaten breakfast."

"Next time I'll know better," Molly said with a grateful smile. "Thank you."

"It's a tough haul if you aren't used to riding," Jessie spoke up from Molly's other elbow as the two women shared the bench with her to eat their lunch. "Guthrie and I spent our honeymoon up here. It was just perfect except for a run-in with a grizzly two nights into the stay. It spooked the horses but Guthrie fired a round from his rifle and scared him off. There was no trouble."

"A grizzly? You mean, a bear?" Molly said, sitting up a little straighter and glancing warily around.

"One of the biggest bears on the North American continent," Jessie agreed. "Beautiful, too, but they can be dangerous."

Molly felt comforted by the solid log wall she leaned against. Surely no bear would attack them here. She thought about taking a bite of her ham sandwich but didn't have the strength to lift it to her mouth. "I don't suppose this honeymoon retreat of yours has a hot tub?"

"No," Jessie said with a sympathetic laugh. "Just a very cold creek, though there's a place about a quarter mile downstream where a hot spring makes bathing quite comfortable."

"That's a quarter mile too far for me, I'm afraid," Molly murmured. The sandwich was so heavy she had to rest it in her lap. Two thick slices of Ramalda's most excellent homemade bread, two equally thick slices of ham bracketing a thick slice of cheese. She was hungry, starving, famished, but her arms, like the rest of her body, lacked all strength. She wasn't at all sure she'd be able to stand up ever again. She was contemplating closing her eyes and passing out when she heard one of the boys shout.

"Buffalo! We found the buffalo!"

She heard the drum of hoofbeats and looked to her right. The boys were racing their horses toward the cabin, Roon in the lead. They crossed the creek in wild plumes of spray and drew rein practically right at their feet, the horses tossing their heads and snorting.

"Where?" Pony said calmly, never flinching.

"In the little valley just above this one. It looks like they're heading over the next pass to Horseshoe Pond and the headwaters of the Silver."

Jessie brightened. "Good news. That's less than a mile from here. Let's eat and ride."

STEVEN SAT OUT in the sun like Molly suggested and even fell asleep like that after eating Ramalda's bounteous lunch. A nap seemed natural, and his body soaked up the heat of the September sun like it was a kind of medicine. Maybe Molly was right. Maybe it would heal up the bruises and cuts on his face. He'd like that. The idea of attending another public meeting while resembling a slab of roadkill was unappealing, especially since he knew there'd be a lot of press there, eager for more bloody pictures, more front-line stories. And so he sat in the soothing warmth and drifted off to the lulling sounds of the Bow and Arrow, and when he woke it was late afternoon and the sun was westering and Molly wasn't back yet.

He pushed out of his chair and stood and looked over at the place where the old Indian trace came down by the creek. The afternoon was warm and sleepy, redolent of ripe blackberries and freshly mown hay, buzzing with crickets and cicadas. It was beautiful and peaceful, but there was no Molly. They should have been back by now. They should have returned while Ramalda was dishing up the lamb stew and yeast rolls that were his lunch. The boys should have been filling his head with visions of wild stampedes and angry grizzlies. Pony should have been quietly amending their fabrications and helping Ramalda with the evening meal. Caleb should have been expounding on the importance of his keeping that old rifle of Luther's clean and safe. Badger should have been leaning back on the wall bench, working on a fresh chaw of tobacco and ruminating on the days when he was young and the West was still wild.

But the place was as quiet as a tomb, and he cat-footed across the porch and sneaked a peek into the kitchen. Ramalda was slicing big ripe tomatoes into a huge pot on top of the cookstove. Steven watched for a moment, and then back-pedaled onto the porch again and stood looking at the place down by the creek where he knew they would emerge when they came. But where were they? They'd been gone since before sunup, and here it was, late afternoon. This was Molly's first time on a horse, and though he'd tried to warn her, she was of the stubborn persuasion that she could handle anything the Bow and Arrow could hurl at her.

And maybe she could. He wouldn't be the least bit surprised. She was tough and fierce and determined, and could probably hold her own in the midst of a tornado, but dammit, he was worried about her. She'd suffered some rough knocks in the past few days, and...

And what was that? A flash of movement where before there'd been none. A bird flushing out of the brush. A horse down by the pole barn suddenly wheeling about, pricking its ears, and whinnying a plaintive welcome. And yes. Here they came, here at last, one by one, threading slowly through the brush along the creek where the trail merged with the beaten cow paths. The horses had their heads down, weary. The riders...hard to tell. Where was Molly? Steven started down the porch steps and heard movement behind him. Ramalda came out onto the porch, knife in hand, squinting her eyes at the same place he'd been studying for so long.

"Biene," she said with a satisfied nod. "They come."

Steven met them down by the corral. He didn't want to appear as if he'd had anything but the laziest and best of times. He leaned against the open gate, waiting until they rode their horses into the corral, all of them, and then he closed the gate behind them and walked up to where Molly sat on the small brown gelding. He stopped by her knee, put his hand upon it and felt her muscles quiver. Her eyes locked with his and she leaned ever so slightly over her horse's shoulder.

"Did you see the buffalo?" he said.

Her expression held an emotion he couldn't quite grasp, but he thought that given enough time, and he craved time with Molly more than anything, he could come to know and love every mystery she embodied. "Yes," she said.

And that was all.

AN HOUR LATER they had said their goodbyes and were leaving the Bow and Arrow. Steven had enjoyed the stay but was relieved to be leaving, if only because it meant being alone with Molly for the drive back to his place. She curled on the seat beneath a blanket he'd pulled out of the back in deference to the chilly evening. Every once in a while she would shift position slightly and the movement would bring a soft moan of agony. "I don't know how I'm going to make it to work tomorrow," she said. "You were so right, Steven. Riding up that mountain today was one of the dumbest things I've ever done."

"But you saw the buffalo."

She sighed. "When they spotted us they moved away and broke into this strange kind of run. Pony said they didn't like having the horses get too near them. She said if we were in a vehicle we could have gotten closer, but I thought we were plenty close. They were huge. And then we came back down the mountain."

"You did well. That was a hard ride."

"My first and last. And Steven, for future reference, I'll be happy with just those two puppies and the cottage by the river. Forget the horses and the buffalo." He glanced at her and she caught his eye. "What are you smiling about?"

"I was just wondering. If you weren't an attorney, what would you be?"

"Definitely not a cowgirl," she responded, flinching as she shifted position. "An architect, perhaps. That was my alternate major, and I actually took a bunch of electives in that field. I'd be designing interesting and unique buildings. On the other hand, maybe I'd be a race-car driver or an astronaut. Then again, I always thought it might be fun to marry a man who was so disgustingly rich that I didn't have to do anything at all but lounge around in expensive clothing, contemplating the next charity fund-raiser or where might be a novel place to summer in Europe."

"Somehow I can't see you living that way."

"Neither can I," she murmured, cautiously propping herself up to look out the window. "So, being that I'm a working girl, Monday I'll go back to work. That is, if I can walk, and if I still have a job."

"If they were going to fire you, they would have done it on Friday after your statement to the press. But if you had lost your job, would it be the end of the world?"

Molly was silent for a long while, gazing out the side window. "Yes," she said. "I think it would be devastating to my career to be fired from such a prestigious law firm."

"Prestigious isn't the word I'd use. You could always resign."

She shook her head. "I made those damning public statements just to keep my job, which I wouldn't have done if I were going to resign. Yes, they threw me to the wolves, but maybe I deserved it for being so ignorant about the road permitting process. I've learned my lesson. This will blow over, and in a week's time nobody'll even remember what all the fuss was about."

"What about next time?"

"There won't be any next time." Molly stared back out the window, her chin lifting in that defiant way.

"You're probably right," Steven said, wishing

he'd never started the conversation that had destroyed her peaceful mood. They drove in silence for a long while, long enough for him to think of a hundred things to say to make her ease back in her seat and relax again, but before he could voice a single one she turned abruptly to face him.

"Steven, if you're so anti-Taintor, Skelton and Goldstein, why won't you talk to me about the lawsuit you brought against the Soldier Mountain mine?"

"Because you still work for Taintor, Skelton and Goldstein, and discussing the Soldier Mountain lawsuit with you would be a definite conflict of interest."

"Mr. Skelton told me that lawsuit nearly landed you in jail."

Her unexpected statement caused Steven's grip on the steering wheel to tighten, but he kept his eyes on the road and made no response.

"If I resigned, would you talk to me about it then?"

Steven groped for the right answer, but the right answer didn't exist. There was just an ocean of murky gray waves that he couldn't begin to navigate. Her question hung in the air and with each passing mile the silence grew more formidable until finally she curled up again, her back to him, shutting him out. "Well, it doesn't matter, Young

Bear. You can keep your all-important secrets forever, because I'm not resigning," she said.

WITH EVERY MILE that brought her closer to her own world, Molly felt the peace she'd experienced at the Bow and Arrow draining out of her. It was late when they reached Steven's place. He parked the Jeep beside Molly's car and cut the ignition. The silence between them filled a universe. Molly could feel her heart beating a rapid, painful cadence in her breast. She drew a deep breath and exhaled slowly.

"For a little while life was perfect, wasn't it?" she said softly.

"Come inside," Steven said. "I'll make a pot of coffee."

Molly shook her head. "I have to get going." She willed herself to move, to get out of the Jeep and leave before she did something weak and silly like break down and cry. She was so tired and discouraged. She reached for the door handle, hoping her legs were up to the task of getting her as far as her car.

"Stay the night."

Molly felt the tears stinging at the back of her eyes and shook her head. "I can't," she whispered around the lump in her throat.

"I'll wake you early. You'll be on the road by

six and in your office by nine. I promise you will, and I'm a man of my word."

Molly nodded in the darkness. "I know that," she said. "But I need to be alone right now to think this through. I'm so confused about us. I don't understand why you would take me to that mine, offer to take me to the reservation, and then slam the door in my face when I want to learn more." She fumbled for the door handle again and this time she wrenched the door open and got out. Her legs screamed silent protest but they did her bidding. She had her car keys in her hand and was in the driver's seat before Steven could reach her. She turned the key in the ignition as he approached.

"Molly, please don't leave like this."

"Like what, Steven?" she said, her voice trembling with emotion. "Like a woman who's been shut out completely by the man she's hopelessly in love with because he so obviously doesn't trust her?" She shifted into reverse. "How do you expect me to feel?"

He braced his hands on her car door and leaned in her window. "I trust you, Molly, you know I do, but the Soldier Mountain lawsuit isn't about trust. Look at me. You think I had a fun time with those truckers? That's the level of blind rage we're talking about here, and it can get much worse, believe me it can. I don't want anything like that ever happening to you. Don't you understand?"

Molly stared at him, shaken by his words. "Oh, Steven," she said softly, broken by the passion she saw in him and the realization that he truly cared for her. "Don't *you* understand that everything that happens to you, happens to me, too?" She shifted into first gear and pulled away before he could reply.

CHAPTER ELEVEN

THE NEXT MORNING Molly's physical and emotional states were at such an all-time low that not even bright sunshine, multiple cups of strong coffee or the long hot soak in the tub could dispel the aches in her muscles or the black depression that shadowed her as she drove to the office. She half-expected to see someone else's name on her reserved parking sign, and her climb up the granite steps was slow and painful. In her office, she was relieved that everything looked the same. Her pictures still hung on the walls, her books lined the shelves, and her desk was just as she had left it—yet everything felt strangely different. The place had changed somehow.

Or perhaps *she* was the one who had changed. Perhaps the time spent at the Bow and Arrow had altered her perceptions enough to throw her off-balance in a world she thought she knew and understood...and wanted to belong to. She sat down at her desk, placed her briefcase on the floor beside her, and drew a deep, steadying breath. It was exactly 9:00 a.m. If the firm was going to ask for her resignation, it would probably happen today, before the public meeting on Tuesday. That way, Taintor, Skelton and Goldstein could wash their hands of her and present a clean slate to the public on the New Millennium Mining proposal. Brad had assured her that this would never happen, but…

There was a tap on her door and Jarrod Skelton entered. Molly felt the pressure building beneath her lungs. It was going to happen, then. Skelton rarely arrived at the office before ten. She pushed painfully to her feet and kept one hand on the desk, steadying herself for what was to come. "Good morning, sir," she said.

"Molly," he said, closing the door gently behind him. "I wanted to see how you were doing." His expression was patronizing and sympathetic. "Friday was no doubt a very difficult day for you."

"Yes, it was." She wondered if this was leading into something sinister or if he was truly concerned about her welfare. "But I'm doing quite well, thank you."

Skelton nodded. "I have every confidence that you'll weather this little setback and become a respected member of this law firm."

"Thank you, Mr. Skelton." She felt the pressure

ease enough to draw a breath. Her job was secure, at least for the time being.

"About the public meeting tomorrow evening. Both Brad and Ken agree that it would be best if you didn't attend, even as an interested spectator. We think a low profile is called for on your behalf, at least for a little while. I have some files you can work on, things to keep you busy...."

Molly nodded. "I understand." She stood for a few moments after he left her office before lowering herself into her chair. She knew beyond a glimmer of doubt that from this point onward, for as long as she worked in this firm, she would never progress beyond the status of being Brad's glorified legal assistant. She was still staring into her bleak future when the phone rang. She resented the interruption, but painful moments meant nothing to an office telephone.

"Ferguson," she snapped.

"Ms. Ferguson, this is Gregory Dehaviland, of Condor International. We spoke briefly last week."

Surprise and shock rocked her back in her seat. "Yes, Mr. Dehaviland," she replied, her voice sounding faint to her own ears. "What can I do for you?"

"I was wondering if you could join me for lunch this afternoon. One o'clock, at the Bistro off Main Street."

"Here? In Helena?" she blurted, then sagged in

her chair. What was the matter with her? The Bistro was in Helena, just off Main Street, not three blocks from the office. Could she have possibly said anything more inane?

"I'm in town for the day and I'd like to meet with you. It will be just the two of us, if that's all right with you."

"Yes, of course," Molly said. "I'll be there." Her hand was trembling as she hung up the phone. Her whole body was trembling. Skelton hadn't fired her, but Gregory Dehaviland would. With a sudden jolt she understood all the stockbrokers who had jumped out their windows when the market crashed back in the twenties. It wasn't just the loss of their fortunes that destroyed all hope of a future, it was the loss of their identities. Molly groaned. She was being foolish. If Dehaviland wanted her fired, he certainly wouldn't dirty his own hands with the task. No, this was about something else, so instead of jumping out her second-story office window and perhaps breaking her leg, she'd meet him for lunch and find out just what it was.

THE BISTRO WAS ALWAYS BUSY for lunch because the food was great, the service excellent, and businesspeople appreciated the fact that they could dine within their time allotments and not feel pressured. Molly arrived a little early and was

shown to a table overlooking the garden court-
yard. The maître d' seated her and took her drink
order, Perrier with lime. She was so nervous she'd
have preferred a gin and tonic, but she wasn't
about to cross any lines with the CEO of Condor
International. She hadn't been seated more than
five minutes before Dehaviland arrived, and she
had no problem whatsoever identifying him the
moment he stepped into the establishment.

It wasn't the way he was dressed, for he was
very casually attired in tan chinos and a dark
green flannel shirt. It was the way he carried himself, with the extreme self-assurance of a very accomplished and powerful man. He was shown to
her table even as she struggled painfully to her
feet, and his handshake was firm and brief.

"Thank you for joining me," he said after intro-
ducing himself, and to the hovering maître d',
"I'll have my usual."

"You come here often, then," Molly said, in-
wardly wincing as soon as the words passed her
lips. So far she hadn't said one single intelligent
thing to this man.

"Yes, as a matter of fact. That's why I'm so interested in New Millennium's proposal." He had
very keen eyes behind the horn-rimmed glasses.
Neatly trimmed salt-and-pepper hair. Clean-
shaven, tanned complexion, very outdoorsy look-

ing, almost as if he could have come straight from herding buffalo on the Bow and Arrow. "I saw the Friday edition of the newspaper. Quite a front-page story you gave them."

Molly felt the heat creep into her cheeks. "I'm sorry. I certainly didn't mean to cast a disparaging light on New Millennium."

"No apologies necessary, Ms. Ferguson. I may only have been CEO for a year, but I've been with the company for two decades and I'm fully aware of how mining companies and law firms operate, which is another reason why I'm here. How long have you known Ken Manning?"

His directness was unsettling. "Less than two weeks," she replied.

"I see." A server delivered his drink, what looked like scotch on the rocks, and he lifted it for a taste. "You must have thought you were going to be fired after all that hoopla. Why didn't you resign?"

"I need the job," Molly replied without hesitation, because it was the truth and because her dander was up. "And besides, I—" Molly stopped abruptly. She took a sip of water to give herself time to collect her thoughts. "I've always tried to do my best, sir. This road-permitting mistake that I made—"

Dehaviland held up his hand, cutting her off. "I think we both know that you had nothing to do with that," he stated briskly. "Let's minimize what happened, fix the mistakes, and move on. Bottom line, I want to change things around here. I want us to begin a positive relationship with the environmental agencies and the public. I want the image of the heartless, powerful oil-and-mining conglomerates to end with the examples that Condor International sets. I want to lead the industry into a new age of cooperation, compromise, and communication."

Molly took another sip of her water, hoping her outward demeanor remained calm because his unexpected declaration had rendered her speechless.

"And I want it to begin right here, right now, with this New Millennium project," Dehaviland continued. He leaned forward on his elbows, his expression animated. "There were two sites originally proposed for the New Millennium mine, one on Madison Mountain outside of the town of Moose Horn, and the other about thirty miles to the west, a place called Butte Mountain, which is located on privately owned property just outside the national forest. Butte Mountain's ore samples actually assayed out richer than Madison Mountain, but the problem was the price of the property. The landowner wouldn't accept our offer, so we filed the claim on Madison Mountain. All of this happened prior to my being named CEO of Condor International."

"I see."

"The test drilling and road construction at the Madison Mountain site has run into a great deal of money."

"I'm sure it has." Molly nodded.

"The board members want to keep on with the project, but I'm trying to convince them that it would be a wiser move at this point to purchase Butte Mountain outright."

The server reappeared to take their order. Molly hadn't even glanced at the menu. "I'll have a house salad, dressing on the side," she said.

"I'll have my usual," Dehaviland repeated, and the server bowed away. "The problem is, not only is the Butte Mountain purchase price high, but we've already invested heavily in the Madison Mountain site."

Molly cleared her throat. "But, sir, the claims filed on Madison Mountain are all perfectly legal, and the permitting process is well underway."

"That doesn't change the fact that those claims are smack-dab in the center of a beautiful national forest, and that Madison Mountain's watershed does indeed flow into the Yellowstone River. Yes, the assay reports were glowing, but is it worth situating an open pit mine in such an environmentally sensitive place, especially in light of the bad publicity we've just been swamped with?"

"Well, sir…"

Dehaviland reached into his shirt pocket and withdrew a folded map, which he spread out on the table. "Okay, this is how things stand. Here's the Yellowstone," he said, tracing the river toward its headwaters in Yellowstone Lake. "Here's Yellowstone National Park. Here's the proposed mine on Madison Mountain. And over here—" he slid his finger to the west and stopped with an emphatic jab "—Butte Mountain. No major watersheds nearby, no natural scenic wonders, no national forest surrounding it, and no Yellowstone National Park. Good, established roads access the mountain from two directions, here and here." He leaned back, lifted his drink for a swallow, and eyed her appraisingly.

Molly met his gaze. "Mr. Dehaviland, why are you telling me this?"

"As you're aware, there's a public meeting tomorrow night in Bozeman regarding the New Millennium project, and after all the publicity it's gotten, I'm sure the meeting will be well attended."

"Yes, but I've been taken off the project. I'm no longer Brad's assistant, and I've also been informed I can't attend the public meeting."

"Ms. Ferguson, believe it or not," Dehaviland said, "I have the power to change all that."

Molly shook her head. "Sir, I don't understand why you'd bother. I'm the least experienced attorney at Taintor, Skelton and Goldstein, and right now my reputation is less than sterling."

"True, but you can still make miracles happen. You can talk to Steven Young Bear. He'll listen to you." He leaned forward again, drink cradled in his hands. Hands which were masculine and strong, not at all the pale, soft hands one would expect of a corporate executive. "I'd like the two of you to work together to broker a deal between Condor International and the people who want to protect Madison Mountain."

"What kind of a deal?"

"We sell the patented claims on Madison Mountain to one of Young Bear's environmental land trusts for two million dollars."

Molly blinked. "Do you honestly think raising that kind of money is doable for a bunch of blue-collar workers?"

Dehaviland nodded. "I also think it's the only way I can push this idea to the board of directors. By selling the mining claim for that price, we'll recoup everything invested up to date and be able to meet the Butte Mountain purchase price."

"How long would they have to raise the money?"

"Six months. That gives them all winter. Young Bear could probably swing it in half that time. He knows his stuff and he's good at what he does."

The server came and silently slid Molly's salad in front of her. Dehaviland's plate held a thick turkey club. He plucked the two toothpicks from either half and laid them aside. "So, what do you say?" he said, startling her yet again.

She picked up her fork and held it poised over her salad, eyebrows drawing together. "You're doing all this just for good publicity?"

Dehaviland picked up one half of the sandwich and a faint grin accompanied his keen glance. "Not quite." With his free hand he shifted the map so she could see it better and traced his finger once again along the river. "Here's Yellowstone Lake, Yellowstone National Park, and the Yellowstone River flowing south into the Missouri." He glanced up. "Did you know the Yellowstone is the longest river without a dam obstructing it in the United States? I also happen to think it's one of the most beautiful as well." His eyes dropped back to the map. "Here's where the river passes through the Madison Mountain watershed and here—" his finger glided to a stop along a seemingly empty stretch "—here's where my cabin's located. I've been going there since I was a boy. When my grandparents died, they left the place to me, and over the years I think I've spent more hours fly-fishing on the Yellowstone than I have sitting in corporate boardrooms. Believe it or not, Ms. Ferguson, I love that river, and I'll help in any way to keep it just the way it is." He took a bite of sandwich and raised his eyebrows. "Does that explain things to your satisfaction?"

Dazed, Molly nodded. "Yes, sir. I'll do everything I can to help."

"Could you run this proposal by Young Bear before the public hearing?"

"I'll speak with him about it tonight," she promised.

"Good. I hope this is the beginning of better times. I see no reason why we can't work together to reach an equitable compromise, and I'd like that to be expressed up front and center Tuesday night, if not by Ken Manning, then by you."

STEVEN SPENT A RESTLESS DAY at his office catching up on work for the Conservancy while fielding calls from journalists interested in the New Millennium mine proposal and how it would impact the Yellowstone River drainage. Some callers were from the East Coast, some from the West, and some from points in between. The interest sparked by the violence on the access road had put the proposed mine squarely in the public's eye, and Steven did his best to keep it there.

That afternoon he fielded a different kind of call from Conrad Walker. "I thought you'd want to know that the second autopsy on Sam Blackmore didn't turn up anything suspicious," Walker said.

"Did his digital camera and briefcase ever surface?"

"Nope. He may have left them at a friend's house. Maybe he was having an affair, who knows, but apparently the fact that they're missing isn't reason enough to open up a murder investigation. His death is being officially listed as resulting from injuries sustained in a car crash. How are your injuries, by the way?"

"Fine," Steven said. "Yours?"

"Better, little by little. The one good thing that came out of getting the stuffing beat out of me is having Amy Littlefield check in on me from time to time. She's a nice girl."

After talking with the sheriff, Steven contemplated phoning Molly but decided against it. She'd been angry with him last night, and he didn't blame her. Somehow he needed to smooth the waters and make it right between them. He needed her to know how important she was to him, and that he was thinking about her. Not being an experienced romantic, the most obvious inspiration took a while to strike, but when it did he reached for the phone book and turned to the yellow pages.

Say it with flowers.

MOLLY'S HEAD WAS still spinning after she returned to her office that afternoon. The conversation had been so unexpected and Gregory Dehaviland had seemed so sincere and been so *nice*. Could this really happen, this compromise between New Millennium Mining and the people from Moose Horn? And could Steven really raise two million dollars in six months? The idea began to excite her. Twice she reached for the phone to call him, but somehow the proposal seemed too important to relay over the phone. "I could sell my car...." she murmured aloud, then laughed. The thought had come out of nowhere. Sell her car, buy a junker, give some money to Steven for the land, for the mountain, and she was the girl who, not that long ago, was arguing that a mountain was just a heap of dirt and minerals. "I could sell my car," she repeated. "Every little bit will help."

She reached for the phone again and then glanced at the clock. Four-thirty. She could drive to Steven's place and tell him about Dehaviland's offer in person. Maybe then he'd realize that she was right, that industry and the environment could coexist in a symbiotic relationship; that people could have steady, good-paying jobs, and the land could be treated with the respect it deserved.

A tap at her door and Brad entered, looking full of something important. "Skelton just called from the courthouse," he said, standing across the desk from her, hands shoved in the pockets of his tailored slacks. "He wanted me to tell you that he's reconsidered everything that's happened and wants you to remain as my assistant on the project. He also wants you to attend the public meeting tomorrow night."

Molly feigned surprise. "Really? What made him change his mind?"

Brad shrugged, his gaze evasive. "I'm not sure. He also said he'd smooth things over with Ken Manning."

"That's going to take some fancy smoothing," Molly said. She pushed to her feet, stifling a moan as her legs reminded her of a horseback ride and a herd of buffalo. "Thank you, Brad. I'm afraid I have to leave the office a little early today, so I won't be able to file these for you." She picked up a thick stack of folders and handed them to him with as sweet a smile as she could manage. "But I certainly appreciate you giving me the opportunity to do so, just the same."

Looking mildly disgruntled, Brad left her office, and not long after that, Molly was in her car. As she was driving out of the parking area she noticed a floral delivery van parking out front. Some lucky person was getting flowers.

STEVEN STOPPED at the grocery store on his way home and invested in some food. His bank account was stretched pretty lean, but it was no great hardship for him to exist on stir-fries and rice, supplemented by the fresh seasonal vegetables with which September was especially generous. He reached home by five-thirty, time enough to cook a quick meal before heading for the special strategy meeting in Moose Horn that he'd promised Amy Littlefield he'd attend. He sipped a beer while he stirred the strips of boneless chicken breast in spicy garlic oil and sliced the vegetables. He wondered if Molly had liked the flowers. He hadn't quite known what to send her but the florist had been very helpful.

"Is this a special occasion?" she'd asked.

"Yes. Her first public reprimand, and her first horseback ride, which happened to be up a very steep mountain."

"All in one day?"

"Near enough. She needs something special."

"Hmmm. Roses?"

"Are roses good for sore muscles and a bruised ego?"

"Roses work for everything," the woman's sage voice pertly informed him. "What color roses would you prefer we send? Yellow is for friendship, white is for purity of spirit, pink is for beauty, red is for love."

He thought about this for a moment and wondered why the wild flowers that colored the prairies and mountain slopes and alpine climbs had not attained such lofty symbolism as roses had since they were by far the most beautiful flowers of all, and tougher than any cultivated rose. But then again, he was a man. What did he know about things like flowers, or a woman's heart? "All of them," he said.

"How many?"

"At least a dozen."

"A dozen is a nice number. Any less, and a woman might feel slighted." Spoken like a true florist, but he heeded her advice. He'd sent Molly two dozen roses, four each of the yellow, white and pink, and twelve of the red, hoping they might help to bridge the gap that had widened between them on the drive back from the Bow and Arrow. It seemed doubtful to him that mere flowers could wield that much power, but time would tell. She'd either call to thank him, or her chilly silence would span the rest of his life.

He spooned the chicken onto a plate and added

the vegetables to the hot oil in the pan. He'd gone without lunch and the food smelled good but he had no appetite, because in Helena there lived a woman who believed that he didn't trust her, and that knowledge preyed on him and stole his hunger and his need for anything but her forgiveness and understanding—though he wasn't sure he was worthy of either.

NO MATTER HOW MANY TIMES Molly drove it, the distance between Helena and Bozeman remained the same, and it took her two hours to reach Steven's house, which gave her two hours to rehearse exactly how she would present Dehaviland's proposal to him. Yet when she turned down his drive, her cleverly rehearsed and passionate presentation fled before the overpowering need to see him again. She climbed from her car, her muscles stiffer than ever after the long drive. He opened the door and stood in the doorway, watching her careful approach.

"You're walking pretty good, for a lame cowgirl," he said. "It's good to see you. Come inside. I'll make a fire in the fireplace and fix you a drink. Have you had supper?"

She paused at the foot of the steps. "Are you going somewhere?" she said, her heart plummeting as she noticed that he held his new leather briefcase.

He nodded. "Moose Horn. They're discussing the emergency zoning they want to put in place, and the meeting starts at seven. I'd ask you to come along, but if we arrived there together they'd probably tar and feather us both. It won't take long. I should be back in a couple hours."

Molly's disappointment was huge. For the past two hours she had envisioned a celebratory evening together, just the two of them. Perhaps they would have shared a bottle of wine in front of the fire, and talked away all the barriers between them. "I guess I should have called before driving all this way. I'll make this quick. I have good news. Great news."

"You resigned your job," Steven said.

Molly felt a rush of anger at his insensitive words. "I met with Gregory Dehaviland this afternoon. He wants the two of us to work together to broker a deal between Condor International and your group. He's offering to sell the patented mining claims on Madison Mountain for two million dollars. That's the amount of money they've invested so far in permitting, road building, test drilling, and site preparation. He's talking about shifting their mining operations to a place called Butte Mountain, which is about forty miles due west of here on privately owned land. You'd have until March to raise the money. I know it sounds like a lot, but—"

"Why would he do that?" Steven asked.

"Because he's a nice man," Molly burst out heatedly. "Because he wants to change things, improve the public's image of the big corporate mining interests—and because he owns a cabin on the Yellowstone River below the Madison Mountain watershed. He wants to protect the natural resources as much as you do."

Steven nodded thoughtfully. "I suppose you saw the legal papers that go along with his remarkable offer?"

Molly felt her anger intensify. "I believe Dehaviland's an honest man, and I took him at his word." She could see his skepticism and her fists clenched involuntarily. "Steven, why can't you believe this is real? If you can come up with the money, which Mr. Dehaviland thinks you can easily manage, there won't have to be any emergency zoning in Moose Horn because there won't be any mine on Madison Mountain."

"Were you the only one present at this meeting with Dehaviland?"

"Yes," Molly said stiffly. "He said he wanted to run it by me first because he trusted me the most."

"Smart man. No wonder he's CEO. And then I

suppose he asked you to come here and fill me in before the public meeting tomorrow night?"

Molly felt the stab of betrayal at Steven's words, drew a sharp, painful breath and blinked back the sting of tears. "I came on my own, but I can see it was a complete waste of my time. You don't believe a thing I've said." She turned abruptly on her heel and started for her car.

"Molly." She felt his hand close on her arm and tried to shrug it off. She stopped, but refused to look at him. "Molly. Stay, please. We need to talk. I believe in you, I just find it hard to believe Dehaviland."

"Well, you know what, Young Bear?" she snapped in a voice that shook with pent-up emotion. "I no longer give a damn what you believe or don't believe. In a one-hour lunch at the Bistro this afternoon, I learned more about Gregory Dehaviland than I would in a lifetime of lunches with you, so you go ahead and attend that ridiculous meeting with those foolish people to discuss your unnecessary emergency zoning laws. I'm through trying to talk to you or understand you, and that's all I have to say."

She wrenched out of his grasp, gained the safety of her car, and was five miles down the road before her emotions finally caught up with her. She pulled onto the shoulder, rested her forehead against the steering wheel and wept bitter tears.

THE MEETING AT THE TOWN OFFICE in Moose Horn lasted forever, the talk droning on and on, with each of the twenty-seven residents needing to have their heated, self-righteous say in every quarter, no matter how irrelevant it might be to the subject at hand. Steven tried to concentrate, tried to moderate and give good input, tried to participate the way he knew they wanted him to, but it was impossible. He should have stopped Molly from leaving. He should have stayed with her and skipped this endless meeting that was leading nowhere. Instead, he'd stupidly said the very worst things he could have, and then gone off about his own business. The two dozen roses he'd sent hadn't helped at all. Their relationship was on rockier ground than ever, and he didn't see any way to right his wrongs.

His first instincts had been to keep Molly's announcement to nimself until he'd had time to speak with Dehaviland himself and make sure the deal with Condor International's board of directors was legally cemented, but when 10:00 p.m. came and went with no end in sight, Steven stood.

"It's getting late. We've laid the groundwork for the emergency zoning, and I can help you get that in place, but before we leave here tonight there's something you should all be aware of," he said, cutting off Amy Littlefield's fiery diatribe. Amy stopped, visibly surprised by this interruption, and then sat down abruptly next to Conrad Walker, who had nodded off early on and slept through most of the meeting.

"Gregory Dehaviland, chief executive officer of Condor International, has made a tentative proposal pending final approval from the board of directors. According to his attorney, if we can raise two million dollars by March, the mining company will sell us the patented mining claims on Madison Mountain. It seems Dehaviland owns a camp on the Yellowstone River and doesn't want the watershed threatened by mining runoff. It also appears that he's trying to work with us and reach a compromise that will make both parties happy."

For a long moment everyone sat in stunned silence. "Two *million* dollars?" Amy said, the first to recover. "Oh, sure, I'll just write him a check. Not a problem."

"That's what they've invested in the mine to date," Steven said. "It's not an unreasonable amount, and it's not an impossible task to raise that much money in six months, but it will take a helluva lot of campaigning. I haven't yet spoken to Dehaviland personally, and I wasn't going to tell you about this offer until I'd seen something in writing, but it's doubtful I'll be able to get in contact with him before the public hearing tomorrow night, and I think this matter might be brought up in front of the media. I didn't want you to be caught off guard."

Another thoughtful silence fell upon the room as everyone digested this information, and then Amy said, "What do you think we should do?"

"Run with it, if the offer pans out," he said. "It's the best option we could ever hope for. If we hold our ground and fight the permitting through environmental litigation, we might slow the process down a lot, but we'll probably lose in the end. Tomorrow night we'll have more media in one place than we probably ever will again. If Dehaviland's attorneys bring up the buyout option, we can announce that we're starting a campaign to raise the funds, emphasizing that any donations will be tax deductible, and that when purchased, the mining claims would become the property of the Madison Mountain Land Trust. I'll start setting up that trust tomorrow morning, first thing.

"And here's something else to think about. Because those claims are already patented, that means the property will become a private inholding in the national forest. It will encompass over five hundred acres, and a board of directors will need to be established to oversee the trust and to decide how to manage the land."

"Manage it? What do you mean? The whole purpose of our protesting the New Millennium mine was because we wanted to keep the mountain wild," Amy said.

"I realize that, but a land trust needs a board of directors and some kind of plan. Let's wait and see what happens at the meeting tomorrow night before we talk about this any further."

Steven drove home faster than was prudent, hoping beyond hope that Molly would have come back and been waiting for him, but the house was dark, his driveway empty, and a bleak, hollow emptiness filled him with her absence and became the full measure of his failure.

CHAPTER TWELVE

MOLLY'S ANSWERING MACHINE was flashing when she arrived home, and while she heated up a can of chicken-noodle soup she played it back. The first message was delivered in a stern, maternal voice: "This is your mother, who loves you. Call me. Your father and I are worried about you." The second was along the same lines. "Hey, it's Dani. It's 7:00 p.m. Monday, where are you? I tried you yesterday, too. Have you eloped with your handsome counselor? Please call." Molly laughed bitterly at the idea of she and Steven eloping. The third message was from Stradivarius John, professor of the violin. "Molly, I've been thinking about you. How about dinner this Saturday?" Fourth message: "Molly? Brad. Something's come up, something urgent. Call me as soon as possible, no matter how late. You have my cell-phone number."

Molly carried the saucepan of hot soup to the sofa and set it on the coffee table. She mixed herself a drink and sat down. She felt completely numb. She should call her mother. She should touch base with Dani. She should find out the urgent stuff from Brad. Later. She'd call them all after she'd eaten. She took a sip of her drink and let her head tip back. What a long day this had been, and from the sound of Brad's voice it wasn't over yet. What could have come up? Could it have anything to do with the public meeting tomorrow night?

Her thoughts drifted back to Steven, in spite of her resolve never to think about him again. Damn the man for being such a cynic. He was stubborn-headed and unswervable and he saw things one way: his own. She glanced at the phone. In spite of her anger with his obstinance, she wanted to call him so badly that her hand began to tremble. She lowered the glass and moaned aloud, "What would I say to him?"

A heavy knock at her door startled her. She wasn't feeling the least bit sociable, but she pushed wearily off the sofa and, carrying her drink, walked to the door and slid back the dead bolt. It never occurred to her to ask who it was, but as she swung the door inward a greater force pushed it hard against her and she staggered back with a cry of alarm, followed by a gasp of surprise. Ken Manning stood in her doorway. He appeared uncharacteristically disheveled and his eyes had a narrow glitter that put her instantly on guard.

"Mr. Manning," she said, gathering her startled wits. "What are you doing here?"

"We need to talk," he replied, closing the door deliberately behind him, a sinister move that immediately caused Molly to retreat several steps but not before she caught a strong whiff of alcohol.

"It's late and I'm very tired. Can't this wait until morning?" Molly's initial surprise was rapidly being replaced by feelings of vulnerability and fear. Manning's eyes were hostile and his body language menacing.

"No, it can't," he said. He was standing in the same spot but the impression he gave was that he was advancing somehow, and Molly took another step back. Her level of anxiety had risen to the point where she no longer felt the pain in her muscles from that long and torturous horseback ride up Montana Mountain, but she tried to maintain a calm demeanor.

"Mr. Manning, I think you should leave immediately. We'll discuss this some other time."

"I've worked for Condor International for fifteen years," he said. "Fifteen years of loyal service, and I'll be damned if I let some two-bit woman lawyer ruin my reputation and cost me my job." He took just one step as he spoke these words, but it was enough.

"Get out," Molly said. She lifted her drink as if

to fling it at him and half of it spilled down her arm, as icy as the blood that ran through her veins. "I'm warning you. Leave now, or you'll force me to call the police."

"You're no threat to me," he continued, taking another menacing step. "No more of a threat than that other flame of Young Bear's. I have connections in high places...."

Molly flung the glass at him but he dodged it easily, and, if anything, her action made things worse. He lunged toward her and she jumped back, bumping into the coffee table. In a flash she whirled, picked up the saucepan of hot soup, and flung it in his face. This time she didn't miss, and while he wiped at his eyes with a bellow of pain and outrage, she flew past him, wrenched open the door and dashed into the hallway. She heard footsteps pounding up the stairs and came face-to-face with a wide-eyed Dani at the top of the stairwell.

"Hurry!" she said, grabbing her friend's hand and jerking her around to follow. "He's right behind me!"

Dani didn't hesitate and when they reached the entry door to the apartments they were both running. They ran straight to Dani's car and jumped in. Dani wasted no time pulling away from the curb.

"Saints preserve me," Molly said, slumping

back in her seat and raising her hands to the sides of her face. "I can't believe what just happened."

"Are you all right? What *did* just happen? *Who* was right behind us? And where on earth have you been for the past two days?"

"Ken Manning just showed up at my apartment. He'd been drinking, and he was behaving in a threatening way, and..." Molly wrapped her arms around herself to try and stop her teeth from chattering as the adrenaline worked through her. "And so I threw my drink at him, followed it with a pot of hot soup, and that's when you came on the scene."

Dani was visibly shocked. "My God, Molly. Why was he there? What did he say? Do you think he was trying to *rape* you?"

Molly shook her head emphatically. "No. He was very angry. He wanted to hurt me, and I think it has something to do with his job. Could I borrow your phone?"

Dani reached in her coat pocket and handed it to her. Molly was so rattled it took her several minutes to remember Brad's cell-phone number. He answered on the second ring. "Molly," he said when he recognized her voice. "Listen, Manning was fired today by Dehaviland himself, and I think Skelton might have inadvertently implied that you were behind it. I just wanted to warn you because Manning was pretty damn ugly when he showed up at the office this afternoon. He made quite a scene."

"I can believe that," Molly replied. "He just made quite a scene at my apartment."

"He went to your place? Are you all right?" Dweeb that he was, Brad did sound genuinely concerned.

"Yes. He was drunk and threatening, and when he wouldn't leave, I left at a dead run. Could you do me a favor? Call the police and have them check my place out?"

"I'll do that right now. Where are you?"

"With a friend who made a very timely appearance. I'm definitely not going back there tonight. I'll see you at the office tomorrow."

Molly folded the little phone up and handed it back to Dani. "Thanks." She slumped back in the seat and drew a deep, albeit shaky breath. "Look at me. I'm barefoot, half-dressed, and didn't even get to eat my supper."

"Yeah," Dani said. "That Ken Manning is definitely lacking in manners."

DANI TOOK HER TO THE HOUSE she and her boyfriend shared five miles outside of town. It was a rambling old place with a big, friendly kitchen and two golden retrievers whose quiet, devoted affections were just what Molly needed. That, and a strong drink, and a bowl of vegetarian chili heated in the microwave. Dani's boyfriend, Jack Richards, was out of town. He was an airline pilot and was gone most of the time, or so it seemed to Molly, but he and Dani had been together for two years and seemed to have a good relationship.

While Molly ate, she filled Dani in on the past weekend, the party at the Bow and Arrow and her horseback ride, which already seemed like another lifetime ago. Then she told her about her extraordinary lunch with Gregory Dehaviland, her subsequent reinstatement to active duty at Taintor, Skelton and Goldstein, and her falling out with Steven. "And you know all about Ken Manning and the pot of hot noodle soup," she concluded, finishing her drink.

"Wow," Dani said. "No wonder you weren't answering your phone. You're a busy lady. So now what?"

"What do you mean?"

"I mean, you and Steven."

"Weren't you listening? It's over between us."

Dani fixed her with a long-suffering expression. "Right," she said, leaning forward to retrieve Molly's empty glass. "I'm going to fix you another drink, you're going to sit here and relax with it, and you're also going to promise me before you creep off to bed that you'll stay right here until this whole mess blows over. I don't want you living all alone in that apartment. My God, Molly, drunk or no, there's no excuse for Manning's behavior. You could have been hurt. You're staying here with us, no arguments."

STEVEN dialed Molly's home phone at six Tuesday morning. He knew the hour was well beyond the boundaries of proper etiquette, but each minute that passed only increased his agony after a long and sleepless night. When she didn't answer, his anxiety grew. He called her again five minutes later. Still no answer. He made coffee, rang her number every five minutes but each time her answering machined picked up, and he felt a growing sense of unease. She'd left in such a distraught state the night before. Had she made it home safely, or was her little red Mercedes piled into another ditch somewhere between Bozeman and Helena?

He barely tasted the coffee, was hardly aware of getting dressed, and didn't even think about breakfast. Called her again at seven. At five past. By seven-thirty he'd given up all hope and was in his Jeep, heading for Helena. She lived on one of those high-end streets, in a fancy brick walk-up that in a year or two would probably have a doorman. Two hours later he was halfway up the entry stairs when a young policeman leaned over the stairwell and said, "Hold on. You live here?"

The sight of the uniform triggered an intense panic in Steven. He rounded the top of the stairs, plowed past the startled officer, and burst into Molly's apartment with a feeling like he'd never experienced before. "Molly?" he called out, as if she would materialize before him, alive and well, when every fiber of his being twisted in silent anguish that something terrible had happened to her, and that he could have so easily prevented it by not going to that damn meeting.

"Steven?" Her voice speaking his name was like sweet music, and he whirled toward the sound. There she was, alive and well, emerging from her bedroom. "It's all right, Officer, he's a friend of mine." She was pulling a shoe on her foot and holding a hairbrush in one hand. Her face was pale and there were dark smudges beneath her eyes. "I'm late for work," she explained, casting him a guarded glance. "The police are just finishing up."

Steven stared, his heart hammering. "Finishing up what?"

"Someone broke into my apartment last night." Molly's eyes dropped and a faint blush colored her cheeks. She laid the hairbrush down on the kitchen counter and began to braid her hair with trembling fingers. With a nod she indicated the three uniformed officers. "They're just making sure they get the story straight from me. So tell me, Young Bear. Did your emergency zoning meeting go well last night? And what brings you to Helena this fine Montana morning?"

Her coolness set him back on his heels; that, and the fact that the police were eyeing him with wary suspicion. "I came when you didn't answer your phone this morning," he said. "I was worried about you."

She neatly bound the end of her braid and her eyes remained downcast. "Well, as you can see, I'm perfectly fine." She turned to one of the officers. "You'll lock up when you leave?" Satisfied with his nod, she picked up her purse and briefcase and walked to the door. Steven followed.

"Who broke into your apartment?" he asked as she started down the stairs.

"I'm just an attorney, not an investigator. Ask the police," she responded, not bothering to look back.

"Molly." His plea for her to stop fell on deaf ears. "Molly, dammit, talk to me."

She paused and glanced over her shoulder with obvious reluctance. Her eyes mirrored an ocean of unspoken hurt. "Why?" she said. "What do you and I have to say to each other, Young Bear?"

Steven didn't care if half the police in Helena overheard. He spoke his mind, and he spoke from the heart. "I love you, Molly Ferguson. I trust you and I believe in you, and when I call you up at six in the morning to make sure you're okay, I want you to answer the phone. That's what I have to say to you."

She dropped her eyes again but not before he caught a glimpse of the tears that flooded them. "Oh, Steven," she said in a voice choked with emotion. "Why couldn't you have told me that last night?" And without another word or so much as a backward glance, she continued down the stairwell, slamming the most painful of emotional doors in his face.

WHEN MOLLY REACHED HER OFFICE, the first thing she saw were the long-stemmed roses on her desk, twelve red and four each of pink, yellow and white. "They were delivered right after you left yesterday afternoon," the secretary said with a wistful smile. "Aren't they beautiful?"

Molly waited until she was alone to read the card that accompanied them.

You were right.
I should have eaten some of Luther Makes
Elk's owl stew.
It might have given me wisdom.
Steven.

"Oh, Steven," she murmured, remembering the stricken expression in his eyes as she turned her back on him and left him standing at the top of the stairwell not half an hour earlier. "We're both stubborn and stupid. We both should have eaten some of your grandfather's stew."

If only there were some way to reach him, to call him and tell him she was sorry, but he wouldn't be back in Bozeman until later that morning. She wouldn't see him until the public meeting tonight, and then they'd be in opposite camps, each fighting for a different cause.

Unless…unless she did what he wanted her to do, and resigned her position with the firm. Unless she picked up the phone right now and called Dehaviland's private cell-phone number and told him she'd failed to persuade Steven to speak with him, and she felt the only recourse was to resign her position with Taintor, Skelton and Goldstein because she felt that remaining in their employ, given what she knew about them, might compromise any future she might have as a reputable attorney….

Molly glanced at the phone. She could do it. She could call Dehaviland. In her heart she knew it was the right thing to do, and she felt sure that he would understand. She flipped through her desk file and found his unlisted number, which he'd given her in the restaurant before parting.

"Call anytime," he'd said. "Tell Young Bear I'll meet with him wherever, whenever. Tell him the ball's in his court and he calls the shots."

Oh, why couldn't Steven have listened to her? Why couldn't he have believed?

Molly reached for the phone and just as her fingers brushed the receiver, it rang. Startled, she lifted it to her ear. "Ferguson."

"Young Bear." Her heart jumped with gladness at the sound of his deep, calm voice. "I just spoke with Dehaviland, and in the course of our conversation he invited me out to his fishing camp. I asked him if I could bring a date, and he asked if you liked to fish."

Molly's grip tightened on the receiver. "Where's his place, and when do we go?"

"About two hours south of here, and how does right now sound?"

"Right now sounds pretty good. Where are you?"

"Parked beside your car in the parking lot."

"Give me five minutes," Molly said, rising out of her chair as she spoke. "And Steven?" she added, her voice softening. "The roses are beautiful. Thank you."

Skelton gave her no arguments about leaving work just minutes after arriving. He'd heard about Manning's visit to her apartment the night before, and when she told him she was on her way to meet with Dehaviland prior to the public meeting, he gave a curt nod. "I'll let Brad know," he said.

Steven opened the passenger side door of his Wagoneer as she walked briskly across the parking lot. The very sight of him made her want to rush into his arms, and it took all her willpower to remain coolly professional. A sudden breeze tousled her escaped curls and she reached a hand to brush them out of her eyes as she came to an uncertain halt. "Shouldn't we take separate vehicles?" she faltered.

He shook his head. "Not until this is over. Until he's taken into custody, Manning's still a definite threat. You should place a restraining order on him."

"He was just drunk, and mad because he thought I had something to do with him being fired. How did you know he was the one who broke into my apartment?"

"I took your advice and asked the investigator. Get in, we can talk on the way."

Steven's expression was uncharacteristically stern and she felt the beginning twinges of indignation give way to a prickle of fear. "He was just drunk," she repeated.

"I'm sure he was, but if you don't place a restraining order on him, I will." Steven continued to hold the passenger door for her and when she continued to hesitate he said, "It's time I told you about Mary Pretty Shield."

With a jolt of surprise Molly stared into his dark eyes. Suddenly breathless, she climbed into the Wagoneer and moments later they were headed south, toward the valley of the Yellowstone. But before Steven would speak a word about Mary Pretty Shield, he made sure Molly called the police and requested them to place a restraining order on Ken Manning.

"MARY WAS ONE OF THOSE PEOPLE that everyone loved," Steven said, beginning her story before the time he met her. "She was class valedictorian. She played basketball in high school. She was captain of the team in her senior year, and they never lost a game. She got a scholarship to go to a good college off the rez, and decided to major in political science. In her sophomore year, she called me out of the blue. I'd never met her before, but she said she'd heard about me through some of the elders on the rez and wanted to intern with me for the summer, if she could. She had changed her major to environmental studies, and was thinking of going to law school."

"And that was when you happened to be involved in the Soldier Mountain dispute," Molly guessed.

"Yes. I was practically living on the Rocky

Ridge reservation. In fact, when I was there I stayed with one of Mary's aunts, though I didn't know it until after I took her on as an intern. Mary dove right into the mine dispute that summer as my intern. She was full of an energy and idealism that captured the hearts of nearly everyone she spoke to about the mine, and Mary spoke to everyone, including the mine workers. She didn't like the things she was learning, and she wasn't afraid to talk about them."

Steven fell silent for a few moments, gathering his thoughts. "I was studying the mining laws, looking for some loophole to use against Soldier Mountain mine to keep them from extending their permits, and I found it in the wording of the mill site law. Apparently I wasn't the only one looking closely at it. The mining industry had been lobbying the government to get it changed, but eventually it was decided that the original mining laws shall stand, which meant that each designated mill site on each mining claim could use no more than five acres for activities associated with mining. Are you familiar with that law?"

Molly nodded. "I'm relatively new to all of this, but Brad's been coaching me. I've read the Emergency Supplemental Bill pushed through by Congress to sidestep the wording in the old law, and I also happen to know the Senate is working for all its worth to overturn the decision and permanently prohibit placing limits on mill sites in the Interior Appropriations bill."

"The House isn't going to let them," Steven said. "They're fighting that Senate amendment tooth and nail."

"If you're right, and the House wins this fight, that old mill site law could do a lot of damage to a whole lot of mining operations. It could cause a whole lot of hate and discontent."

"Yes," Steven said. "I looked into Soldier Mountain's permitting and found that they'd filed for only ten mill sites for a total of fifty acres, yet over the years they'd been dumping waste rock and contaminates on well over three hundred acres, all of which was contributing to the contamination of the groundwater. Bottom line, they were in gross violation of their own laws, so I decided to bring that to light.

"The day before Mary died, I ran the idea past her. She was sharp, and I often used her as a sounding board. I explained to her about mill sites, about how the whole permitting process worked in regards to them, and about how we might be able to make that same process work for us. If we could prove that Soldier Mountain was operating in noncompliance of the mill site law, which it was and in fact still is, we might have the edge we needed to prevent their ten-year permitting extension. I cautioned her not to speak about it, but I could see that she was excited by the idea. She was young and naive and still believed that good always triumphed over evil. She said, 'We'll beat them with their own rules and regulations, won't we? We'll stop them from poisoning our water and killing our people!' She told me I was brilliant, and then she left.

"That was the last time I saw her alive. She called me the following evening, a Saturday, all excited about a message she'd found in her car, put there apparently by a whistle-blower willing to talk to her about illegal dumping at the Soldier Mountain mine. When Mary told me where and when the note said she was supposed to meet him, I told her that I'd follow up on it, that it wasn't safe for her to go alone, and I told her to go home."

"But she went anyway," Molly said.

"Yes. I was late getting there, half an hour later than the message requested. It was a long drive from where I was staying. Mary's car was there, and I found her lying facedown in the shallow water near the river's edge. Her body was still warm. I called for help on my cell phone, tried CPR until I was exhausted, cursed the gods that let this happen, and was sitting beside her when the tribal police showed up, followed closely by the feds. They trampled the ground enough to obliterate any evidence, asked a lot of questions, and I spent the rest of the night answering them. Are you following me?" he said.

"Yes," Molly said faintly. "Someone murdered her to shut her up, and you walked right into it. Did you have legal representation when you were questioned?"

"I didn't think I needed it."

"Do you think Ken Manning was somehow involved?"

"He was the one pushing the hardest for my arrest. When the feds could find no motive that would fly in court, and my character was vouched for by too many reputable people, including a congressman and a heavy-hitting California senator I worked for while I was in law school, they finally let me go. They listed her death as an accidental drowning. I told Mary's father about the message, and her meeting with the supposed whistle-blower, and my belief that her drowning had definitely not been accidental. I asked him to push for a forensic autopsy. He looked me in the eye and said that if I didn't stop what I was doing, if I didn't stop trying to shut down the uranium mine on Soldier Mountain, more innocent people would be hurt or killed. He knew Mary's death hadn't been an accident, and he knew I hadn't killed her, but he was scared, and clearly he held me responsible for the loss of his daughter.

"So I told the tribe I couldn't help them anymore, and without any legal representation they had no choice but to drop the lawsuit against Soldier Mountain. The feds immediately sealed the files, so who knows? Maybe by backing off I kept my own people safe. My sister Pony, for one, and my brothers and their families, but I betrayed the tribe, and I betrayed Mary Pretty Shield.

"And Mary's father was right. I was responsible for her death. That innocent girl died because after she left my office that afternoon she said the wrong things to the wrong people. She died because suddenly she was a threat to the federal government, to the corporate bank, and to corrupt tribal members. She died because I told her something I shouldn't have. She died because of *me,* and she died for nothing."

Steven kept his eyes fixed on the road ahead, taut with pent-up emotion. He was unprepared for the touch upon his arm and Molly's gentle voice saying, "No, Steven, that's not true at all. Mary Pretty Shield died fighting for something she truly believed in, and that's truly the noblest death of all."

CHAPTER THIRTEEN

GREGORY DEHAVILAND'S fishing camp was located at the very end of one of the worst stretches of dirt road Molly had ever seen. Five miles passed at the unheard of speed of five miles per hour. They could have walked the distance faster. She clutched the dash as Steven eased through another deep washout and then stared at the sky as he climbed in low gear out the far side. "This *can't* be right," she repeated for the umpteenth time. "Dehaviland owns and flies his very own Learjet. He certainly wouldn't have a cabin on a cart path like this, and there hasn't been another building for the past forty minutes."

"These were the directions he gave," Steven said, unperturbed. "He warned me the road was rough and the camp remote."

"Yes, but 'remote' to a man like him doesn't have anything to do with this, Young Bear. I think we're hopelessly lost."

"This isn't exactly wilderness, and we're not

lost," Steven said. "There are other vehicle tracks in the road. Have patience."

"Hasn't anyone ever told you that redheads have no patience?" She studied him at the next stretch of level road. "Steven, did you call Dehaviland today, or did he call you?"

"I called him. I wanted to be sure he knew about Ken Manning breaking into your apartment."

Molly paused, then said, "Manning was so angry. He said that I was no more a threat to him than that other flame of yours. Was he talking about Mary Pretty Shield?"

Steven kept his eyes on the road but she saw his knuckles whiten as his grip tightened on the wheel. "I don't want you staying alone at your apartment."

"Dani's already made me promise to stay with her. She and Jack have a big house with lots of room and two wonderful golden retrievers. Steven, were you in love with Mary?"

Steven's glance was fleeting but Molly was jolted by the depth of expression in his eyes. "I've only ever been in love with one woman," he said. "Her name is Molly Ferguson and she's the red-haired daughter of an Irish laborer and a Scottish dreamer."

Molly stared, overcome with emotion at Steven's statement. When he said, "Here we are, the end of the road," she jerked her eyes to the front and was astounded to see an old cabin of rustic, weather-bleached logs that looked as if Butch Cassidy and the Sundance Kid might have holed up there a time or two, in another century.

Steven parked beside a late-model pickup and cut the ignition. They sat for a few moments in silence, studying the cabin and the sparkling dance of sunlight on the river just beyond, and Molly was about to reemphasize that no way on earth a man of Dehaviland's wealth would live in a place like this when the cabin door opened.

"Saints be praised," she breathed. "Sure and it's *himself*. It's Dehaviland."

DEHAVILAND WAS CLAD in blue jeans and a red-and-black buffalo plaid flannel shirt. He was filling a pipe with tobacco from a small foil pouch and looked as if he had no more pressing business in the world than to read a good book beside the banks of the Yellowstone and ponder which fly to use at his favorite fishing hole. "The fish are biting today," he said by way of welcome as Steven and Molly approached. "I'd have kept a few if I thought you liked trout rolled in cornmeal and fried in bacon fat, but I keep more conventional fare on hand."

"Thanks," Steven said. "But we didn't come to eat your food, or fish the river."

Dehaviland tamped the tobacco down in the

bowl of his pipe, tucked the foil pouch in his shirt pocket, struck a match on his thumbnail, and puffed on the stem while blue smoke curled into the air. "No," he said amiably. "You came to save Madison Mountain, but that doesn't mean we can't eat lunch. I think we could manage both quite nicely."

"I'm starving," Molly said, casting Steven an apologetic glance.

"So am I," Dehaviland said with a grin, his strong white teeth gripping the pipe's stem. "How about a pepper-steak sandwich and a cold beer?"

They ate lunch on a rickety porch that practically hung out over the river, affording them a breathtaking view of the rugged Rocky Mountains. Steven grudgingly felt his cynicism dissolving as he shared Dehaviland's humble fishing camp, ate his home-cooked and very good pepper-steak sandwich, and drank a cold, bitter Heineken. Dehaviland, in spite of his enormous wealth and power, seemed like the genuine article. He talked straight and didn't beat about the bush, repeating almost verbatim everything he'd said to Molly.

"I travel all over the world meeting with businesspeople, diplomats, and politicians," Dehaviland said. "I've dined in some of the swankiest restaurants, slept in the fanciest mansions and palaces, but this—" he raised his beer bottle to indicate in one broad sweep the river, the mountains and the wilderness "—this place is what keeps me sane. When I came back from two tours in Vietnam I retreated here and hid from the world for nearly a year. I want to preserve the wildness as much as you do, Young Bear. Bottom line, my interest in your cause is purely selfish, but that's okay, because if by making Madison Mountain off-limits to mining operations we protect this river's watershed, we all come out winners. Even more important than that, this compromise could mark the beginning of a new environmental policy amongst gas, oil and mining interests.

"If the biggest, toughest, wealthiest corporation starts greening up, the other players are going to sit up and take notice, and more than a few will follow suit. The public is focusing more and more on environmental concerns, and rightly so. Even money-hungry corporate entities can't continue to ignore the fact that this planet's resources are finite. We need to look at the big picture and change our way of life to develop and promote renewable energy sources. We need to make sure our grandchildren and great-grandchildren will be able to breathe clean air, drink clean water, and experience places just like this."

After a brief silence Steven said, "Who wrote that speech?"

Dehaviland laughed. "My daughter. She's in her final year of law school, and there's no doubt in my mind that she'll be following in your tracks, Young Bear. She loves me, but lets me know often and in no uncertain terms what she thinks of who I work for and what I represent."

"She might soften up a bit when she learns about this," Molly said.

"What if we can't raise the two million dollars in time?" Steven asked.

"You'll raise it." Dehaviland drained the last of his beer and set the bottle on the porch railing. His eyes were keen. "I've studied up on you, Young Bear. If you make your pitch tonight in front of the media, you'll probably have a good chunk of that money in hand by the end of the month."

"And if we raise the funds, the sale of your patented mining claims on Madison Mountain to our group is guaranteed?"

"I have the agreement in writing." Dehaviland pulled a sheaf of papers from his jacket pocket and handed them to Steven. "The board of directors faxed me a copy last night, before I drove in here. We can sign these papers tonight at the meeting. I've arranged for a notary to be present."

"What about Ken Manning?" Steven said, his eyes scanning the legal forms.

"He's permanently out of the picture as far as

Condor International is concerned," Dehaviland replied. "I've known him long enough to realize that I don't want him in my corner. He's blatantly bent every law, bribed every politician, and he let Molly take the public hit for his own transgression. I fired him because he deserved to be fired." He shifted his gaze to Molly. "If Manning comes anywhere near you again, if he so much as calls you on the phone, you let me know."

"I've placed a restraining order on him, but I don't think he'll try anything," Molly said. "He was drunk, that's all."

"Being drunk doesn't excuse him from threatening you," Dehaviland said. "As far as I know, the police are still looking for him, but when they find him they'll charge him with criminal threatening. I doubt he'll bother you again."

A pair of ravens flew over, wings swishing in strong, purposeful strokes as they headed toward the wall of mountains to the west. Steven watched them for a moment and then glanced at Molly. "Well," he said, pondering the infinite mysteries of the universe. She just gazed into his eyes and smiled.

IT WAS MID-AFTERNOON when they left Dehaviland's cabin on the banks of the Yellowstone, Steven still mulling over the conversations they'd had, rehashing them, searching for hidden deception but finding none. He'd met with Dehaviland expecting political duplicity and gotten straight talk instead. Molly sat smugly in the passenger seat, looking well pleased with how the meeting had gone.

"Admit it, Young Bear," she said before they'd even navigated the first of the many treacherous washouts. "I was right. Dehaviland's a genuinely nice person, and he's going to help you save Madison Mountain."

In spite of himself, Steven felt a stab of jealousy. Molly was clearly taken with the power and importance of the man, and he couldn't blame her, but the fight for Madison Mountain had begun long before Dehaviland had flown his Learjet into Helena to meet with her over lunch. What Dehaviland had done had been effortless; a few phone calls, a few political strings pulled. What Steven had done had been grunt work, thankless and unpaid. Yet if Dehaviland hadn't happened on the scene, all that thankless and unpaid work might well have saved Madison Mountain, too. At least, Steven liked to believe as much.

"Not that you couldn't have done the same," Molly added as if reading his mind, instantly easing the twist of tension within him. "But he saved you so much work."

"Yes," Steven admitted.

"Soooo much work," she repeated.

"Point taken."

Molly kicked back in the seat and smiled. "I think it's wonderful. It proves that Big Business isn't made up of a bunch of heartless monsters."

"It proves that *Dehaviland* isn't a heartless monster," Steven amended.

"But for all intents and purposes, Dehaviland *is* Condor International," she said. "He's CEO of one of the most powerful companies in the world."

"He hasn't held that job very long, and they could give him the boot if they don't like how he's steering their boat."

"Still the cynic, eh, Young Bear?"

"I've been in this business for a while, Molly. I like the man, don't get me wrong, but I still find it hard to believe that all of a sudden we're standing in the shadow of a rainbow."

Molly shifted in her seat to face him. "Sometimes you just have to believe. It's all about faith. Your grandfather knows that far better than you. We both should have eaten some of his owl stew."

Steven felt the Jeep begin to dip forward and he braked, his eyes locked with hers. "We still could."

"Think there's any left?" Her eyes reflected a depth of mysticism and spirituality that far exceeded his own.

"He's probably expecting us for supper," Steven said.

"Do we have time to go there before the meeting tonight?"

"Yes." The Jeep was idling. Molly's eyes were soft and bright with a myriad of emotions, and she leaned toward him even as he reached for her. Her lips moved against his, warm and soft and sweet, and her fingertips brushed his cheek in a tender caress. She drew back to regard him somberly.

"Then let's go."

THEY DIDN'T REACH Luther Makes Elk's shack beside the little-traveled dirt road until late afternoon. Luther was sitting in his customary place, wearing his old wool peacoat and dark hat and watching the sporadic traffic go by. He was silent as they approached. Steven held up a paper sack. "We brought you some Chinese food."

"I was hoping you would," Luther said. "I've been thinking about Chinese food all day. They say that kind of cooking makes you hungrier, but I like it." He nodded at the shack. "I saved some of that owl stew for you. It tastes better, now that it's aged some. I put the pot on the stove a while ago. It should be hot by now." This last he spoke to Molly, who nodded and went into the shack to dish up the stew, leaving the two of them alone.

Steven lowered himself onto the bench and leaned back against the tar-paper wall of Luther's shack. In spite of his reticence with Luther, being in this place always made him feel as if, in the end, when all the battles had been fought, victory would fly its noble flag upon the pure mountain winds. The slanting rays of sunlight felt good. He half closed his eyes, imagining Molly's bewilderment inside the cluttered shack. "Grandfather, there's something I need to ask you," he said.

"I know." Luther broke into the bag and pulled out the containers of food, setting them side by side on the bench. "Boy, this smells good. Did you get egg rolls?"

"Yes."

"Good. I like egg rolls with that sweet sauce on them."

"About the owl stew…"

"You should have had some when you came the other day." Luther dug deeper into the bag. His ancient brow furrowed with concern. "Did you get the sweet sauce?"

"It's in there somewhere." Steven shifted on the bench. "Molly had a dream about an owl just before we came here the other day."

Luther held something up and shook it. "Good, it's a big container. There's nothing worse than running out of sweet sauce for the egg rolls."

"The owl flew through her dream, and last night, a man broke into her apartment. She might have been hurt if she hadn't run away."

"Did you get fried rice?" Luther interrupted.

"Fried rice, egg rolls, beef with pea pods, chicken lo mein, and there are plastic forks and paper napkins."

"Yeah. I got 'em." Luther sat back with a contented sigh. "Boy, this stuff smells good." He began to eat. "And so," he said after a couple mouthfuls. "You think she got in trouble because you didn't eat the stew?"

"You told me once that an owl was an omen of death."

Luther took another forkful and chewed slowly, with obvious relish. "And you are afraid Red Hair will die?"

Steven watched an old pickup whip past. Dust swirled and was whisked away on the light wind. He shook his head. "Ken Manning's a dangerous man. If there's anything you can do to protect her…"

Luther opened a different box and poked inside it with his fork. He sampled the contents of the new box and grunted with satisfaction, sitting back again. "Red Hair doesn't need protecting. But you?" He shook his head. "You should eat a lot of that owl stew. Are you carrying that pouch I gave you?"

Steven reached to tug the leather thong that hung around his neck and showed Luther the pouch.

"Good. That's big medicine."

Molly emerged from the shack, carefully balancing two tin bowls of the stew. She handed one to Steven, then perched beside him on the bench and balanced her bowl on her thighs. "Sorry it took so long. I could find only one spoon."

"That's because I only need one spoon," Luther said.

"We can share," Steven said, handing her the spoon that she'd nestled into his stew. Molly smiled her thanks and then tasted Luther's cooking for the first time. Her expression remained unchanged. She hesitated only fractionally before diving in and rapidly finishing off her portion, after which she handed Steven the spoon and raised her empty bowl with a smile of gratitude.

"That was good," she said to Luther.

Luther nodded. "A man living alone learns to be a pretty good cook."

"Well, thank you. That was delicious," Molly said, "but I couldn't help but notice that you don't have a refrigerator. How do you keep things from spoiling?"

"I don't worry about stuff like that," Luther told her. "I'm too old. You know, I'm so old that tonight, I could die in my sleep. And so. I'll eat all this Chinese food first, before it has time to spoil."

Steven regarded the spoon Molly had handed him. He dipped it into the stew and took the obligatory taste, swallowing quickly. "Grandfather," he said, feeling sweat prickle his forehead as his stomach turned, "you may be old, but you can't die in your sleep until you've married my sister." He rose to his feet, setting his bowl upon the wall bench. "We have to go. We have a meeting to attend tonight."

"Another meeting." Luther shook his head. "It would be better if you went on a vision quest instead."

"I'll go soon, Grandfather," he said. "We can't be late for this meeting tonight. It's very important. Thank you for the stew."

"You go to your meeting if you have to, but climb the mountain soon. There is much wisdom that needs to find you, but when you hide yourself in the white man's world, the spirits get confused." Luther shifted his solemn gaze to Molly. "You have already had your vision, Red Hair," he said, "but you don't know what it was you saw. The owl sees in the night and flies on silent wings to bring you his message. And so. If you want to come here again, that would be okay."

"THAT WAS JUST LUTHER'S WAY of saying you didn't bother him too much," Steven said in response to Molly's prodding questions as they drove away. "He was telling you that he liked you. You cleaned your bowl. You ate all your stew."

"And that was enough to make him like me?" Molly said.

"Yes. Like I said before, most white people think he's a crazy old man."

"But he told me himself that he was a good cook," Molly pointed out. "It shouldn't have surprised him that I cleaned my bowl."

"If it weren't for his friends bringing him food to eat on a regular basis, Luther would probably starve to death. All the meals he cooks for himself taste like that owl stew."

"That's because he's poor. He doesn't even have a refrigerator, or a bathroom with running water. I looked while I was inside, and that shack of his isn't fit for a junkyard dog—"

"Luther wouldn't live any other way," Steven interrupted. "He has no need for what he calls all your modern inconveniences. He'd live in tepee, go back to the old ways and the time of the buffalo, and be happy. That's why Pony wants to be married by him. He's the last of his kind, and she's the last of hers."

Molly frowned. "What did he mean about the owl?"

"I told him about the dream you had on the way to the Bow and Arrow. An owl is a powerful omen."

"Yes, but what was the message I was supposed to learn?"

"Luther speaks in riddles, but I think he meant that you should listen to me, and obey me at all times."

Molly glanced at him. "Nice try, Young Bear. So when are you planning to climb *Cante Tinza?*"

"Not tonight."

"Can I come with you when you go?"

"A man can't have a vision unless he's alone. Besides, you're still lame from your ride." Steven concentrated on the road. "Don't worry. We'll climb a mountain together, but we should start with one that's not as tall as Brave Heart."

Molly's chin lifted. "I can climb your spirit mountain, Young Bear. Just tell me when, and I'll be ready."

THE PUBLIC MEETING in Bozeman was so well attended that afterward, the media dubbed it opening night on Environmental Broadway. All the major TV news crews were on hand, as well as a whole slew of journalists from across the country who'd had the time to hop a flight to Montana. The only person missing was Dehaviland.

At first his absence was hardly noticed. There were enough diversions to shift the attention of the crowds who jammed the room, spilled into the hallway and stood outside the court building, waiting and hoping for some positive glimpse into the future or a bloody feud between opposing factions.

Amy Littlefield was the spokesperson for the citizens of Moose Horn, giving her presentation with a poignant naïveté and passionate innocence that couldn't help but move the most hardened of journalists present. Following on her heels, Steven delivered his own summation of the New Millennium project on Madison Mountain. His delivery was calm and deliberate, and everyone present, whether for or against the mining project, hung on his every word.

Molly listened to both deliveries with a pounding heart. She was next up, but where was Dehaviland? Why wasn't he here? She caught Steven's eye as he stepped down from the podium and could read nothing in his expression. She glanced at Brad and he nodded that it was time. She stood on trembling legs, hoping that her fright was well hidden as she approached the podium, and gazed out at the sea of faces. So many people had come to hear what was about to happen to the place they lived in, the land they loved. She drew a deep breath to calm herself and released it silently.

"Good evening. My name is Molly Ferguson, and I'm the attorney representing Condor International and New Millennium Mining Company. A few short days ago I was drawn on the carpet for pushing this project forward without waiting for the proper permitting. I stand humbly before you tonight and ask your forgiveness for my inexperience in these matters. Having come to know some of you personally during the past few weeks, I can only hope that my track record will improve.

"This is a great state, and she has great champions, many of whom are in this room tonight. Two of those champions, Steven Young Bear and Amy Littlefield, have helped me realize that a mountain is far more than just a pile of rock, dirt and minerals, that a national forest is more than just a green spot on a topographical map, and a river is more than just a blue ribbon of water that ends its journey in the sea."

Molly paused, scanning the crowd, searching for some positive reaction to her words. "I'll be the first to admit that I'm a city girl. I don't know the first thing about trees and rivers and mountains. I moved here to take a job in a law firm that represents companies who specialize in extracting minerals from the earth, and my interests were necessarily with the law firm's clients.

"What's wrong with that? Nothing. The minerals are there, the need for them exists, and they possess tremendous value. But how we go about mining them makes all the difference. My client, Condor International, believes that mineral extraction can be accomplished without the destruction of precious natural resources like the Yellowstone River. In fact, they want to guarantee that the river is protected. How? By not creating an open pit mine anywhere within the river's watershed." Molly paused for a moment and glanced at Brad, who responded to her raised eyebrows with a negligible head shake. Her interpretation: Dehaviland had not yet arrived. *Where could he be?* Dare she discuss his proposal in his absence?

She gripped the sides of the podium, drew a steadying breath, and stepped off the edge of the cliff. "The CEO of Condor International, Gregory Dehaviland, has urged his board of directors to ensure the preservation of the greater Yellowstone ecosystem for generations to come, and to that end they voted just yesterday to suspend the Madison Mountain project."

There was an audible murmur of surprised exclamations from the crowd. Only the citizens of Moose Horn had any inkling of what her statement might contain, and even they seemed startled to be hearing it from her, as well as visibly pleased and relieved. Applause rippled through the room and gained volume as the reality of her words sunk home.

"There are conditions, of course," she continued, leaning toward the microphone and raising her voice until the applause died. "Condor International has invested a lot of money to date in establishing the New Millennium mine on Madison Mountain, over two million dollars in the past year and a half. The board of directors passed a vote that gave the option to purchase the patented mine claims to a land trust set up by Steven Young Bear's constituents. The purchase price is two million dollars, and the land trust has until March to come up with the funds to save Madison Mountain."

A journalist in the front row stood, pen poised over notebook. "Excuse me, Ms. Ferguson, but two million dollars seems like a pretty big chunk of change for twenty-seven blue-collar workers living in Moose Horn to raise in six months."

"Indeed, it is a great deal of money," Molly replied smoothly, "but Madison Mountain is part of our national forest, and therefore its fate lies in the hands of all the people of this nation, not just the citizens of Moose Horn. Surely a country as great as this one can rally around such an important cause."

Amy Littlefield stood up with her hands clasped

tightly before her and said, "I have a question for you, Ms. Ferguson. Condor International is a pretty big company, is it not?"

Molly nodded, her eyes scanning the room as her heart hammered and her mouth grew dry. Where on earth was Dehaviland? "Very big," she said.

"I guess the point I'm trying to make is, two million dollars is peanuts to an outfit like that," Amy said. "If they're suddenly so anxious to color themselves green, can you explain to me why they wouldn't just forfeit the patented claims to a land trust in the name of good publicity?"

"Two million dollars is two million dollars," Molly said briskly. "We're talking about a corporation here, with stockholders that demand fiscal profits. What Condor International has offered is a compromise that will benefit both parties and serve as a blueprint for future interactions with environmental interests."

"I think what your client has offered is a cheap way out of an embarrassing situation," Amy challenged. "Condor International broke a whole slew of laws trying to push the New Millennium mine down our throats, and several people were seriously injured as a result of those laws being broken. Isn't there the possibility of a big lawsuit being brought against them, a lawsuit that might cost them well over two million dollars? And where is their CEO, anyway? Wasn't he supposed to attend this meeting tonight? Maybe his board of directors had a change of heart. Maybe there *is* no compromise, and that's why he's not here."

CHAPTER FOURTEEN

WHEN PONY TOUCHED Steven's shoulder, he was just rising from his seat to go to Molly's aide. He turned, startled, then relaxed when he saw it was his sister. She leaned closer. "Steven," she murmured in his ear. "The lady in the reception area took a phone call a few minutes ago from Gregory Dehaviland. He's on his way but he had some trouble and is going to be a little late."

Steven nodded. "Good," he said, relieved that Molly didn't have to face the crowd alone. "I hope he gets here soon."

"And Caleb has some important information for you about Luther Makes Elk's rifle," Pony added before returning to the rear of the room.

As Steven approached the podium, Dehaviland himself entered the room. The CEO of Condor International shouldered past the onlookers standing at the rear of the hall and strode up the aisle to the podium. He glanced at Steven with an apologetic expression, turned to Molly and said, "Did you make the announcement?" and when she nodded, swung to face the room.

"Good evening. I'm Gregory Dehaviland, and I'm sorry I'm late. My attorney has outlined Condor International's proposal, so I won't beat around the bush while you wonder why in hell Condor International would suddenly give up an enormously profitable venture just to appease a handful of protesters. My initial reason for proposing this compromise was selfish. I own property on the Yellowstone River. I want the fishing to remain great, and the wilderness around that old cabin to stay the way it is. While I strongly believe it's possible to extract mineral resources from the earth in a safe and responsible manner, I also believe that when the proposed mine is being situated on public lands, the people of this nation should decide whether or not the permits are granted.

"Bottom line, Condor International is willing to work with local communities and environmental groups to ensure that the land gets the respect it deserves, and we want our stewardship to reflect our belief in a future that allows all of us to experience the power and the beauty of the wilderness.

"Perhaps Thoreau said it best when he said, 'In wildness is the preservation of the world,' but I think my daughter said it even better when she told me, 'Dad, you owe me and my children and my grandchildren a world that has at least as much to offer as yours did. The air and water should be as clean, or better yet, even cleaner, the forests as full of trees, the wild places just as wild.' And she's right. We need to think about the resources we're using and how we're using them. We need to think about what we're leaving behind for future generations.

"I'm seeing a lot of skeptical faces out there," Dehaviland said, drawing a fold of papers from inside his parka. "I have the papers with me, and there's a notary here to make it all nice and legal." He held them up. "So here's the deal, in black and white, waiting for signatures. This is for real. The price may seem steep, but it's fair, and I'm sure that Steven Young Bear is the man who can make this all happen. He's a fighting man, as you can tell by the bruises on his face, but hopefully the fight to protect the Yellowstone watershed from this moment forward will be a good, peaceful, and positive fight." He lowered his arm. "If the notary could please come forward, we can get these papers signed."

Dehaviland gestured for Steven to stand beside him as a stout gray-haired woman stood and made her way to the podium. While she watched, both parties signed the documents, after which she added her own signature and stamped them with her notary seal. Steven held the papers as she left the podium, then shook hands with Dehaviland and allowed himself a rare smile.

"The Madison Mountain Land Trust has been given six months to raise the money necessary to buy the patented leases from Condor International," Steven spoke into the podium microphone. "Two million dollars is a lot of money, but it's just money. Money passes through our hands like water, and when it's gone we don't even remember the measure of it, but the measure of the land is timeless and infinite. A mountain and a river live forever. This is a gift we can give to future generations. One day they might look back at the place we once stood and say, 'Thank you.' That would be a good epitaph for all of us—that together, we cared enough to make a difference."

MOLLY FELT HERSELF MELTING as Steven spoke, felt a growing warmth and softness battle with her cool and impersonal professional image. When he finished speaking, he glanced at her and she felt herself falling ever more deeply in love with him. She was uncomfortably warm, almost dizzy. A hand touched her arm and she jerked her eyes upward to meet Caleb McCutcheon's.

"May I say a word or two?" he said.

"Of course." She nodded, and Steven, who had

overheard the exchange, gestured for McCutcheon to take over the mike. He stood in front of the podium, a tall, handsome man equally as self-possessed as the two who had preceded him.

"Good evening. My name is Caleb McCutcheon, and I live at the Bow and Arrow Ranch, outside of Katy Junction. Some of you might know of the place, but for those of you who don't, it's one of the most beautiful ranches in the West. My opinion, of course, but as a matter of fact that's why I'm here tonight. I think Montana truly is one of the last great places, and I believe we should try our best to keep it that way. Like Steven Young Bear said, money is just money, but a river and a mountain live forever. We can raise that two million dollars one dollar at a time, and I'm going to start the process here and now with a contribution of five thousand dollars.

"Furthermore, I'll match any contributions made here tonight dollar for dollar, and be glad to do it. I'm thinking that almost everyone in this room is here because they care about this land, so if you can kick in five bucks tonight, I'll match it. Five hundred and I'm right here. One thousand? Better and better. Think about it. Alone, we don't stand much of a chance, but together we can raise this money. We can leave a helluva legacy for our children and grandchildren." McCutcheon's keen gaze scanned the room. "So come on. This is your chance to make a difference. Get your checkbooks out and write a big one. Help save a small but precious piece of the wilderness we all belong to."

Molly felt her eyes sting with gratitude. She moved to the microphone, and, in a voice that trembled with emotion, said, "I pledge nine hundred dollars," which was the total sum of her savings account, and amounted to more than what she could have gotten for her car after paying off the loan.

THE MEETING, for all intents and purposes, might have ended then and there with people rising from their seats in response to McCutcheon's words and reaching for their purses and wallets, but at that moment a journalist rose from his seat and said in a loud western twang, "Mr. Young Bear, you were the attorney who tried to shut down the Soldier Mountain mine two years ago, were you not? Doesn't Condor International own that mine as well? And what was the outcome of that law suit?"

Steven paused for a moment before stepping up to the podium to respond to the question. His dark eyes gazed out across the room. "It's true that Condor International also owns the Soldier Mountain mine just outside of the Rocky Ridge Reservation," he began slowly. "And yes, I was involved in the lawsuit that attempted to close that mine down. For those of you who might not be familiar with it, Soldier Mountain is an open pit uranium mine situated on federal land that's been in operation for over twenty-five years. Two and a half years ago, the mine petitioned to extend its original permitting for another ten years. Tribal members approached me and asked me to fight this extension, because they believed that over the years the mine had contaminated their water sources, and that people on the reservation were getting sick from drinking that water."

People were settling back into their seats with interested expressions and the journalists resumed scribbling in their notebooks. Video cameras zoomed in as Steven spoke. He didn't look in Molly's direction, though he was very much aware of her. He met Dehaviland's questioning eyes only briefly before continuing. "At the time, a geologist by the name of Ken Manning was managing the Soldier Mountain operation. Manning was also actively involved in raising funds to combat the environmental roadblocks we were putting in his path. Condor International paid out considerable sums of money over an equal number of years to a nonprofit right-wing antienvironmental lobby called the Wise Use Movement, a group dedicated to protecting the interests of oil-and-mining industries by thwarting local environmental efforts."

Steven paused for a moment, carefully considering his words. "During my research into the Soldier Mountain mine I uncovered copies of two interoffice memos, both from the Department of Health and Environmental Studies, dated two and a half years ago, and both sent to Ken Manning at Soldier Mountain, with copies forwarded to the headquarters of Condor International and the law offices of Taintor, Skelton and Goldstein. These memos confirmed high levels of radioactive contaminants found in the groundwater surrounding the mine, and growing complaints of illness, particularly organ cancers, in young people on the Rocky Ridge Reservation.

"Twenty-three officially documented cancer deaths are mentioned. The memos concluded that if Soldier Mountain intended to extend the operating life of its uranium mine, future permitting would be directly contingent upon the defeat of the Clean Water Initiative, a bill proposed by powerful environmental lobbies.

"This bill was defeated at the ballot box six months later, after the mining industry kicked in over two *million* dollars to campaign against the initiative." Steven paused for effect before continuing. "There's no question that it's hard for ordinary citizens to fight the corporate giants, especially when our own government backs them at the expense, and often the health and well-being, of its own people. But I believe that together, with the help of honorable and powerful people like Gregory Dehaviland, we can overcome the greed, corruption, and legalized murder that has prevailed in the mining industry.

"I believe that with a strong enough voice we can amend current mining laws, which allow mineral exploration and development on public lands. Saving Madison Mountain is only the beginning. It's a great beginning, but we have a long, hard road ahead of us."

Steven stood back to a swelling murmur of voices. He was turning from the podium when a reporter called out, "What exactly do you mean by legalized murder, Mr. Young Bear?"

He turned back. He thought of Mary Pretty Shield, and a shadow on hushed wings flew through his consciousness. He hesitated briefly, glancing at Molly and noting the paleness of her face. "Changing the laws to allow continued contamination of the drinking water on the Rocky Ridge Reservation, and accepting the resulting illnesses and deaths as a justifiable cost of doing business, can be construed as nothing less than legalized murder."

"Then am I to understand, Mr. Young Bear," another journalist asked, "that both Condor International and the law firm of Taintor, Skelton and Goldstein were fully aware of the repeated violations of the clean water act at Soldier Mountain and the high cancer rates on Rocky Ridge Reservation from contaminated groundwater and were also actively involved in the push to repeal legislation that would have corrected those wrongs?"

Steven paused only momentarily before speaking into the microphone. "Montana's Department of Health and Environmental Studies was equally aware. I have no further comments," he said, and then, amid a burgeoning onslaught of queries from other reporters and attendees, he turned, and without so much as a glance toward Molly or Dehaviland, departed the meeting.

EVERYTHING HAD GONE so well up to this point. Molly listened with growing dismay as Steven told the crowd just how dark and political the environmental arena was. He spoke simply and eloquently, and when he fielded the question about legalized murder she felt her heart skip several beats as she waited for him to tell the world about the death of Mary Pretty Shield. She knew he desperately wanted to avenge her death, but she hoped just as desperately that he didn't. As if reading her thoughts, he had caught her eye, then concluded by damning both the law firm she worked for and the corporation Dehaviland spearheaded.

Chaos erupted when Steven stepped away from the podium, and the triumph of Madison Mountain might have been eclipsed by the travesties of the Soldier Mountain mine had not Dehaviland smoothly taken over the microphone and said, with a grace that bespoke both his power and his blunt honesty, "Thank you, Mr. Young Bear, for beginning this new age of enlightenment so boldly. I fully intend to do my best to pick up the gauntlet you've thrown down, and work toward righting any wrongs and clarifying any misconceptions, real or perceived, that may or may not have been perpetuated through ignorance, misinterpretation, or deliberate actions on behalf of the mining industry and its supporters."

McCutcheon, as if on cue, took over the meeting, refocusing the crowd's attention on the two-million-dollar fund-raising effort. He announced once again his intention to match every donation that was made there and then. "Don't forget that your donations are tax deductible. I've already been pledged nine hundred dollars. Come on, everyone. Let's show the world how much spunk a bunch of Montanans have."

Molly watched the people rise out of their seats

and approach the podium, but all she could think about was Steven's voice as he stood before God and country and so calmly destroyed her career and her life. She was suddenly desperate to escape the confines of the room. In her blind haste to flee she bumped squarely into Dehaviland, who steadied her with a hand on her arm. "I'm sorry," she said, overcome with humility and perilously close to tears. "What Steven said here tonight… I had no idea…."

Dehaviland nodded wryly. "It seems I have a lot to learn about the Soldier Mountain mine, as well as the law firm of Taintor, Skelton and Goldstein. Young Bear sure as hell opened Pandora's box tonight. I was hoping we could catch up to him and talk about what other surprises might come out of it. The sooner I find out what I'm up against, the better. Come on, let's go hunt him down."

They didn't have very far to look. Steven was waiting outside by his Jeep. He straightened at their approach and his calm deportment infuriated her, but before she could speak he said, in that deep voice of his, "I'm sorry. I didn't intend for that can of worms to be opened. It wasn't planned."

"No apologies necessary," Dehaviland said. "I understand how the media works. If tonight marks a new beginning of honest and open communications between mining interests and environmental lobbies, then I can assume all past transgressions will be brought to light sooner or later. I'd just as soon have all the cards laid out on the table." Dehaviland rubbed the back of his neck as he spoke. "Look, I haven't had supper yet. There's an historic railroad station close to here that seconds as a pretty good eatery. What do you say we start charting the waters over a few beers and steaks?"

The last thing Molly wanted to do was fraternize with the man who had just announced to the entire world that the law firm she worked for was corrupt, but when Dehaviland looked at her with raised eyebrows she couldn't think of any graceful way out of it. "That sounds fine," she said.

HALF AN HOUR LATER they were being served drinks at the old train station, a charming restaurant that Molly might have enjoyed under different circumstances. As it was, she lifted her gin and tonic and studied the menu to avoid Steven's eyes. Dehaviland was the most gracious of hosts. Ignoring the tension at the table, he talked about fishing, about the trout he'd caught and released that day and the flies he'd used to catch them, and about the old man in Livingston who'd tied them for him.

"His great-grandfather was one of the first explorers to this area. Wasn't with the Lewis and

Clark expedition, but should have been if history could be rewritten," he said with a grin. "That old man knew his stuff, too. He took me to all his special places and taught me how to use the flies he tied. We camped out on the banks of the river and he cooked sourdough pancakes for breakfast. I'll never forget those times. He died this past summer, but for the past two years I was just too busy to touch base with him." Dehaviland stared into the amber sparkle of his beer for a moment, then straightened and said to Molly, "Steaks are the specialty here."

They all ordered steaks and a house salad. Molly started on her second gin and tonic. Steven was quiet while Dehaviland expounded on a horse he'd once owned, a retired world-champion cutting horse. The salads came. Molly poked at hers, Steven didn't touch his, and Dehaviland was now talking about a racehorse named Kola, who could drink beer out of a bottle and outrun a cheetah.

The steaks came, sizzling and cooked to perfection, with sides of baked potato and roasted vegetables. Molly poked at hers, Steven didn't touch his, while Dehaviland devoured every last morsel with the enthusiasm of a starving man. "Damn," he said, pushing his empty plate away and picking up his beer. "Lunch seems like it was a long time ago. Nothing like being outdoors all day to put an edge on a man's appetite." He took a deep drink of his brew, then set his mug down on the table with a sharp thump and leaned forward on his elbows.

"The reason I was late getting to the meeting was because I was paid a visit by Ken Manning. He showed up a couple of hours after the two of you left and asked for his job back. When I told him no, he got a little ornery. He had more than a few things to say about the two of you, then he made some nasty comments about my performance as CEO. All in all, he said too much that I found offensive, so I interrupted him and asked him to leave."

"Did he?" Molly asked, feeling the blood drain from her face.

Dehaviland nodded. "He did, after making some ugly threats, which I took as empty gestures of anger because I'd had him fired. But on the way to the meeting, before reaching the main road, I got a flat tire. The thing I noticed right away about that flat was that the hole was in the sidewall, so I got in my truck and called the state police, then took my sweet time changing the tire. Until the police arrived I pretty much stayed under the truck trying to get the spare tire unbolted from the rear frame."

Molly's fingers tightened on her glass. "It was

Manning, wasn't it? He shot your tire and he was trying to shoot you."

Dehaviland shrugged. "It's possible he shot my tire, but I doubt he'd have shot me. He was pretty irrational, but not crazy enough to want to spend the rest of his life behind bars. Anyhow, the cops showed up in about thirty minutes. They didn't find Manning hiding in the bushes, but they did find where someone had pulled off the road in a spot that gave them a good clear shot. No proof, of course, but I'm hoping if Manning was anywhere in the area, he saw all those badges and decided to leave the country. Anyhow, two of the state cops helped me change my tire or I never would have made it to the meeting. I couldn't get those damn lug nuts loose for the life of me. Not as young as I used to be."

"What about Manning?" Steven said.

"They're still looking to charge him for criminal threatening, breaking and entry, and serve him with your restraining order, but when I told them about the new rash of threats he'd made, they beefed up their all points bulletin to bring him in for questioning. They staked out the meeting tonight, thinking he might show, but so far as I know he didn't. I wanted to give you a heads-up because I think he has the potential to be dangerous. Environmentalists and Native Americans are definitely at the top of his black list, as well as anyone who hangs out with them or negotiates with them." He reached for his beer, took a swallow, then sat back in his chair. "Okay, I know it's late and the two of you don't really want to be here, so I'll wrap things up as quickly as I can," he said.

"A man in my position meets a lot of people, day in and day out. Most of them think they're important. A few of them are. Very few of them are honest. I believe both of you are." He glanced between them. "I also believe that in spite of all the negative things that have happened in the past, we can work together to create a better future."

Steven tilted his head very slightly to one side, a subtle but skeptical gesture that brought the blood back to Molly's cheeks. She took a big swallow of her gin and tonic. "I believe that, too," she said.

Dehaviland looked squarely at her. "The law firm of Taintor, Skelton and Goldstein has done its last work for Condor International," he said.

Molly felt the bottom drop out of her world. "But…"

Dehaviland raised his hand to silence her. "Would you be willing to leave them and come work for me?"

"Work for you? Doing what exactly?" she asked, her heart pounding.

"You'd be in charge of coordinating all of the

environmental impact data collected by our staff, and you'd report on all existing or potential environmental problems as and when they apply to all of our mining projects, past, present and future. Think carefully before you respond. We're talking worldwide. Condor International holds active mining leases in over twenty countries. The position would involve extensive travel and long, insufferable dealings with more than a few uncooperative old-school staff members."

Molly sat back in her chair, momentarily paralyzed as her mind scrambled to process what Dehaviland was saying. He was handing her an unbelievable career opportunity, one that she was hardly qualified to accept. "Well, sir, I—"

"Don't give me your answer now," Dehaviland interrupted, raising his hand again. "Take your time and think about it. As for you," he said to Steven, "I'd like you to think about this. Everything Molly learns, all the information she compiles, she brings to you. Together, the two of you prepare briefs for me, and I do mean briefs. I'm a busy man and don't have time to wallow through mountains of chaff just to find a grain of wheat." He raised his beer and drained it.

"I realize the two of you are in opposite camps right now," he continued, "and I also realize this partnership might not work, but I can't think of another way to break through the concrete wall that's been built by generations of corporate execs who only knew how to do business one way. My daughter's counting on me to change the world, and I need some help." He broke off abruptly and regarded Steven with a calculating eye. "You're going to tell me no," he stated flatly.

"I can't accept," Steven said with a brief head shake. "It would be a definite conflict of interest."

"It doesn't have to be," Dehaviland said.

"I'm sorry."

Molly set her glass down on the table with a sharp rap. "I'm sorry, too," she said. "Mr. Dehaviland, I don't need any time to think about your offer. I accept, with gratitude. I'll hand in my resignation to the firm tomorrow, and be available in two weeks." She pushed her chair back abruptly and stood. "It's getting late, and it's been a very long day. If you don't mind, could you drop me off at the airport hotel?"

"Of course," Dehaviland said. "I'll get my truck warmed up." He rose to his feet and shook hands with Steven. "It's been quite an evening, Young Bear. Good luck with your fund-raising, and if you should change your mind at any time, please give me a call."

After Dehaviland left the table, Steven stood.

"Come home with me tonight," he said. "We need to talk."

"About what?" Molly stared him in the eye. "I think you've made it perfectly clear how you feel about helping to change things for the better. It would be a definite conflict of interest." She retrieved her coat from the back of her chair and when Steven tried to help her into it, she shrugged away from him, her eyes blurring with bitter tears.

"Damn you, Young Bear," she choked. "That man's offering you the best opportunity you'll ever have for a good-paying job that would let you make the kind of difference you want to make, and you throw it right back in his face. And...and you made a fool of me tonight at that meeting, and..." Tears spilled over as she struggled with the coat. Steven reached to help her again, and again she pulled away. "I don't understand you at all," she said, turning blindly for the door because she knew if she stayed a moment longer she'd never find her way out. As she left the eatery and walked rapidly toward the headlights of Dehaviland's waiting vehicle, she heard Steven call her name, but she didn't look back.

CHAPTER FIFTEEN

THE BLEAK EMPTINESS Steven felt watching Molly drive off in Dehaviland's truck became an unbearable ache as he headed home. If only he'd been able to talk her into coming with him, maybe they could have made things right between them, but he knew nothing he could have said would have penetrated the depths of her anger. She felt betrayed by him, and she'd never understand why he couldn't work for Condor International. Perhaps time would dull her hurt, but he doubted it, just as he doubted that all the roses on the planet could smooth over the giant rift he'd created between them.

He pulled into his drive, parked, and sat in the darkness listening to the tick of the hot engine as it cooled. In two weeks Molly would be gone. She'd move to Texas and he'd never see her again. The thought burdened him with an almost suffocating sense of loss, and he climbed out of the Jeep slowly, weary to the depths of his soul. He moved to go into the house when a sharp explosion rent the darkness and something struck him hard in the chest, knocking him back against his Jeep. The blow drove the air from his lungs and he twisted as he fell, hitting the ground facedown. He lay motionless, stunned, feeling only the cold sharpness of gravel digging into the side of his face and an intense burning pain in his chest. He struggled for breath and finally felt an easing, felt air trickling back into his lungs with agonizing slowness as his fingers closed around handfuls of gravel.

Over the thunder of his heartbeat, he heard approaching footsteps and remained still, silently breathing through cracks in the pain. The footsteps moved closer, pausing frequently, cautiously. He knew who it was, knew even before the expensive leather shoe tentatively prodded him, knew before the hand reached down to roll him onto his back, knew before the starlight gave substance to Ken Manning's features. He knew the way Mary Pretty Shield must have known, two and a half years ago, on the terrible night she'd died.

"I would have done this years ago, Young Bear," Manning said, his voice chillingly calm and matter-of-fact, "but back then I had a lot to lose. Now I have nothing. Before you die, know that you've failed, you and Dehaviland both. Without you to raise the money, the patented claims will remain the property of Condor International, and the New Millennium mine will be in full operation on Madison Mountain before the end of next year. You just fought your last fight, and you lost. Not even that powerful California senator friend of yours can help you now."

As Manning spoke, Steven felt his strength returning with every shallow breath he drew. The crushing burn in his chest was easing. Manning's bullet had struck him squarely, but somehow he was still alive—if only temporarily. Manning still held a pistol in his hand, and if Steven didn't die in a timely fashion he had no doubt that Manning would shoot him again.

"You killed Mary Pretty Shield," Steven said.

Manning's smile was without remorse. "It was the only way to get you to drop the lawsuit. Killing her was risky, but it worked like a charm."

"And Sam Blackmore?"

"A shame about him. I heard he was driving too fast."

Steven flung the fistful of gravel upward with all his strength, but that compromised strength wasn't enough to propel him off the ground. Manning's well-placed kick easily leveled him again and he found himself staring point blank into the face of death as Manning pointed the pistol at his head.

"You're a tough bastard, I'll give you that much,

Young Bear. You're going to die as hard as she did," Manning said. "It took her a long time, too. She was quite a fighter."

Even as Manning spoke, Steven's thoughts blurred on Molly and he was glad, so damn glad, she hadn't come home with him. He wished he could tell her how much she meant to him… waited for the gunshot and heard a sudden rush of wind…no, not wind, swift movement, footsteps rushing out of the darkness behind Manning, many people moving, swift and silent and deadly, a sudden swarm descending. There were sounds of weapons being readied, sounds of Manning being grabbed, struck, driven hard onto the ground beside him, so close Steven could reach out and touch him, and a voice, taut with the stress of the moment, saying loudly, harshly, *"You are under arrest!* You have the right to remain silent, you have the right…"

Another voice, closer, a familiar voice saying, "Young Bear? It's over. We have Manning and an ambulance is on the way." Sheriff Conrad Walker bent over him as he spoke, a dark figure blocking the starlight.

"I'm all right," Steven said, dazed and shaken. He parried Walker's hands and tried to sit up, but Walker pressed his shoulders firmly down onto the ground.

"Sure you are. You're going to be just fine. Just lie still. The ambulance is on its way."

"How did you know Manning was here?"

Walker was unzipping Steven's jacket, fumbling in the murky light. "Somebody get a light over here!" he shouted over his shoulder. Then to Steven he said, "I was listening to the police radio and I heard a report that Manning's vehicle had been spotted in Gallatin Gateway. I called the state cops to tell them where you lived but Dehaviland had beaten me to it. We all got here about the same time, which was about two minutes too late to stop Manning. Stop moving. Lie still."

"Did you hear what Manning said?" Steven asked, trying to sit up again, and again being pressed back down.

"Something about you fighting your last fight, and dying as hard as she did," Walker said, unbuttoning Steven's shirt. "I sure as hell hope he wasn't talking about that red-haired lawyer friend of yours."

"No. It was someone he killed over two years ago." Steven slumped back, relieved that Manning had implicated himself, that someone had heard him, and that Mary Pretty Shield's death would finally be avenged.

Someone trotted up with a flashlight, holding it while Walker peeled opened Steven's shirt and stared at the place where Manning's bullet had struck. "I'll be damned," the sheriff muttered beneath his breath. "You're a lucky bastard, Young Bear. No doubt you have one hell of a bruise and probably some cracked ribs beneath that T-shirt, but there's not a drop of blood. You've cheated death tonight." Walker held up the remains of Luther Makes Elk's pouch, which had been torn apart by the bullet. "What's this thing?"

"An amulet containing powerful medicine," Steven said.

Walker upended the shredded remains of the pouch and shone the flashlight on what dropped into his palm. "An old rifle cartridge," he mused aloud, "and two equally old silver dollars, an 1879 Morgan and a 1921 Peace. If they were in mint condition before tonight, Young Bear, they sure as hell aren't now. Take a look." He held out his hand. "You can see how the bullet struck them. Lying together the way they were in that pouch, they saved your life. You're a lucky bastard, Young Bear," he repeated, shaking his head.

Steven touched his fingers to his T-shirt, felt the large tender swelling on his chest and winced. Dead center, right where Luther's powerful medicine had hung. Keep it close, the old man had told him. Man.

It was another thirty minutes before Manning

had been carted off and the last of the police had gone. Walker stayed long enough to make sure Steven's refusal to be checked out at the hospital wasn't going to end in his untimely demise, then followed the ambulance down the drive. Steven stood in the doorway until the sounds of both vehicles faded into silence, then closed the door, locked it, and retrieved a beer from the refrigerator. His message light was flashing and he played back the tape, hoping it was from Molly.

"Sorry I didn't get a chance to talk with you tonight before or after the meeting," McCutcheon's voice said, "but we were late getting there and things got a little hectic afterward. This news is too damned exciting to wait until morning. That rifle Luther Makes Elk gave you was issued to an officer by the name of Captain Myles Keogh, who died at the battle of Little Big Horn. And get this. A similar weapon from that battle, which was issued to an unknown soldier, sold at auction last year for nearly seven hundred thousand dollars. The person who gave me this information, and he's a highly respected expert in his field, said that once the documentation is verified, he thinks that rifle of yours could bring well over a million dollars. Thought you'd want to know, just in case you were using it as a doorstop."

Steven walked into the living room, sat down on

the couch, and took a sip of cold beer. He swallowed a mouthful of foam, lowered the bottle. His hand was shaking so badly that the beer was sudsing up. He wedged the bottle between his knees and sat in contemplative silence, but he wasn't thinking about the worth of Luther's old weapon. He was thinking about how close he'd just come to death, and how much worse things might have been if he'd been able to persuade Molly to return home with him. He sat like that for a long time, pondering life's dark mysteries, thinking about Luther's owl stew, and overwhelmed by a cold fear like he'd never known.

MOLLY SPENT THE BETTER PART of the night alternately seething with anger at Steven and anguishing over the look in his eyes as she told him what she thought of him, and the sound of his voice as he called after her at the restaurant. She drifted off briefly into a troubled sleep just before dawn and saw the owl sitting in a tree, watching her in the darkness, but her 5:00 a.m. wake-up call interrupted any message the owl might have given her. She caught the first commuter flight back to Helena and took a cab to the office, dressed in the same clothes she'd worn the day before. A part of her felt so adrift and disconnected from the corporate world that she scarcely cared if her suit was rumpled. There were things in life far more important than that.

First on her agenda of those far more important things was to meet with Jarrod Skelton and tell him of her decision to accept the position Dehaviland had offered her. She would then touch base with Dani, call her mother and fill her in on the latest, play catch-up with some office work, and begin planning a future that involved extensive travel, intensive research…and had very little to do with Steven Young Bear.

Skelton's secretary gave her a startled up-and-down once-over that reflected Molly's mildly disheveled appearance. "Good morning, Mrs. Lancing, is Mr. Skelton in?"

"Yes, but he only just arrived, and…"

"Thank you." Molly forged boldly forward, rapping once on his door before opening it. Skelton was seated at his desk reading the front page of the daily paper, which explained the thunderous expression on his face as he lurched to his feet uttering what sounded like a very unprofessional profanity. "And good morning to you, too, Mr. Skelton," Molly said, closing the door firmly behind her. "I see you've read the headlines. The public hearing was very interesting."

Skelton's countenance darkened. "That public hearing was a travesty. Young Bear's overstepped his bounds, and this firm intends to bring charges of slander against him for those damning public statements. Furthermore, I can't believe you actually stood up in front of that pack of bloodthirsty media wolves, while representing both this law firm and Condor International, and pledged nine hundred dollars to Young Bear's cause. I'm afraid your actions go way beyond mere apologies."

"It was Mr. Dehaviland who put forth New Millennium's buyout proposal. The idea wasn't mine, and the cause isn't exclusively Young Bear's. I was merely supporting my client's proposed compromise. And actually, I'm not here to apologize." Molly stood before his desk, curiously calm in the presence of a man who, until yesterday, had intimidated the hell out of her. "I'm here to tender my resignation. I'll work out my two-week notice if you wish, but I've accepted a job offer from Gregory Dehaviland. I want you to know that I appreciate the opportunities you've given me here during the past year. I've learned a great deal, and I'm grateful to you for that."

"Dehaviland won't last out the month as CEO of Condor International," Skelton said, his upper body rigid with anger. "He sealed his fate at that meeting last night when he sided with Young Bear's camp."

"I happen to disagree, Mr. Skelton. Dehaviland

may be ahead of his time, as all truly brilliant men are, but I admire his vision of the future and I want to help make it a reality."

Skelton blinked, then shook his head as if he couldn't believe what he was hearing. "You may vacate your office immediately, Ms. Ferguson. We no longer require your services."

Molly met his flat stare for a moment longer before turning to leave, still infused with that strange calm that allowed her to exit Skelton's office with measured grace, nod to Skelton's secretary, and pass Brad in the corridor with an almost beatific smile. Brad fell in behind her as she returned to what would remain her office for a perilously short time. "Have you read the morning paper?"

"Yes, on the plane this morning," she replied.

"And I suppose you already got it from Young Bear that Manning's been taken into custody."

Molly masked her surprised relief with a brisk nod. "Of course." There was no need for Brad to know that she and Steven were no longer communicating.

"What did Skelton say to you just now?"

"He told me to clear out, and that's exactly what I'm going to do," Molly said, and left him standing slack-jawed behind her. Once inside her office, she closed the door and leaned against it, waited for the spell of weakness to pass, then moved to her desk, picked up her phone and dialed. Dani answered on the second ring. "I have some important news," she said, sinking into her chair for perhaps the last time. "Can you meet me for lunch?"

Within two hours Molly had cleared the last of her things out of what had once been her office and packed them with some difficulty into the small confines of her car. She met Dani for lunch at their favorite deli and after their sandwiches had been delivered Dani said, with long-suffering patience, "Well, are you planning to keep me in suspense forever?"

Molly drew a deep breath. "I've resigned my position with Taintor, Skelton and Goldstein and accepted a job working for Dehaviland as an environmental consultant."

Dani paused, sandwich halfway to her mouth. "You're kidding, right?"

"It's an unbelievable opportunity for me. I'll be traveling all over the world."

Dani gave her a quizzical look. "Wow. I guess I was way off base. When you asked me to meet you for lunch, I assumed it was because you were going to tell me that Steven had popped the question." She laid her sandwich back down on the plate. "I'm usually right on the money with these affairs of the heart. What happened?"

Molly's shoulders rose and fell around a dispirited shrug. "Dehaviland was generous enough to offer Steven a position, too, but he declined, so I guess that's it."

"That's *it?* Don't give me that, Molly Ferguson. For a woman who's supposed to be all excited about landing the career opportunity of a lifetime, you're looking pretty miserable."

"I'm not the least bit miserable," Molly said.

"Right." Dani sat back in her chair with a frown. "I watched the late news last night and read the paper this morning. Was it what Steven said at the public hearing?"

"He's completely unwilling to accept the fact that the mining industry can be beneficial in any way, shape, or form," Molly said, wishing she felt as cool and logically detached as she sounded. Wishing she'd never met the man who'd made her heart ache so badly. "He's stubborn and set in his ways, and there's no way we'll ever see eye to eye on any of the important issues."

"Don't forget that he's had years of negative experiences dealing with those big mining companies," Dani reminded her. "Look, I'm glad you have such a good rapport with Dehaviland, but you have to admit that there's an excess of shady politics involved in any high-stakes money-making endeavor. Why is Dehaviland being so nice?

Maybe he knows that two million dollars is too much money for a little group like Steven's to raise. Maybe he made that offer just to take the heat off Condor International and give the press something warm and fuzzy to write about, instead of illegal road building and rioting truck drivers."

"Dehaviland is being so nice because he has a daughter that's forcing him to become environmentally responsible, and he has a fishing camp on the right river. I believe he's genuine in what he's trying to do." Molly pushed her plate away. "But what I believe doesn't matter. It's pointless, don't you see?" she said, her throat squeezing up and her eyes burning. "Steven and I are so different there could never be anything real and lasting between us."

Dani reached across the table to squeeze her friend's arm. "Of course there could be, Molly. There already is. Go see him. Talk to him. Don't leave him wondering and waiting and hoping. At the very least, have the decency to tell him goodbye."

At Dani's words, Molly lost the last of her composure. "I can't," she said, the bitter tears spilling over before she could hide her face in her hands. "I just can't."

"Then maybe you'd better reconsider taking that job," Dani said.

STEVEN SLEPT POORLY, was drinking coffee long before the first light of dawn paled the sky to the east, and was on the road well before the sun rose over the Beartooth range. It was a Wednesday, a workday, but after the previous night of mayhem and sleeplessness, he deemed a day off was in order. Besides that, he hurt all over, though the worst of the pain was definitely localized in his heart. He headed east, toward the reservation. He brought the rifle with him, and wasn't surprised to find Luther Makes Elk sitting on the wall bench outside his shack, wrapped in his old wool pea-coat, bare headed in spite of the cold.

"You should have gone on the vision quest, like I told you," Luther said as Steven joined him on the bench, balancing the rifle across his knees.

"Maybe, but the meeting last night was important," Steven said, the vibration of his voice causing an equal vibration of pain in his bruised chest. "Grandfather, I have some information about this rifle of yours."

"I already told you about the rifle," Luther said with an impatient wave of one hand. "And so. Maybe today you should climb Brave Heart. Maybe the spirits are ready to talk to you."

"This weapon could be worth a great deal of money, as much as a million dollars. Maybe even more."

Luther nodded, gazing out across the distance. "So you should sell it, if money is what you want. But go on your vision quest first."

"Grandfather, the money from selling this rifle could make you a wealthy man. You could live in a real house with running water and electricity, and have a television, and someone to cook your meals. You could eat Chinese food every night if you wanted."

"I gave you that rifle," Luther said, his ancient eyes softening on the beauty of the morning. "I don't need the white man's money like you do. You can use that old thing to prop your door open, like my father did, or sell it and buy a television, if you want to sit and get fat and lazy, like Charlie Three Dogs did. But go on the vision quest before you do. Are you still wearing the big medicine I gave you?"

Steven nodded. He tugged on the leather thong and showed Luther the new cloth pouch. "The leather pouch broke last night," he said, "but the medicine inside is still good."

"Medicine that strong will always be good. One day, I will tell you about those two coins, and that old rifle cartridge." Luther's eyes narrowed on Steven's. "We should smoke the pipe before you go." He pushed off the bench and moved slowly, his joints stiff with arthritis, into the shack, re-emerging with the pipe and the foil sack of tobacco. "There is one thing I want, if you sell the rifle," he said, settling back on the bench and unwrapping the pipe. He laid it across his knees and opened the tobacco pouch. "I want a dark suit, like the ones you wear to work."

Steven studied Luther's face for some sign of humor, but the old man was intent on packing the bowl of the pipe with tobacco. "Grandfather, why would you want a suit?"

"Because," Luther said. "Your Red Hair will want me to dress fancy for her wedding. She's that way."

STEVEN DIDN'T WANT TO GO on a vision quest, but neither did he want to dishonor Luther Makes Elk, and so he smoked the pipe with the old man and departed Luther's shack still in possession of an extremely valuable rifle that he didn't know what to do with. Luther Makes Elk had to be one of the poorest Indians on the rez, but his poverty was measured by the white man's yardstick, a measure that was wrong in so many ways. Luther had told him to go on a vision quest, and so he would do Luther's bidding. He would climb *Cante Tinza,* Brave Heart Mountain, and wait there until he learned what he needed to learn, and maybe then the path before him would be clear.

From Luther's shack it was an hour's drive to the parking area that led to the trailhead, and from there it was another two hours of steady climbing to reach the summit. He carried Luther's sacred bundle in a borrowed backpack, along with his heavy parka, two liters of water and a bottle of aspirin that was stashed in the Jeep, half of which he had already consumed. He also carried the rifle, because he didn't dare leave it behind, though the weight of the weapon cost him dearly on the climb. His chest burned with every breath he took, until he half expected fire to pour forth, dragon-like, from his flaming lungs. He reached the summit before noon and shrugged off the pack, taking a long appreciative moment to drink in the high beauty that surrounded him. The wind pushed against him and hissed through the stunted growth that clung to crevices in the rock.

It was cold, but there was a sheltered spot in the lee of a granite outcropping where he could spend the night and greet the dawn. He placed his stakes there as best he could in the shallow, flinty soil, the strips of red cloth flagging in the chill wind. He made sure to place them correctly, in the four directions, to mark the boundaries of his vision quest, but he knew the spirits would not speak to him. These things took time and patience, and he had already lost his focus.

He was thinking not of the sacredness of the place or the spirituality of his purpose for being there, but of the red-haired woman who had taken such a strong hold of his heart. He wondered if she thought of him at all, or if Dehaviland had already swept her into his own powerful, corporate world. Perhaps she was flying back to Texas with him in his Learjet even as he sat on this lonesome mountaintop. Accepting Dehaviland's job offer had been the smart thing for her to do, but a part of him, a big part, hoped she would change her mind and decide to stay here in Montana.

Steven laid the rifle down, burdened by a weariness that had nothing to do with the steep climb. He knew Molly wouldn't stay. She'd leave just to prove to him that Dehaviland was the man who could change the world for the better. She'd leave because she was angry and hurt, thinking he'd made a fool of her at the public meeting. She'd leave because that job offer had been the opportunity of a lifetime, and he'd never see her again.

His desperate love for her had driven him to this mountaintop to kindle a tiny fire, burn the sweetgrass and sage smudge that Luther Makes Elk had given him, and purge the fever of wanting her from his blood. But it was his equally desperate belief in that same love that, two hours later, made him pull up the four stakes with the red strips of cloth flagging in the wind and pack them away. He shouldered his pack, picked up the rifle and, in the strong golden sunlight of the September afternoon, began his rapid descent of *Cante Tinza*.

It was foolish, he knew, but if the rest of his life must be spent apart from that wildly beautiful woman, then he must see her one last time, if only to say goodbye.

CHAPTER SIXTEEN

MOLLY LEFT THE DELI after not eating any of her lunch and pointed her little red Mercedes south, spending the early hours of the afternoon driving across the vast Montana landscape as if gradually emerging from a thick fog and seeing everything clearly for the very first time. She drove straight through Bozeman, past the turnoff to Gallatin Gateway, and the road to Steven's place. She knew he wouldn't be home. He'd be at his office, hard at work trying to raise two million dollars in a mere six months. She turned around and headed back toward Bozeman, intending to stop at his office, but instead took the highway back to Helena. She just couldn't do it. She could say goodbye to all of Montana, but she couldn't bring herself to say goodbye to Steven Young Bear.

Her cell phone rang, and she answered it. "Ferguson."

"Molly? Dehaviland here. I just this moment arrived in my office and listened to my messages.

One of them was from a Sheriff Walker. Have you talked to Young Bear today?"

"No. Why?"

"Ken Manning paid him a visit last night. Apparently Manning's been arrested for attempted murder, in addition to his other charges. Young Bear's okay, but I thought you'd want to know. I've been trying to reach him at home and at his office, but he's not answering."

As Dehaviland spoke, Molly felt waves of shocked disbelief tingling through her. Heart hammering, she pulled over to the side of the highway, struggling to catch her breath. "He's okay? Steven's all right? Are you sure?"

"Yes. Sheriff Walker was there when it happened."

"What did Manning do?"

"Waited in the shrubs beside his house and took a shot at him after he got out of his Jeep, but apparently the bullet hit something Young Bear was wearing around his neck."

"Oh, dear God," Molly said, leaning her forehead against the steering wheel. She felt very close to passing out. Her mind raced. She thought of Luther's owl. The stew. The pouch with the powerful medicine. Her dream. Steven…

"He's okay," Dehaviland repeated emphatically. "The sheriff made sure he was checked out by the EMTs."

"How did Sheriff Walker know that Manning was going to try to kill Steven?"

"He had a hunch, same as I did. I called the state police last night just after I left you at the airport hotel. Manning was so worked up and on edge when he was at my cabin earlier I thought Young Bear should have police protection until Manning was brought in for questioning. They told me that Manning's vehicle had been spotted headed for Gallatin Gateway and they'd already put two and two together, with a little prompting from Walker. Apparently the sheriff heard the radio transmissions and drove to Young Bear's place on his own."

Molly closed her eyes and drew several deep breaths. Her stomach was doing flip-flops and a cold sweat filmed her brow. She sat like that long enough for Dehaviland to say, "Molly?"

"Thank you for protecting Steven," she said, her voice sounding faint and faraway. "And thank you for calling me. I didn't know about any of this. I'm on my way to see him right now, and Mr. Dehaviland, about that job offer... I know I told you last night that I accepted, but—"

"Say no more," Dehaviland said. "The job will always be here for you, if you want it. And when you see Young Bear, tell him I said he's a lucky man, in more ways than one."

Molly hardly remembered the drive to Steven's place, only the bitter disappointment that when she arrived at his house, his Jeep wasn't there. She called his office number and got his answering machine. She called his cell phone and got his answering service. She called the Bow and Arrow and got Caleb McCutcheon, who told her in a non-stop enthusiastic diatribe about the estimated value of Luther Makes Elk's rifle, believing that's why she'd called. When she could get a word in she informed McCutcheon about Ken Manning's attempt on Steven's life.

McCutcheon swore softly. "I'll tell Pony. You might want to check out Luther's place. Steven might have gone there to tell him about that rifle. When you catch up with him have him call Pony. She'll be worried sick."

Molly gassed her car up in Livingston and headed for Luther Makes Elk's shack, hoping that McCutcheon was right and Steven would be there, and if he wasn't, that Luther could tell her where he was.

IT WAS LATE AFTERNOON when Steven returned the rifle to Luther. At first he thought his adopted grandfather was napping on the wall bench outside of his shack, chin tucked to his chest and hat tipped over his eyes, but at his approach the old man made a small gesture with one gnarled hand, and Steven joined him. After a while Luther roused, studied him for a few moments from beneath the hat brim, and said, "I may be near the end of my days, but I still remember how it felt to be young. I remember that kind of pain."

"I came back to tell you that I'm not selling the rifle," Steven said. "I'm leaving it here with you, where it belongs."

"The spirits didn't tell you to do that," Luther said. "They chased you off the mountain because you went looking for something that wasn't there. Keep the rifle. I gave it to you because you needed it."

"Grandfather, I've had enough of guns and violence. If you don't want to keep the gun yourself, give it to the tribal elders and let them decide what to do with it. A million dollars could do a lot for the people on the rez. They could set up a scholarship fund and send a lot of kids to college."

"To learn the white man's ways?"

"To learn how to survive in today's world, and make life better for the rest of the tribe. And I'll buy you a fancy suit like the ones I wear to work, but you won't be wearing it at Red Hair's wedding. She's taken a job in a far place, and chances are I won't be seeing much of her."

"Your Red Hair's not so far away as you think," Luther said. "I think maybe you'll see her again, probably soon."

Steven leaned against Luther's shack. He ached all over, physically and spiritually, and felt beyond all hope. "Sometimes I wonder if it's worth it," he said. "Sometimes I wonder if all the struggle makes any difference at all."

"The white man struggles all the time and does little that matters, but what you do makes a difference," Luther said. After a brief pause he added, "Does Red Hair drive fast?"

"Too fast."

"And so. I think maybe you'll see her even sooner than I thought." Luther was squinting at a ribbon of dust being thrown into the golden September air by a rapidly approaching vehicle on the reservation road. It was a small vehicle, sporty, and the sudden thump in Steven's chest made him wince with pain. Was the car truly red, or was that just the reflection of the setting sun? He pushed to his feet, fixing his eyes on the approaching dust cloud and struggling to catch his breath. Dare he hope?

"I remember how it felt to be young," he heard Luther Makes Elk repeat, "and I think maybe you better get me that fancy suit, pretty quick."

MOLLY SPOTTED STEVEN'S JEEP parked in front of Luther's shack and felt an overwhelming surge of relief. Dry tears stung and her throat squeezed up as she braked hard, parked and got out, her eyes riveted on the tall, broad-shouldered man who stood beside Luther Makes Elk. For the life of her she couldn't move, couldn't speak. Steven walked toward her, halting an arm's reach away. He studied her in a cautious silence that Molly found unbearable.

"Dehaviland called me this afternoon and told me what happened last night, about what Manning did," she finally managed to say, the words tumbling out. "I went to your house as soon as I could, and when you weren't there I called your office, and when you weren't there, I came here...." She choked back a strangled sob and raised her hand to her mouth, overwhelmed with emotion.

He took another step, reached out and cupped the side of her face as she spoke. His hand was large and strong. She leaned her cheek against its warmth, closed her eyes briefly, and drew a shuddering breath.

"I'm glad you did," he said.

She covered his hand with her own, not caring that he felt the trembling in hers. "Are you all right?"

"Manning's bullet hit the pouch Luther gave

me. I wasn't hurt, and Manning's in jail where he belongs. He's no threat to you now, and that's all that matters to me." His thumb caressed her cheek as he spoke, and for the first time she thought she could read the expression in the dark eyes that quietly searched her own.

"Luther said there was strong medicine in that pouch, but how could it have stopped a bullet?"

Steven loosed the thong from his neck and upended the contents of the pouch into his palm. Molly touched the two old coins, warm from the heat of his body, and felt ice water flood through her veins as she laid them one on top of the other in her palm and studied how the bullet had struck them dead center. "What were the odds of Manning's bullet hitting these coins?"

"You'll have to ask Luther that, but I think he'd tell you they were pretty good." Steven returned the coins to the pouch and looped the thong around his neck.

"Dehaviland wanted me to tell you that you were a lucky man," Molly said.

"I know. I owe half that luck to Luther, and the other half to him."

"I resigned my job with the firm this morning," she said, aching deep down inside. "I came here to say goodbye."

"I know," he repeated.

"Last night, I was so hurt and angry with you that the only thing that mattered to me was proving that you were wrong about Dehaviland and Condor International," she said.

"I'm sorry that I ever made you feel that way."

Molly shook her head, her eyes filling with tears. "Today, all day, I've been wondering what would happen to us if I took this position with Dehaviland. At first I tried to convince myself that I didn't care, that our relationship was over, but then..." Molly stopped before her voice could break.

"Molly..."

"No, wait," she said, no longer caring that her voice betrayed the depth of her emotions. "Let me finish. Today, after driving around aimlessly for hours, I realized that as good as I felt about Dehaviland's job offer, it couldn't begin to compare with the way you've made me feel in the short time we've known each other. What we've shared together has made me realize that being with you is far more important than accepting the most prestigious position in the most powerful company on the entire planet."

Steven's eyes held hers. "Dehaviland sees something in you that I saw from the very beginning. Think about what you could accomplish working for him."

Molly touched her fingertips to his mouth to

hush him. "I already have, and I've made my decision. Besides, we both know that it was *you* Dehaviland was really angling for. You're the one with all the know-how and experience he needs, not some inexperienced attorney fresh out of law school. And...and I was hoping you might want some help raising two million dollars."

"I've never refused an offer of help." His hand closed over hers, warm and strong.

"Caleb told me about the rifle. You're already halfway there."

Steven shook his head. "I'm not selling Luther's rifle. You might think it sounds crazy, but that old gun is part of our history, and if anyone benefits from selling it, the tribe should."

"I don't think that's crazy at all," Molly said. "I love you even more for feeling that way. We'll raise that two million before the March deadline."

"With your help, we'll probably beat Dehaviland's deadline by a good three months."

"I'll help you in any way I can. I could help you at your office the way I helped Brad. I could learn so much working with you, Steven. Maybe one day I'll really be capable of the kind of position Dehaviland offered me."

"My law practice isn't exactly lucrative," he cautioned.

"I don't care."

"Molly, you're used to so much more than I could ever offer."

She reached up and shushed him again. "I love you, Steven Young Bear, and I don't ever want to say goodbye to you again. I can only hope you feel the same way about me, but even if you don't…" Steven drew her into his arms and kissed her into silence, kissed her until no doubt remained as to how he felt, kissed her until she was breathless in his arms. Molly knew her feet were on the ground but she felt as if she were floating, ascending to a level of joy that surely no other woman on earth had ever experienced. "So, when do I start?"

"Right after we climb Brave Heart Mountain," Steven replied. "But in the meantime, there's one other important matter I could use your help with."

"You name it."

Steven brushed a stray tear from her cheek. "Luther wanted me to buy him a suit, and I could use some help picking it out."

Molly glanced over her shoulder to where the old man sat dozing on the wall bench, seemingly oblivious to the moment. "What on earth does he want a suit for?"

"He told me you'd want him to wear one at your wedding."

Molly wondered if her feet would ever touch ground again as she gazed into the eyes of the man she loved. "He's right," she said. "Luther would look very handsome in a suit. Come on." She reached for his hand. "Let's go find out exactly what he wants. And who knows? If we're lucky, maybe he'll tell us how many children we're going to have, and what color their hair will be."

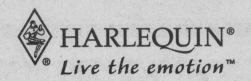
HARLEQUIN®
Live the emotion™

Upbeat,
All-American Romances

flipside
Romantic Comedy

Harlequin Historicals®
Historical,
Romantic Adventure

INTRIGUE
Romantic Suspense

HARLEQUIN ROMANCE®
The essence of
modern romance

HARLEQUIN®
Presents
Seduction and passion
guaranteed

Emotional,
Exciting, Unexpected

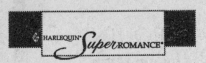
Sassy, Sexy, Seductive!

SUDDENLY A PARENT

Family at Last
by K.N. Casper

Harlequin Superromance #1292

Adoption is a life-altering commitment.
Especially when you're single. And your new
son doesn't speak your language. But when
Jarrod hires Soviet-born linguist Nina Lockhart
to teach Sasha English, he has no idea
how complicated his life is about to become.

*Available in August 2005
wherever Harlequin books are sold.*

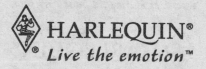

HARLEQUIN®
Live the emotion™

DEAR CORDELIA

by Pamela Ford

Harlequin Superromance #1291

"Dear Cordelia" is Liza Dunnigan's ticket out
of the food section. If she can score an interview
with the reclusive columnist, she'll land an
investigative reporter job and change her boring,
predictable life. She just has to get past
Cordelia's publicist, Jack Graham, hiding
her true intentions to get what she needs.
But Jack is hiding something, too....

*Available in August 2005
wherever Harlequin books are sold.*

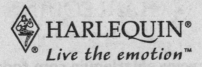

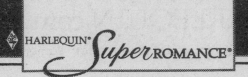

HARLEQUIN *Super*ROMANCE

ANOTHER WOMAN'S SON
by Anna Adams

Harlequin Superromance #1294

**The truth should set you free.
Sometimes it just tightens the trap.**

Three months ago Isabel Barker's life came crashing
down after her husband confessed he loved another
woman—Isabel's sister—and that they'd had a son
together. No one else, including her sister's husband,
Ben, knows the truth about the baby. When her sister
and her husband are killed, Tony is left with Ben,
and Isabel wonders whether she should tell the truth.
She knows Ben will never forgive her if her honesty
costs him his son.

*Available in August 2005
wherever Harlequin books are sold.*

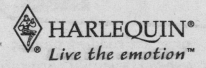

HARLEQUIN®
Live the emotion™

HSRAWS0705